TRIAL BY BLOOD

A Daniel Pike Novel

WILLIAM BERNHARDT

D0862233

BABYLON
BOOKS

PRAISE FOR WILLIAM BERNHARDT AND THE DANIEL PIKE NOVELS

"I could not put *Trial by Blood* down. The plot is riveting —with a surprise after the ending, when I thought it was all over....This book is special."

> — NIKKI HANNA, AUTHOR OF *CAPTURE LIFE*

"*Court of Killers* is a wonderful second book in the Daniel Pike legal thriller series....[A] top-notch, suspenseful crime thriller."

> — TIMOTHY HOOVER

"Once started, it is hard to let [*The Last Chance Lawyer*] go, since the characters are inviting, engaging and complicated....You will enjoy it."

> — *CHICAGO DAILY LAW BULLETIN*

"William Bernhardt writes fast-paced thrillers with lovable characters and many twists and turns. He inspires me to write better."

> — DAN FRIEDMAN, AUTHOR OF *DON'T DARE TO DREAM*

"Bernhardt is the undisputed master of the courtroom drama."

> — *LIBRARY JOURNAL*

TRIAL BY BLOOD

For Lara
again and again and again

Memory believes before knowing remembers.

— WILLIAM FAULKNER, *LIGHT IN AUGUST*

IDENTITY CRISIS

CHAPTER ONE

Fourteen Years Before

Ruby slid the steel-gray handgun into her beach bag, so grateful, so sure this would be the solution she and her son desperately needed. For the first time in ages, she saw a way out. Day One of a better chapter in a bitter life.

She felt a tear snaking down her cheek, but she wiped it away before the boy could see. "Do you remember your name?"

He scrunched his eyes. "Of course I do. I'm four fingers old."

"I mean your new name."

"Aw, that."

"Do you remember?"

"Yeah."

"And where you're from? And your mama's new name? And why we're traveling?"

"I wanna go home."

"We can't, son. Ain't safe for us."

"Are we safe now?"

Here? In a twenty-year-old Yugo GV that barely started,

barely ran, and looked like hell? Were they safe when the most powerful person she had ever known hunted them? She didn't know what the word *safe* meant any more. "You just stay close to your mama. Mama gonna take care of you."

She felt him scoot a little closer. Good. I can take care of you. I can stop the bad from coming.

"Mama, are we almost there?"

"Almost, baby boy. Almost. We're like Moses. Mostways to the Promised Land, standing outside the gate, hopin' someone will let us in."

"I'm hungry."

"I am too, son, but we gotta keep movin'. There's people lookin' for us and we don't want them to drag us back where we come from."

She slowed for a stop sign. The car choked, shuddered, then died.

She swore under her breath, hoping the boy didn't notice. She had no time for this. She turned the key in the ignition.

Nothing happened.

She tried it again. Barely even a churning sound. She let up, not wanting to flood the engine. Hard as it was, she made herself count to thirty before she tried again.

Nothing. This sorry excuse for a car wasn't going anywhere anytime soon.

"Come on." She tugged her boy's arm and together they slid out on the passenger side.

"Mama, I need my box."

"We'll come back for it later."

"It has all my stuff. My Power Rangers and my drawing book and—"

"We'll come back for it later." She pulled hard on his arm. "You be a big boy. You be the man Mama needs you to be, understand? We can't be sittin' still. We got to move."

She felt her heart pounding inside her chest. Her pulse

raced. She had never felt so afraid in her entire life. Please, dear Lord, just give me a chance. Just one chance.

She looked both ways down the street. Her car had stalled in the worst possible place, one of the dirtiest parts of St Petersburg. Mostly industrial, with a few taco stands and massage parlors and other places she had no intention of visiting. Southside Imports had a big ugly warehouse to the north. Gossips said that was a front for drug-runners. Best to stay away. She needed someplace they could hide till she found a ride out of town.

She couldn't afford the Tradewinds or one of those rich white-people places in the tourist district. But there were some cheap motels nearby where they could hole up. They needed to get off the street and they needed to do it fast.

He was looking for her. And she knew what he would do if he found her.

"Come on." She jerked the boy forward, not permitting any resistance.

They had barely walked a hundred feet when she heard tires squeal. A car barreled down the road, straight toward them.

Was that him? Or someone working for him? So soon?

Nowhere to hide, no way the driver could miss them. Maybe she shouldn't have worn this bright yellow dress, but she had few choices. Since Carl died, she couldn't afford to do much shopping. She knew that bastard wanted to get rid of her, to take her boy and send her somewhere she would never return from.

The car slowed as it approached...

Then turned left. She felt the air rush out of her lungs. It wasn't him. Not him and not nobody working for him. They were safe. A little longer.

But that wouldn't last long.

"Mama! You're bleeding!"

She looked down, just above her waist on the right side. Sure enough, blood stained her dress from the inside out. Damn yellow. It didn't hide anything. Looked like he'd cut her worse than she'd imagined. She told him she was taking the boy and leaving. He tried to stop her and they both got hurt. She didn't mean to push him but he got in her way and—

He'd hated her before, but now—she didn't even know a word for it. He would do anything to find her, stop her. Maybe kill her, just to tie up the loose ends.

Not that it mattered. He could cut off her head and she would keep moving forward. Her boy didn't have no one, not one soul in the world he could trust, except her. She was gonna do what she should have done a long time ago.

"It's nothing, darlin'. Just a cut. Don't worry yourself none over it."

In the distance, she spotted a Motel 6 sign. That would do. She could afford that, just, with the money she'd stolen from his wallet. Hole up a little while, then once the heat died down, get out of here. Leave Florida. Go someplace her boy could be the man he deserved to be, safe from the ugliness and pain she'd dealt with for so long. Just a few days and—

Another car careened around the corner behind them.

And she recognized it.

"It's Derrick. Run, boy. *Run.*" She squeezed his hand and together the two raced down the asphalt. She knew she was holding the boy back. Her feet didn't move the way they once did.

The car sped around them, then spun directly in front, blocking their path.

A second later, a wiry man covered in tattoos and wearing a torn tank top crawled out of the driver's seat. "Where you goin' in such a rush, Ruby?"

She stood her ground, took in a deep breath, and faked courage she did not feel. "Don't you mess with me, Derrick. We're leaving."

"I know someone who doesn't think that's such a good idea. Especially not with the boy."

"He's my son. I'm the one that makes decisions 'bout where he goes and what he does."

"Well now, there's a strong difference of opinion on that point."

"We're gonna walk down this street, Derrick. We're gonna walk down this street and you ain't gonna do nothin' to stop us."

"Not after what you did to the boss. That changed everything." Derrick pulled a baseball bat out of the front seat of his car. "Don't want to do this, Ruby. But I got no choice about it."

"We all got a choice, Derrick. We decide who we are and who we wanna be. You're making a choice right now. A bad one."

He walked closer, swaggering and swinging the bat. "You two get in my car peaceful-like and we won't have any problems. You know you can't get away with this. Make it easy on yourself."

The boy stepped forward. "You stay away from my mama!"

Derrick grinned. "What have we got here? A little hero?"

Ruby laid a hand on the boy's shoulder. "He's got more courage than you ever thought about having."

"Courage can be a dangerous thing." Derrick stepped closer, staring into her eyes. "Do you want your boy hurt? Hurt bad?"

"You wouldn't do that."

"I'll do whatever it takes." Before she knew what had happened, he brought his hand around and hit her hard across the face, knocking her to her knees.

She steadied herself, rubbing the side of her cheek.

The boy ran forward, screaming. Derrick knocked him to the ground with a single swat.

"You're just making this unpleasant, Ruby. You're both gonna end up banged up and bleeding. And you're still goin' back with me. Just banged up and bleeding."

"Maybe not." There was only one thing she could do. And if she hesitated, he might talk her out of it.

She reached into her bag and pulled out the gun.

Derrick held up his hands. "Whoa. Hold on there. Where'd you get that, Ruby?"

"Doesn't matter."

"Don't do anything you'll regret later."

"I won't. Should've done this months ago." She pulled the trigger.

Derrick looked stunned, but he did not fall.

She shot him again.

Derrick crumpled to the pavement.

She put the gun back in the beach bag and did her best to remain calm. She looked every which way but didn't see anyone. Maybe no one saw or heard. Maybe she was lucky just this once. But someone would find the body. She had to disappear before the cops arrived.

The boy looked stunned, frozen. She took his hand. "We need to get off the street."

A few minutes later she was at the registration desk for the Motel 6. The clerk gave her a funny scowl when she offered him cash, but he took it.

"Just you and the boy?"

"Just us."

The man was obviously suspicious, but he didn't say anything. He slid the key across the counter with two dingy brown towels.

Two minutes later, they were in their room. Ruby sat on the edge of the bed. All at once, tears sprung from her eyes. It was like a waterfall, pent up for so long, then finally released all at once. Her whole body shook. She had been through so much. And there still was so much left to do.

"It's okay, Mama. It's okay." The boy wrapped his arms around her ample frame. "We made it. We're safe now."

She didn't say anything. She couldn't. Her throat was choked and dry. But she knew they weren't safe. She had bought them a little time, but as soon as he heard about Derrick, he would send someone else after them. Or the police would find them.

They would never make it out of town. She knew that now. Never.

She heard a rustling sound outside on the sidewalk.

There was only one way she could save her boy now.

She reached for her bag and slowly withdrew the gun.

"Mama, what are you doing?"

She raised the gun, her hand trembling. "What I have to do."

"No, Mama!"

Tears streamed from her eyes. "I don't wanna do it. Don't you see that? But I have to. We've run out of choices."

"You said everyone has a choice."

She nodded, wiped her nose. "I just got the one now, boy. So I'm taking it." She tried to concentrate, tried to stiffen her arm.

"Mama, don't point that thing at me."

"Don't you see? It's the only way. The only way left."

"Mama!" The boy was crying and shaking, terrified.

"Goodbye, son."

"Mama, *no!*"

The room was paralyzed by the crash of thunder.

CHAPTER TWO

Dan knew a defense lawyer's primary goal in any trial, and especially a bench trial, was to elicit the judge's sympathy. That was crucial—and exceptionally challenging in the present case, since his client was an alcoholic homeless man with 174 priors. The first time he saw that on the rap sheet, he thought it must be a typo, but it wasn't. Henry Bates had been arrested on 175 occasions. This time he'd been brought in for the usual misdemeanor—disturbing the peace—but also on a felony charge—resisting arrest. Judge La Costa made it clear he'd had enough, and if the defendant were found guilty, the sentence would not be merely another night in jail. Henry would get a lengthy prison stay. One Dan knew Henry probably wouldn't survive.

To people on the outside, this might look like a minor case. But he knew the stakes were as high as they came.

He knew the prosecutor assigned to the case was a young man named Brad Phelan, barely out of law school. He'd hoped his friend

Jazlyn Prentice would be assigned the case, but these days she only handled major felonies. The sole witness for the prosecution was the arresting officer, James Voight, as young as the prosecutor and about as experienced. They wanted Henry Bates out of the way, but never once considered the personal consequences to the troubled man they manipulated. They were a bunch of bullies, albeit bullies with the official sanction of the US law enforcement system.

He hated bullies. He'd spent most of his life fighting them.

Today would be no exception.

Before he rose from the defendant's table and started his cross-examination, he patted Henry on the back—showing the judge he liked the man. "Keep your hands under the table."

He strode to the witness stand. His Air Jordans always put a spring in his step, not to mention an additional half-inch in his height. "Officer Voight, did you consider escorting my client to another location?"

"No. The owner of the restaurant preferred charges."

"Did you attempt to talk him out of it?"

"That's not my job."

"Did you offer to get my client help?"

"Also not my job. He appeared to be intoxicated."

"So take him to an addiction treatment center. Or at least an AA meeting. They were holding one at the Methodist church just a block away."

"Our protocol for dealing with public disturbances is to place the offenders in custody and take them back to the station. Unfortunately, when I attempted to arrest the defendant, he became violent."

He watched the officer testify. Many years before, a law professor had trained him to watch people carefully, observing everything. Even if the details meant nothing at the time, they might later. That advice became the foundation of his success. Many a case had been resolved favorably when his subconscious finally "connected the dots" and put those observations together in a meaningful way.

Current observations? Officer Voight didn't seem able to sit still. He shifted his weight from one side to the other constantly. Perspiration on the back of his neck. Rumpled collar. Visible tan line across his right wrist.

"You claim he became violent. What did Henry actually do?"

"He made loud and aggressive remarks."

"That's not resisting arrest."

"He fought with me. Threatened to hit me."

He allowed himself a small smirk. Voight outweighed Henry by at least thirty-five pounds. Henry looked like he hadn't had a non-liquid meal in years. "You must've been terrified," he deadpanned.

"That's not the point. The man threw a punch at me. I was forced to restrain him."

"Henry tells me he didn't resist at all, except to say that you had no right to arrest him because he hadn't committed a crime."

"He'd been asked to leave. He wouldn't."

"It's a public place, isn't it?"

"For customers."

"Does it say that on the door? Paying customers only?"

"It's understood. I was forced to remove him."

"You were forced, or you were asked?"

Voight hesitated. Still shifting. "I don't understand the question."

"I've eaten at Chez Guitano, Officer. Great Lobster Thermidor. It's a nice place. Henry's clothes are dirty and he smells a little, and I think the managers didn't want him hanging around the front lobby. They ugly-shamed him, basically, and called the police. I think they invented the disturbance to get rid of him, and I think you invented the resistance because you're sick of hauling him downtown."

"You're right about the last part," Voight muttered. "You'd think even a drunk could learn a lesson."

"Unless of course he has a disability. Does the defendant have a disability?"

"Well...I know he drinks a lot."

"Anything else?"

"I don't know."

"You've arrested him eight times and you don't know if he has a disability?" He glanced at the judge. "Seems like that might be worth finding out."

"Not my job."

He walked back to the defense table and pulled a file folder out of his backpack. He preferred backpack to briefcase—less strain on the shoulders and more manageable when you're moving fast.

He glanced at the papers in the file. "So you don't know that his disability payments were interrupted by his constant visits to jail. You don't know about his head injury, his history of mental illness, his addiction issues, or the fact that he's homeless and has no one to look after him. And the worst part is—you don't care."

Phelan finally got in the game. "Objection, your honor. This is not relevant."

"I think it's keenly relevant, your honor. It's the whole reason we're here. Everything I just said my investigator learned in less than an hour—and he doesn't have access to police data-bases." In truth, Garrett did—but he wasn't supposed to. "If the police had taken ten minutes to investigate, they might have ended this pointless and expensive pattern of arrest, jail, out in twenty-four hours, arrest, jail, rinse and repeat."

Judge La Costa cleared his throat. "The objection concerns whether your question is relevant to the charges of disturbing the peace and resisting arrest."

"And I say it is. These people don't wait for Henry to disturb the peace anymore. They arrest him on sight. The police are supposed to serve and protect, but they've become bullies clearing Henry out of the way to appease wealthy businessmen who have political influence and make contributions to the police pension fund."

The judge looked at him sternly. "I sense you're arguing the case, not the objection."

He shrugged. "Might as well save some time…"

"Let me make a different objection," Phelan said, pressing his hands together. Phi Beta Kappa tie pin. French cuffs. Furrowed brow. "That last question wasn't even a question."

"Sustained. New question, counsel."

He turned back to the witness. "Did you see the alleged disturbance my client made at the restaurant?"

"No, but the manager told me—"

"That he wanted Henry gone. But did he describe an actual disturbance?"

"I…don't recall."

"So we have no witness present who can testify about disturbing the peace and hearsay isn't good enough. Your honor, I move to dismiss that charge. That leaves us with resisting arrest. You claim my client threw a punch at you?"

Voight leaned back a bit. "Yes."

"Which hand did he use?"

"Uh…sorry?"

"Stop stalling for time. Which hand did he use when he allegedly took a swing at you?"

"What difference does it make?"

"All the difference in the world. Which hand?"

Voight thought for a moment. "His right."

"Bad choice. Henry's right hand was injured when he served in Iraq. He lost two fingers. He can't clench that fist and he can't raise that arm above his waist. That's documented in this file, which I will be happy to make available to the court. What you just described is physically impossible."

"I guess it was his left—"

"No, sir, you do not get to change your testimony after I've proved you're lying. Your honor, I've got a medical report that will confirm everything I just said. I move to dismiss all charges. And I respectfully request that in the future, instead of this revolving door non-justice, the police be asked to perform perfunctory background checks. Almost half of all homeless people are veterans and they deserve better. We should take care of our people who have served."

Judge La Costa nodded. "I don't have the power to set police department policy. But I do have the authority to rule on this case. The charges are dismissed. Mr. Bates, you are free to go. And—" he added, pointing, "I hope I don't see you again."

The judge left the courtroom. Phelan looked as if he were about to vomit. Was this the kid's first time in court? He hoped so. Everyone's first time in court should be disastrous. Toughens you up.

He clasped Henry's hand. "Did you hear that? You're free."

Henry did not seem elated. "Free to go where? I appreciate what you did for me, but—"

"Hold that thought." He pulled his phone out of his pocket. He had a text from Camila Pérez—the mayor of the city and, as of last weekend, his official girlfriend.

Found him a place at the Crislip shelter. Ready when he arrives.

He texted back. *Thx luv. C U at prty.*

"Got a place for you to stay, Henry. It's billed as a women's shelter, but their approach is non-binary these days. They're specifically planning to offer services to vets, and addiction services to people dealing with opioids and other addictive substances. You can stay there as long as you need to. Get back on your feet and get back to work."

Henry looked incredulous. "Really?"

"They'll get you the help you need. You won't have to loiter in restaurants or get arrested just to get a meal."

Henry's eyes widened. "I—don't know how to thank you."

"Thank me by putting your life back in order. I know you've seen some hard times. But you have to move on. This is a golden opportunity—so I'm expecting you to make the most of it."

Henry squeezed his hand. "I won't let you down."

He squeezed back. "I know you won't."

CHAPTER THREE

DAN WAS BARELY THROUGH THE DOOR WHEN A TEN-YEAR-OLD girl raced toward him.

"Dan!" She wrapped her arms around his waist, hugging him tightly.

Camila gave him an arched eyebrow. "Should I be jealous?"

"No." He crouched down till he was eye level with the girl. "Happy birthday, Esperanza." He handed her a gift wrapped in bright pink paper that matched her dress. "This is for you."

She took the package, looking excited beyond words. "A present? For me?"

"It is your birthday party."

"Is it Hello Kitty? Is it something with Hello Kitty?"

He frowned. Camila laughed. "I told you not to be so predictable."

"But it was so cute…"

Esperanza took him by the hand. "I'll put this with the other presents. Come inside. We've already started playing games."

He followed her lead. "Pin the Tail on the Donkey? Musical Chairs?"

"Dan, I'm ten years old!"

"Well...yes..."

"We're playing Never Have I Ever." In the living room, he found six girls sitting in a circle while an Amazon Echo played boy band music. He wasn't sure which group—they all sounded alike to him. And standing by the punchbowl was his friend Jazlyn Prentice, assistant district attorney for Pinellas County—and adoptive mother. Baby blue party dress. Red eyes. Loose gait. Had she spiked the punch?

"Never Have I Ever?" he asked.

"Oh whatever," Jazlyn said. "It won't take long. They haven't ever done anything. And if they have to take a drink—it's prune juice."

"Still enjoying motherhood?"

"I'm not sure *enjoying* is the right word." She allowed herself a small smile. "But it's the best decision I ever made."

Dan had represented Esperanza—and her then-guardian—during a previous case. Esperanza was slated to be deported after the US revoked Protected Status for El Salvadorian emigres, but he managed to get the girl citizenship and even better, convinced Jazlyn to adopt her.

"I hear you trounced our new hire in court this morning," Jazlyn said.

"The judge dismissed the charges. Your hire didn't have much to do with it."

"All I know is he came back to the office, crawled behind his desk, and curled up in a fetal ball. I think he may be catatonic."

"First time in court?"

"Yup. And it was a crushing defeat."

"Adversity is good for the soul. My client should have been assigned a public defender—175 times. If he had, this situation wouldn't have arisen. But the court says they can't afford to assign lawyers in misdemeanor cases, so Henry got the revolving-door treatment. Mr. K called last night and asked me to take the case, just to put a stop to it."

"I think Brad Phelan feels like you put a stop to him."

"It wasn't his fault. The police officer lied. I would suggest you be careful about using him as a witness in the future."

"Voight may have exaggerated—"

He cut her off with a shake of the head. "He lied. Deliberately. And I detected no remorse. He's dangerous. The kind of officer who damages the reputation of the entire force."

"I'll make a note." She turned to Camila. "How is the mayor of our fine city doing?"

"Keeping my head above water. That's about all I can expect at this point." Camila had recently been framed for a horrible multiple murder, but Dan had managed to not only exonerate her but finger the true culprit. "Not everyone is happy about my return to public office. But not everyone was happy when I arrived in the first place."

"You're still running for the open Senate seat, right?"

Camila hesitated, tucking her hands inside her jeans pockets. "I haven't made an official announcement yet, but...since I'm among friends...count on it."

"I'm very glad."

"What about you? The rumor mill says DA Belasco plans to run for mayor. Which means there will be a vacancy that no one is better qualified to fill than you."

"I have given it some thought. I would hate campaigning, but if I were elected, I could make some positive changes. It's no secret Belasco has made a mess of things. Tarnished the whole system. He's too tied to the city's big money. We've become dependent on plea bargaining, charging people on thin evidence because we know they'll cop a plea to lesser offenses rather than risk a longer sentence. And the racial balance of our defendant roster is embarrassing."

"Tell you what—you endorse me and I'll endorse you. Girls rule."

They shook on it. "Deal."

Jazlyn turned to Dan. "Hope you're not feeling left out."

"Feeling lucky to know so many strong intelligent women."

"I wasn't at all sure you'd find time in your busy schedule for a little girl's birthday party. Not enough wind for kitesurfing?"

"Nonsense." He glanced at the girls sitting in a circle. The one facing him asked if anyone had ever swallowed a Tide pod. "Anything for Esperanza. That little girl changed my life. For the better."

She squinted a bit. "You're still a bit of a mystery to me, Mr. Pike."

"Me? I'm an open book."

Jazlyn and Camila both laughed out loud.

"What? I am."

Camila covered her mouth. "Sure. An open book with mostly blank pages."

"Honey, I have no secrets from you."

"Maybe. But you're not volunteering anything, either."

"You know everything about me there is to know."

"I know as little as you've bothered to reveal. You grew up in Florida. You went to law school and became arguably the best—certainly the flashiest—criminal defense lawyer in town. You left the big firm and joined that wacky outfit run by Mr. K—a pseudonym for a boss you've never met. And you do this crazy thing with your tongue—"

"Whoa. Let's not get too personal here."

"Just wanted to see if I could get a reaction out of you."

"And he has a passion for justice," Jazlyn added. "Which I admire. Even if it is usually a thorn in my professional side."

"I've earned that passion." He saw no need to repeat what they already knew. His father was wrongfully convicted of murder when he was young, then died in prison when Dan was just seventeen. He'd spent most of his adult life making sure others weren't railroaded in the same way.

"So who are you, Daniel Pike?" Jazlyn asked.

He took a step back. "Is this a birthday party or a therapy session?"

"Yes. Deflecting the question with a joke. One of your favorite tactics."

He glanced toward the girls. "Esperanza looks like she's struggling to come up with a question. You think they've asked about sexting yet?"

Camila slapped his arm. "Dan! They're ten!"

"And every one of them has a cell phone."

"And once again," Jazlyn said, "you've managed to change the subject."

"I just don't want Esperanza to lose the game at her own party."

"Well," Camila said, "suggest something other than sexting."

"Never have I ever gotten a sleeve tattoo?"

"No one's going to drink on that one."

"Never have I ever done a risqué TikTok?"

"No one will know what you're talking about."

Jazlyn tilted her head. "Unless it's been on the Disney Channel. And it probably has."

CHAPTER FOUR

Dan removed the lid from his Instant Pot and peered inside.

He didn't have to taste it. One sniff was enough to tell him the risotto was perfect—just the way he liked it. The broccoli and mushrooms and tarragon and turmeric perfectly enhanced the Arborio short-grain rice. He felt guilty about not preparing something more elaborate, but between the emergency hearing this morning and the birthday party, the conference call with Mr. K had already been delayed longer than the boss liked.

He scooped the meal out of the slow cooker and set out Jimmy's favorite plates, the ones featuring the chest emblems of various DC superheroes. He'd been thrown when he first saw this Snell Isle mansion they called their "office" but had to admit there was an advantage to a workplace that came with a fully equipped kitchen.

He didn't have to ring a dinner bell. The aroma was sufficient to bring his partners out of their private offices upstairs.

Jimmy Armstrong was first. African-American, plus-sized cardigan sweater, aficionado of all things nerdist. "You're using the best plates! I call Wonder Woman."

Dan smiled. "First here, first pick."

Maria Morales entered the kitchen jogging, wearing a gold lamé top and Gucci jeans. "Does this have kale in it?"

"Broccoli."

She scrunched her nose. "Not the same."

And a few seconds later, Garrett Wainwright emerged, completing the team roster. He was sporting a Rays t-shirt and humming a jazz riff—but stopped when he spotted the food. "Does this have meat in it, Dan?"

"You know it doesn't."

He looked disappointed, but nonetheless scooped a hearty portion onto his Green Lantern plate. "My luck to be stuck in a firm full of bleeding-heart vegetarians."

"A vegetarian diet is good for you," Maria insisted. "And it's good for the planet. Reduces our carbon footprint dramatically."

"Liberal propaganda," Garrett grumbled. "Let's take it to the living room. Mr. K is getting antsy. He wanted to start this meeting a long time ago."

The others followed his instruction, sitting on the semi-circular sofa facing the television, as was their tradition—even though nothing was going to appear on the screen. All they would receive was Mr. K's voice.

Garrett opened a Zoom event on his laptop, then used Airplay to send it to the screen. A few seconds later, they heard a familiar voice crackle from the television speakers. "Hello, team. How's everyone doing?"

They all shouted positive thoughts. "Dan made risotto," Jimmy said. "Mouth-watering. Don't tell my husband I said this, Dan, but you make the best food I've ever eaten."

"I'm glad you like it."

"Great idea adding Dan to the team. We got a decent trial lawyer—and more importantly, a gourmet chef."

He tucked in his chin. "This is just a little something I whipped up on short notice…"

"And it's delicious. I don't normally go in much for rice—but Dan makes it a delicacy. How do you do it?"

"Well, for starters, that's Arborio rice that's been slow cooking, not Uncle Ben's."

"I'm glad you're all eating well," Mr. K said. "You're going to need lots of energy for your next case. Dan, I heard you scored a victory in court today."

"And more importantly," he replied, "got Henry some professional help. K, what would you think about setting up a robo-lawyer service to help people like Henry who get slapped with misdemeanors but can't afford a lawyer?"

"Robo-lawyer?"

"Yeah. We design a computer program that can provide online assistance. Not actually practicing law, but telling people where to go and what to do."

"Is that viable?"

"The UK has a robo-lawyering computer program that has handled more than 10,000 traffic cases—and has a success rate over 90%. It's a great way to treat cases that are not important enough to hire an attorney for, but can still cost people lots of money or lead to a loss of driving privileges. Some US cities have a similar service to help inmates file prisoner grievances. We could bring the same concept here to deal with all these misdemeanors. I think Jazlyn would cooperate. We could set up free-access computer terminals for people like Henry, with someone to help them use them. Maybe law students who want a taste of the real world."

"I like that idea very much," K said. "Draft a proposal for me."

"I'll get right on it."

"Well...maybe not right on it. I've got a case that needs your immediate attention."

He always did. "You mentioned that before. Something about a disappearance?"

"A notorious disappearance," K said. "One of the most

famous missing-persons cases in St. Pete history. Happened about fourteen years ago. Anyone remember a kid named Ossie Coleman?"

Maria's hand rose to her mouth. "OMG. I do. The little boy. I was a teenager when that happened. It was all over the news. His photo was on every corner and every telephone pole."

Garrett agreed. "And not just locally. All across the country. I was in the prosecutor's office when that case broke."

"Am I remembering this right?" Maria continued. "His mother took him to a motel and was found with a bullet hole in her head. Everyone assumed she shot herself. The boy disappeared and hasn't been seen since."

"That's the case," Garrett said. "And the mother left a note behind. It read, *You will never find him.* It was bizarre. You've lived around here all your life, Dan. You must've heard of it."

"I remember that creepy note. I don't suppose the envelope was addressed?"

"No. No one knows who she was hiding the boy from. Or where he went. The police did everything possible to find him. The FBI got involved too. They looked at everything—cell-phone logs, email accounts, every scrap of forensic evidence found in that motel room. They decided the mother's death was suicide, but there was another man murdered not far from the motel by the same gun. Very confusing. And none of that explains what happened to the boy. Every now and again we got reports, sightings. But they all turned out to be false."

"Was the mother running from an abusive husband?"

"No. She was a widow and she lived alone."

"I remember it too," Jimmy said, swallowing a bite of risotto. "It was the talk of the town. Lots of charity fundraisers. They created a Find Ossie fund." He paused. "But this was apparently a problem money couldn't solve."

"Why does this need our attention now? Do we have a lead?"

"Even better," K said. "We have a boy."

Maria lowered her plate. "Someone found him?"

"He found himself," K said, "or got free, or—something. The details are sketchy and it hasn't hit the media yet. He showed up last week and the police have kept a lid on it so far. They're hoping to investigate more before it becomes a media firestorm. But unfortunately, some of the boy's relatives—assuming he is Ossie Coleman—found out. They were called in to offer an opinion on whether he really is Ossie. And they are not happy he's resurfaced. Expect it to be all over the internet soon."

"Is money involved?"

"Tons of it. An estate of something like a billion dollars, plus intangible assets that are difficult to value. Ossie's grandfather did very well in the tourism industry. Came up from nothing, built one little hotel into a chain. He had four sons—and the eldest married Ossie's mother, after Ossie was born. Ossie would stand to inherit a fourth of the estate, if his identity is verified."

"What does Grandpa say about this claimant to the family fortune?"

"I haven't talked to him," K replied, "but my sources tell me he's guardedly optimistic. He hopes this kid is the real deal—but he's also aware that there is a strong motivation for someone to pretend to be Ossie."

"There must be DNA records on file somewhere. Blood. Or dental records. Or baby footprints taken at birth."

"You'd think, but apparently all such records either never existed or disappeared."

"Or have been disappeared."

"Very possibly."

"Given how antiquated some of the record-keeping in this town is," Jimmy said, "anything is possible."

"Sounds like this is a case for forensic detectives," Garrett said. "Not lawyers. And I don't see why this would be urgent. No one inherits while the grandfather is alive."

"But the grandfather is in poor health," K answered. "He has COPD. Smoked as a young man, I gather. Has been in a wheelchair for years. No one can say for sure, but—his days are numbered."

"And if there's an unproved claimant when he dies," Garrett added, "the estate will go into probate and it could be many years before anyone gets anything."

"Yes," K said, "unless the new heir apparent is either included or specifically excluded before Granddad dies. That's why one of the heirs has filed a suit requesting a declaratory judgment that this young man is not Ossie Coleman. He's hoping to get this matter resolved before the grandfather dies."

"Is he likely to succeed?"

A long pause. "Now you're getting to the heart of the problem. All my sources say the young man seems genuine. He looks like a member of the family and there's not a hint of dissembling or sham about him. If he's not Ossie Coleman, he's the Meryl Streep of pretenders. But he's having severe memory problems. Interested, Dan?"

"You think he's the real deal, don't you?" In the past, Mr. K had always steered them toward people who needed help, deserved help, and couldn't get it anywhere else. He had to assume this case was more of K's humanitarian intervention. "That's why you want us to handle this, right?"

"I want to know the truth. The lawsuit isn't about truth. It's about rich relatives using their economic advantage to push the court into a hasty decision that cuts the kid out before he can do anything to stop it. The court might appoint a guardian ad litum for the boy, but they won't appoint an attorney. Not for a civil suit."

Maria smiled. "So we're going to be his attorney, aren't we?"

"That's the assignment. How do you feel about helping this boy fight off a pack of relatives who don't feel a quarter of a billion dollars is enough?"

Jimmy grinned. "Sounds fun. But what if he turns out to be an imposter?"

"Learn the truth, Jimmy. If he's a fake, you drop the case."

"Understood."

"Dan, are you in? You're going to face some serious opposition on this one. Probably some big-firm lawyering. Endless discovery and motions practice. The Coleman family is resourceful and well-connected."

He shrugged. "You're the boss."

"Is that a yes or a no?"

"Can I meet the kid before I commit? Then I'll have a better sense of how I feel about this."

"Agreed. I've emailed my file to Garrett. He can make copies for all of you. Garrett can start the research and Jimmy can talk to everyone he knows, everyone who's had any contact with this case. Which will be a lot of people. But Dan—let me tell you one other detail before you see it in the file. The Coleman family has an expert. His name is Bradley Ellison."

His lips parted slightly. "*The* Bradley Ellison?"

"I'm afraid so."

Maria looked at them blank-faced. "Am I supposed to recognize this name? Is he a famous chef? Extreme sports nut like you, Dan?"

He shook his head. "He's the detective whose testimony put my father behind bars. For a crime he didn't commit."

Her eyes widened. "Oh. Wow."

"He's retired from the force now," K said. "But he stays active. Investigates cold cases. Get this—he's a crony of Conrad Sweeney."

"Why am I not surprised." Sweeney was the most prominent power broker in the city, wealthy and influential. He and Dan had crossed paths more than once in the past. Sweeney tried to railroad Camila with a trumped-up murder charge. He wanted her out of the way because she wouldn't be his puppet. Of course, Sweeney always worked through minions, never doing anything that might blow back to him.

"I have that from several sources," K continued. "I don't know all the details, but Sweeney and Ellison have worked together more than once."

"So they might be working together now."

"There's a lot of money at stake. Anything is possible."

His brain raced, putting the pieces together. "Was Sweeney involved in what happened to my dad?"

"I don't know, Dan." Long pause. "But I can't eliminate the possibility."

He set down his plate. "We'll take the case. When can I meet the boy?"

"He's staying at a foster home. The address is in the file. Are you going to be able to stay objective, Dan?"

"Of course. I'm a professional."

"Yes...but—that's not all you are. You were shaped—"

"Let me talk to this kid. We can go from there."

"Very well. Let's talk again tomorrow."

Maria placed a hand on his shoulder. "Dan, if you need to—"

"Let's get to work. Garrett, I want to read that file before we talk to the boy."

"Already in your inbox."

"If we hurry, we can talk to the kid first thing tomorrow morning. Let's all rendezvous again tomorrow evening."

"Dan," Maria said, "you don't have to bury—"

"We've got work to do, team," he said, carrying his plate back to the kitchen. "There's a young man who needs our help. Let's make sure we don't let him down."

CHAPTER FIVE

HARRISON COLEMAN CLOSED THE MEDICINE CABINET. THE FACE in the mirror stared back at him.

Is this what it's come to? Is this the only way you can get through the night?

The answer was a resounding: Yes. He picked up the water glass and downed two X-embossed pills, fast. Then catching his reflection again, he held up his right hand, making the shape of the letter "L" with his thumb and forefinger, and pressed it against his forehead.

Loser. Weak loser. You pretend to be a good person, but when it comes time to take a stand, you buckle. You caved all those years ago. And you caved just now, when someone told you he desperately needed your help.

Coward.

He stepped out of the bathroom, wringing his hands. He had to get his head together before the show started. He was the chief production officer these days, and at the Gresham Theater, just down the street from the Mahaffey, one of St Petersburg's top performance venues, that meant something.

He stepped out of his office and was soon backstage. All

kinds of crewpersons bustled about, taking care of business. He could see the plush seating, the elegant European-style loge seats. This was a fine theater, and his association with it gave him pride. *All the world's a stage, and all the men and women merely players...*

He knew some people assumed he got his job through money or connections, but the truth was, he had worked hard and earned this.

Except he didn't deserve it, did he? He didn't deserve anything, except to die like a dog, which was what he was. Why keep dragging it out? *To be or not to be, that is the question,* right? He didn't need to be.

He strolled through the backstage area, technically checking to make sure all was as it should be, but in reality, barely paying attention. Everyone had signed the call board. Everyone knew their jobs. They were brimming with talent—unlike him.

"Showtime in ten, boss."

He nodded at the stagehand passing by, smiling a little. They tolerated him, even humored him. But they did not love him. They never would.

Why should they?

He could go outside, watch the crowd arrive, or better yet, return to his office. No one needed him.

The only time anyone had needed him—he'd been a complete failure.

When he returned to his office, he noted the chess table beckoning, urging him to make the next move. He needed to play more often if he wanted to maintain his grandmaster rating. He moved his remaining rook to an appropriately threatening position. That would do for now. Later he'd come back and play the other side. He was nearing the famed Lucena endgame, and he wanted to explore the possibilities.

He stepped into the bathroom and disrobed. It had been a long day and he needed a shower. That was why he'd had this tub-and-shower combo installed in the bathroom adjoining his office. He needed it. Sometimes he showered twice, even three times a day. He tended to sweat and sticky clothes and musty smell were not the ticket to success in the theatrical world.

After he finished, he dried off, wrapped a towel around his waist, and stared at himself in the foggy mirror for far too long.

Who the hell are you, anyway?

He left the bathroom and entered his main office, thinking he would pour himself a drink. He didn't notice at first. He walked to the desk, shuffled papers pointlessly for a moment or two.

Then he looked up.

He was not alone.

By the pricking of my thumbs, something wicked this way comes.

"How long have you been there?"

"What difference does that make, Harrison? I'm here."

"I don't suppose you've come hoping for complementary theater tickets."

"No."

"There's no need to be rude."

"That remains to be seen."

He stayed behind his desk, as if a rectangle of plywood would somehow protect him.

He could see his visitor staring at the theatrical posters on the wall. "Are these all plays you've put on?"

"Yes. Not all here."

"You go in for all that Shakespeare stuff."

He stifled a smile. "You could put it that way."

"I can't understand what people are talking about when they talk Shakespeare. Seems pretentious, if you ask me."

"You're not the first to say so." Because insecure people always criticize what they don't understand.

"You must like that Henry VI." He pronounced it, "Henry Vee-Eye." "You've put it on often enough."

"No, you—" He swallowed his original response. "That's four different plays. Parts 1-4."

"Four plays about one guy? You'd think if Shakespeare was so great, he could tell the story in one play. Just leave out the boring parts."

"Shakespeare's audience loved history plays. A series of four plays was an artistic triumph—and also a great commercial success. Shakespeare was quite the businessman, you know."

His visitor turned. "If people can make money with these stupid plays—why are you such a loser?"

"I—I don't—Look, why are you here? I have work to do—"

"I doubt it. You look completely unnecessary from where I'm sitting."

"I'm the chief production officer."

"Meaning you don't do squat." He pivoted. "What would your pal William Shakespeare say about your miserable life?"

His voice choked. "A tale told by an idiot, signifying nothing."

"That sounds about right. I think it's time that miserable tale ended, don't you?" The sound of music outside boomed. The overture was underway. "Good. That will cover the noise."

He saw his visitor approach but did nothing to stop him. His hands trembled. "The play's the thing, wherein I'll catch the conscience of the king."

"Your conscience has finally caught up with you, Harrison. Now it's time to ring down the curtain."

CHAPTER SIX

DAN SAT IN THE PASSENGER SEAT READING FILES WHILE MARIA drove the company car—a Jaguar F-Pace SVR that Mr. K provided for their business use. She preferred to drive and he'd gotten used to it—but he would be happier if she weren't constantly distracted by the black band on her right wrist.

"Fitbit chastising you?"

"I'm way behind on my steps for this week."

"It's Tuesday."

"And I'm already behind."

"If you'd rather, you can get out and walk."

"It's twelve more miles to the foster home."

"That would put you ahead. For at least a few days."

"Dan, I feel you do not support my desire to remain fit."

"Is it that you want to be fit, or that you want to fit into your skintight designer jeans?"

She smiled a little. "Well…both. Is that a problem for you?"

He shrugged. "If you're going to pay for those overpriced Gucci jeans, you might as well get the maximum benefit."

"My sentiments exactly."

"So—no freakshake after the interview?"

"Now you're being cruel."

"I hate to see you controlled by wearable electronics."

"Don't be so judgy. I saw you looking at your phone a few minutes ago."

"Because Garrett sent me more research. Some of it is startling. I had no idea kids disappeared as frequently as they do. Did you know over 25,000 children were reported missing last year? According to the Center for Missing and Exploited Children."

"How many of those turned out to be runaways?"

"Most." He pulled out his phone to refresh his memory. "About sixty percent. Most of the rest were abducted by relatives. About 3000 have been found, though only sixteen of those were abducted by non-family relatives."

"But that's what happened to Ossie Coleman?"

"Apparently. No other relatives have disappeared."

"I ran away from home once." Another small smile played on Maria's lips. "My dad wouldn't let me stay up to watch some nonsense on Nickelodeon. So I said I was leaving. I was six at the time."

"Did he try to stop you?"

"No, he helped me pack."

"Ouch."

"He knew I wouldn't go far. I walked around the block twice till I cooled off, then I came home. He didn't even look up. 'Maria Morales,' he said. 'It's your night to do the dishes.' And that was it."

"Sounds like he handled it perfectly."

"I loved my daddy." She suddenly started, as if catching herself. "Oh—I'm sorry."

"Because you loved your dad?"

"Because—I know how you lost yours."

He shook his head. "Old news."

"Sounds like it might be coming back to the surface."

"Just a coincidence, probably."

She hung a sharp right. "Must've been a hard thing to deal with. Like at school. Everybody knowing your dad…"

"Is in the big house? Yeah, not a walk in the park. Especially since I knew he was innocent." He paused. "But nobody else did."

She parked the Jag on the street. "That must've been hell for a young boy."

His face remained phlegmatic. "You know what Nietzsche said. That which does not kill us makes us stronger."

"Nietzsche had syphilis, mental illness, pneumonia, and died at age fifty-five."

He stepped out of the car. "So I guess that didn't make him stronger…"

JOAN AND MARJORIE REYNOLDS HAD BEEN TAKING IN SHORT-TERM foster kids for more than a decade. The stipend was puny, so Dan knew they could only do it out of a genuine love for children. The authorities weren't sure what to do in this case, since Ossie Coleman would be eighteen and technically an adult, but since they had no other ideas, they put him here until his identity could be legally determined.

Ossie was in a room he shared with another boy, but the roomie wasn't home, so they had a little privacy. He looked thin but healthy. Light African-American complexion. Curly hair. Blinked a lot. His clothes were pure Walmart—standard jeans and a solid blue t-shirt. He seemed open and eager to please.

He introduced himself and Maria and asked if the boy wanted them to represent him in the declaratory judgment suit.

He did. Mr. K had already sent the paperwork, so there were no surprises.

"I really appreciate you guys helping me out with this," Ossie said. "That guardian tried to explain it all to me, but I didn't follow it much."

"Understandable," Dan said, smiling. "I don't always understand everything judges say, and I went to law school. Would you mind telling us your story? I know you've already told the police, probably several times, and we can get copies of those reports. But I'd like to hear it from you."

"Sure." Ossie sat on the edge of his bed. "What do you want to know?"

"I hear you're having memory problems?"

"Yeah. Major league. I remember my mom—barely. But everything between then and now is mostly gone. I get flashes, images—but not much else. I don't know why. When the cops found me, I didn't know where I was or how I got there. I knew my name and that was about it. They say my memory might come back in time, but so far—nothing."

There were many possible reasons for memory loss, of course. Everyone's memories of early years tend to be spotty and unreliable. A blow to the head could cause memory loss— and when he was found, he was treated for a serious head injury. Or stress could do it. Alcohol abuse. Malnutrition. Emotional duress. And he couldn't rule out the possibility of neurological damage, given how little they knew about him. "Let's start at the beginning. Are you Ossie Coleman?"

The boy looked back at him quizzically. "Of course I am. That's my name. Always has been."

"Do you know what happened to your mother?"

"No, sorry. Must've blocked that out. If I ever knew."

"Where did you go after you were separated from your mother?"

"Or to put it differently," Maria said, "where have you been the last fourteen years?"

"Someplace remote. Lots of trees. Woods. No neighbors. No television. No phone."

"What woods? This is beach country. Are you talking about the Everglades? Something like that?"

"I'm not sure. Tall trees. Lots of green. I'm sorry—I don't know where it was. I never left, till the very end. We lived in a cabin."

"Why do you call it a cabin?" Dan asked. "Was it made of logs?"

"No. Wood and stone, I think. But it was out by itself."

"Describe the cabin."

Ossie thought for a moment. "It was just a place. It had a wood porch. A rocking chair. You could sit out there and watch the sun set."

So it faced west. "Go on."

"It had a number carved on that big thing hanging over the front door."

"A gable?"

"I dunno. I guess so."

"What number?"

"1-9-8-0."

A street address number? The year it was built? "What color?"

"Kind of a dark brown. Except for a yellow triangle on the gable. Bright yellow."

A brown cabin in the woods with a spot of bright yellow paint? "You told the police about a guy named Joe."

"Yeah. He lived with me. Fed me. Taught me to read and stuff. He had a phone, but he didn't let me anywhere near it."

"An adult?"

"Yeah. Way old. Older than you even."

Practically decrepit. "You called him Joe?"

"Yeah. I dunno if that was his real name or not. He had big bushy hair. Spots of gray. Lots of tattoos, all up and down his arms."

"Describe the tattoos."

"Jeez, I dunno. I never really thought about it. There was some kind of flower on his right arm, just above the bicep. Lots of ivy or green stuff streaming down from it. A heart. And letters—but not normal letters. I think maybe they were Russian or something. They looked weird."

"Like the Cyrillic alphabet?"

"I...don't know what that means."

"Doesn't matter. What else?"

"He had tattoos on his legs, too. I saw them when he wore shorts. Never really thought about what they were."

"Was he strong?"

"Very. Pumped iron. Had a lot of barbells in his bedroom. Big muscles. Kinda scary."

"You look pretty strong yourself."

"He let me use them sometimes. When he was in a good mood."

"How did Joe support himself?"

"Uh...sorry?"

"How did he pay the bills?"

"I dunno. I don't think he had many bills."

"He must've fed you."

"Yeah. We always had food. Mostly frozen meat and Cheerios."

"You had a refrigerator?"

"Yeah."

"So you must've had electricity."

"He had a generator thing behind the cabin."

"And you were in this place for fourteen years?"

"I guess. I didn't know much about time. I didn't have any way to keep track of it."

"Any other visitors?"

"No."

"You seem well spoken." That was an understatement. He wouldn't expect someone raised in isolation to sound like an urban street kid. But this boy, despite his past, had the vocabulary of a college student. "Did you...go to school?"

"No. Joe taught me. From books. We had lots of books in the cabin and he made me study. Punished me if I didn't. Said he didn't want me to grow up sounding like ghetto trash. I didn't even really know what a ghetto was, but I knew he wanted me to read and talk proper English."

Sounded like a nightmare. Isolated, home-schooled, and punished by his abductor. And he had barely begun to scratch the surface of the horrors that might have taken place in this cabin. "Was Joe...nice to you?"

Another shrug. "He fed me. Played checkers with me sometimes. Or poker with matchsticks. Cut my finger once chopping wood and he took care of it."

"But did he ever..." He swallowed. This was beyond hard. "Did he hurt you?"

"He made me work. Do chores."

"Did he...take advantage of you?"

Ossie thought for a moment. "He would go away for a long time. Leave the cabin. Said he was going for supplies. And he had a room in the back that he kept locked all the time. Sometimes I heard weird noises when he was back there."

"Human noises?"

"Maybe. Sometimes."

"Did you ask him about it?"

"Yeah. He said I heard the radio."

"But you haven't answered my question about—"

"You know, when it's all you've ever known, you just get used to everything. It might seem weird to someone else, but when it's what you do, what you always do, day after day for years, it just seems normal."

"That doesn't mean it is normal," Maria said, leaning toward Ossie a bit.

"It's over now. And there's some stuff I'd rather not talk about. You know what I mean?"

His jaw clenched tightly together. Yes, he certainly did understand what the boy meant. He understood all too well.

CHAPTER SEVEN

DAN DECIDED IT WAS TIME FOR A SHORT BREAK. MARJORIE brought in lemonade and they all stretched their legs a bit. Ossie showed Maria how to play Fortnite.

He took advantage of the break to speak to Marjorie. "I'm guessing you've seen all kinds of kids come through here."

She nodded. Blonde. Braids. Late 40s, early 50s. Gap between her front teeth. "You would be right about that."

"Including kids who've been abused."

"Sadly true."

"What do you think about Ossie?"

"Do you mean, do I think he was abused, out in that remote cabin he told the police about?"

"That's what I'm wondering. He doesn't seem to have much to say about this Joe, even though Joe was the only person he saw for years."

"Ossie doesn't display the classic signs of abuse, the prevaricating and hiding. The secretiveness. The fear of being alone. But I do sense there's something he's not telling anyone. Of course, that's not uncommon with kids placed in foster homes. They all think they've done something wrong, even if they haven't. They think they're being punished. They've learned to believe they're inferior, don't deserve better than they've gotten. And Ossie is older than most of the kids that come through here. Legally speaking, assuming he is Ossie Coleman, he's eighteen."

"Does that make him more likely to recover? Or just more damaged?"

Marjorie shook her head slowly. "I don't know."

Ossie and Maria finished their Fortnite grand combat. Ossie explained that he had only learned the game a few days ago. Maria hadn't played before at all, but she proved frighteningly talented at it. All that Fitbitting must improve the hand-to-eye coordination, Dan reasoned.

He noticed that Ossie seemed a bit more at ease. Maybe he was getting used to them. "How did you get away from Joe?"

Ossie shook his head. He looked as if he were trying to recall, trying to haul a memory out of deep storage, but it wasn't coming. "I don't remember. I think we had...some kind of fight."

"Like...a physical fight?"

"Yeah. I think he hit me—pretty hard." He pointed to the left side of his head. "That's how I got this." A serious head wound. "My clothes were covered with dried blood. Enough to cause a girl to scream when I ran up to their car."

"The police say they found you at a downtown crossing."

"Yeah. I saw a group of people. I ran up to them and told them who I was."

"You said, 'Hello, I'm Ossie Coleman.'"

"Actually, my first words were, 'Can you give me a ride home?'"

"And by home you meant—"

"The cabin. I didn't know anyplace else. Then I told them my name. The man's eyes bugged out. I guess he remembered when I disappeared, way back when. He called the cops."

"After you told the police who you were, they tried to

confirm your identity." But they were unsuccessful. And they still hadn't been able to confirm that he was or wasn't who he claimed to be. They hadn't found the cabin in the woods, either. The problem was, they had no location, not even a rough geographical area, which made searching almost impossible. "So they contacted the Coleman relatives. Your grandfather. Your uncles."

"Yeah." A grin broke out on his face. "I never knew I had relatives. I never thought I had anybody."

"Your grandfather has a ton of money," Maria said, with her usual bluntness.

The smile faded from Ossie's face. "Yeah."

"That doesn't make you happy?"

"Seems like that makes everything more complicated. If there was no money, no one would care if I was really Ossie. But since there is, they're suing me."

That summed it up accurately enough. "They want to be sure, that's all. It's not impossible that...an imposter could come along and pose as you to get the inheritance. It's been tried before."

"Yeah. I get that. It sucks. But I don't need a lot of money. Just enough to do what I want to do."

He cocked an eyebrow. "And what is it you want to do?"

Ossie looked embarrassed. "Aw...you'll think it's stupid."

"I won't."

"You'll tell me I'm just dreaming."

"Every great career starts with a dream."

"Well...if I had my druthers...if I could do anything I wanted —I'd be an astronaut."

Hadn't seen that coming.

Ossie leaned forward, excited. "You know, they're training new people right now, out at Cape Canaveral. Not far from here. The president says we're going back to the moon and then Mars. Man, I'd give anything to be part of that. Sailing through the stars. Bein' a hero. Someone people admired. Wouldn't that be awesome?"

He didn't answer for several moments, because he knew if he did his voice would betray his feelings. "If that's what you want, then that's what you should go for. Never let other people crush your dreams."

"But for that, you have to go to college. You have to get trained."

"You're going to need some money."

"Maybe a little, yeah."

"Did you tell your grandfather about your dreams?"

"No. I don't think he's made up his mind about me yet."

"He's afraid he'll get his heart broken," Maria surmised.

"I'd never want to do that." Ossie paused, his eyes turning downward. "When I found out I had family, I was thrilled, you know? I thought they'd be just as excited as I was. I was wrong."

"I'm…sorry."

"That's why I want you to handle this case for me. I don't care about the money. Just give me enough to go to school— they can keep the rest. But I want them to know I'm part of their family. I like them and I want them to like me. You know what I mean?"

"I sure do," he replied quietly.

"I guess, growing up with just Joe, I didn't know what I was missing. But now I do. I want to belong."

He bit down on his lower lip. "Everyone should have family." He pushed to his feet. "Let me start investigating this, Ossie."

"So you'll represent me?"

"Rest assured, Ossie. We will do everything we possibly can for you." He paused. "I know how important family is. I'm not going to let anyone take yours away."

CHAPTER EIGHT

Detective Major Jake Kakazu bent down to scrutinize the powder in the bathtub. It seemed so innocuous. But according to the CSI experts, that powder, as small and insignificant as it appeared, proved a murder had occurred. And somehow, he had to solve it—even though he didn't have a corpse.

He'd been called in when the theater staff reported that Harrison Coleman had disappeared. Turned out, there was a reason for that.

"Medical examiner is on his way," his young fresh-faced sergeant said.

Kakazu nodded curtly. Enriquez—wasn't that the kid's name? He thought so, but why take a risk? The grunt would suffice. He wasn't a gruff person by nature, but sometimes you had to fulfill people's expectations, mostly formed by years of watching bad television programs. "And the rest of forensics?"

"All *en route*. Hair and fiber. Videographers. Do you think the murder happened here?"

He knew why the lieutenant asked. There was no sign of a struggle in the office. No sign of forced entry, no overturned tables or chairs.

This crime scene had been an unending source of confusion since they arrived. Kakazu knew Harrison Coleman, barely, not so much because of his work as an impresario as because he was wrapped up in this business with the missing kid who suddenly appeared a few days ago. Coleman was one of the relatives.

The door to Coleman's private bathroom was open, but there were no signs of a confrontation. He spoke briefly to others who worked there, but so far, no one had seen or heard anything suspicious. Coleman hadn't been spotted since shortly before last night's performance. That in itself was unusual— Coleman had a habit of thanking the crew and making sure the power was turned off every night after the show. He was usually the last to leave, but no one thought anything of it when he didn't appear. Just assumed he had other things to do. An urgent appointment, maybe.

He did have an appointment. The final one. The one nobody can avoid forever.

Kakazu walked into the bathroom. Using a gloved hand, he pried open the swinging mirror to reveal the contents inside the medicine cabinet.

Filled to the brim. With enough drugs to stock a pharmacy. Except some of them didn't look like they came from a pharmacy.

"We're going to need photos in here too."

Enriquez nodded and made a note.

Some of the drugs were the normal OTC items you'd expect to find in anyone's bathroom—Aleve, Tylenol, Band-Aids, Q-Tips. A small bottle of Just For Men. Touched up his sideburns and eyebrows, perhaps? Several bottles of prescription medicine. And several bottles that were not marked.

That was what attracted his attention most.

He carefully removed one of the unmarked bottles and poured a pill into his hand. He couldn't be certain without testing, but he'd spent enough time on the street to recognize Molly when he saw it. Ecstasy. MDMA, for the sophisticated.

Beside the Ecstasy rested a small bottle containing a yellowish liquid. He opened the lid and took a whiff.

Again, impossible to be certain without chemical testing, but he thought it was morphine.

"Something else to bag and tag, sergeant. Every single bottle. After you've photographed it *in situ*."

The lieutenant did as instructed, using his phone to take the shots.

Was Coleman in pain? Or was he a functioning drug addict? There were probably thirty problems with that theory already evident to Kakazu's trained brain. Coleman held down a job. He functioned. That did not sound like someone on the brink of an OD. This cabinet suggested he was an experienced user. Maybe he needed a little something to get him through the day. Maybe he micro-dosed more than he should.

It was a puzzlement, to quote his favorite musical, one he noted had played here only a few months ago. He couldn't be sure—but he didn't believe it was any kind of OD. That didn't explain what had been done to the body. Someone else had been in this room last night, someone other than Coleman. Who?

And something about this room troubled him. Something he hadn't nailed down. What was it?

Why was the bathroom door open? All the other evidence suggested Coleman kept a meticulous office. Maybe he had gone in to get something. Or did he go in for a shower? Entirely possible, given the hour.

And what happens when you take a hot shower?

He went back to the medicine cabinet and stared at the mirror. Was he imagining it, or could you see something there? Just barely. The faintest traces of...letters.

On a sudden impulse, he reached into the shower stall and

turned on the hot water. Then he closed the bathroom door. And waited.

Steam filled the small bathroom. And a few minutes later, he had what he wanted. The mirror fogged up. And the letters emerged.

At the bottom of the mirror, someone had scrawled five letters.

OSSIE.

"Enriquez!"

The lieutenant rushed into the room. "Yes?"

"Call downtown. Get the DA on the line, then start lining up a judge. I want an arrest warrant within the hour."

Enriquez appeared amazed. "Yes, sir. I mean—really? That was fast. Who are we arresting?"

"The murderer."

"How do you know who did it?"

Kakazu removed his phone and took a photo of the mirror. "Because the victim told me."

CHAPTER NINE

Dan didn't know what to think of Judge Fernandez. He had no prior experience with the elderly jurist. He was usually on the criminal side of the courthouse, not here in the civil division. To him, civil suits were mostly businesspeople arguing over piles of money, delaying payment or welshing on agreements. Didn't interest him. But this case was different. A big pile of money was involved, to be sure. But Ossie had much more than that at stake.

Judge Fernandez was of mixed descent—part Hispanic, part Hawaiian. How did he ever end up on the Florida bench? He was said to be on the conservative side, pro-business, not the person you wanted to approach for a handout. He had no idea how that would play out in this case—the normal dichotomy of liberals and conservatives didn't have much relevance. If no one found any forensic evidence, it would simply be a matter of whether people believed Ossie's story. He knew he had to do more than convince the court Ossie was the real deal. He had to make the jury *want* to rule in his favor, to feel they were doing the right thing by helping a young kid who deserved it and would do good by it.

He told Ossie to stay home. All they would cover today were preliminary and administrative matters, and courts typically preferred that the lawyers handle those without clients hanging around. When clients were present, everything took longer because lawyers tended to put on shows to impress the people paying their bill. Better to save Ossie for later. Let Maria buy some decent clothes for him. Let Jimmy spread some positive gossip. What people said about first impressions was true—you only get one. They would make it as good as they possibly could.

The plaintiffs' team was represented by two lawyers from Dan's former firm, Friedman & Collins. He knew them well enough to call them by name, but he'd never spent any time with them. Linda Caldwell and Richard Drake, both senior partners. That meant the Coleman family was spending major moolah on this litigation.

He spotted people he believed to be members of the family in the gallery. They didn't sit at counsel table, but they were present. The oldest man was confined to a wheelchair. That had to be Zachary Coleman, the man who made the millions. He looked weak, feeble, unhappy. The oxygen tank under his chair reminded one and all that he was dying of COPD. On the bench nearby were two adult men with a middle-aged woman who seemed to chatter nonstop. She was probably married to one of the men, but she seemed to address both equally so he couldn't be sure which. His impression was that she wasn't there so much because the lawyers wanted her as because she refused to stay away.

He decided to plant some seeds and see if he got a reaction. He approached Linda Caldwell, the friendlier of the two opposing lawyers.

"Hey, Linda. Long time no see." Scarf tie. Jade-colored pendant. Three rings on three fingers of her left hand.

"I'm surprised to see you, Pike. Are you still practicing?"

He tried not to roll his eyes. "Yes, there is life after Friedman & Collins."

"Making ends meet?"

"Making twice what I did at your factory." Not quite true, but it sounded good. "You should consider going out on your own."

"Leave the most prestigious firm in the city? No thanks. It's all downhill from here."

"Might come a time when you want to be your own boss."

Drake inserted himself in the conversation. "Except that's not what you did, is it, Pike? Word on the street is that you're a hired gun for some weird disembodied voice—and you don't even know who he is."

"I know the cases he brings me are worthwhile. That's all that matters."

Drake smirked. "Fighting for truth, justice, and the American way, are you?" He lowered his voice. "Because this case looks like a bunch of relatives squabbling over the patriarch's portfolio."

"This case is about my client establishing his identity. To him, it has little to do with money and everything to do with family."

"Oh, I'm sure," Drake said, grinning from ear to ear. "It's just the principle of the thing."

"Yes, actually. That's exactly right."

"Whatever. Your guy is a desperate grifter who thought he'd take a shot at a fortune. Like that guy who claimed Howard Hughes left him a bundle because he gave him a lift one night."

"My client was abducted as a child. Held captive for years."

"And then magically appeared in time to get in the will before the old man clocked out? Please. Total con man. Did you get the DNA report, Pike?"

He tugged a file out of his backpack. "Yeah. Compares

Ossie's DNA to the rest of the Coleman clan. They say Ossie could be a member of the family."

"The operative word being 'could,'" Caldwell replied. "The expert couldn't eliminate the possibility, but the commonalities aren't sufficient to prove unquestionably that he sprang from the Coleman bloodline."

"We'll have to rely on something other than DNA."

"Is there anything else?"

"Yeah. Good lawyering."

"You know..." Drake lowered his voice. "This is all very preliminary, but I have been authorized to offer your guy a little...settlement package."

"How little?"

"Ten thousand bucks."

He tried not to laugh. "That's not a settlement offer. That's go-away money."

"Frankly, that's all you're entitled to. You don't have much of a case."

He smiled and offered a little salute. "We'll see. My partners are gathering evidence as we speak. Let me know if you ever have a real settlement offer. If you wait too long—it will no longer be an option."

That sounded sufficiently ominous, even though he hadn't a clue what it meant. This conversation was going nowhere, so he grabbed the opportunity to get away from these smug losers. Had he been like that, back in the day? Thank God he got thrown out of that firm. That wasn't who he was at all.

Was he?

Or is that who he was then, but now—?

The bailiff entered the room and brought the court to order. A few moments later, Judge Fernandez took his seat at the bench. He pushed on a pair of reading glasses, stared at a stack of papers, then called the case. Hunched slightly. Almost completely bald. Liver spots on his hands.

"I note that both parties are represented by counsel. Are there any motions or discovery issues we should take up at this time?"

Drake took it upon himself to answer. "No, your honor. We'll be sending the normal motions, but we're ready to proceed when the court is ready. We'd be good to go to trial today."

The corner of the judge's mouth turned up slightly. "Nice bravado. But I think we'll give the parties time to do a little discovery first. My docket is relatively open though. Would anyone object to this case being set down four months from now?"

Four months? For a civil case, that was the equivalent of being tried tomorrow morning. Was there a reason the court was fast-tracking this? The publicity? Or was someone pushing his buttons, encouraging him to resolve this fast. Like before Grandpa kicks off?

He made a mental note to ask Garrett to investigate whether Judge Fernandez had any ties to the family.

"I'll have my clerk issue the usual deadlines," the judge continued. "But I see no reason why we can't handle this expeditiously. I assume that's in everyone's best interest. Ossie Coleman has been a source of controversy for too long. Let's see if we can give the family some peace."

He didn't know what to make of that completely unnecessary speech. He didn't like it, though.

After the schedule was agreed upon, the clerk issued a form and all parties signed it. He would've liked to speak to the family members in the gallery, but he knew their lawyers wouldn't approve. Jimmy was setting up interviews. He'd wait until it could be done in the court-approved manner.

He was surprised to find Jazlyn waiting outside the courtroom doors. Her lips were pursed and she looked tense.

"I assume this is not about the birthday party."

"No. Though Esperanza loved your gift. Where do you get all this Hello Kitty stuff?"

"Japan."

"Of course you do. Look, this is really none of my business, but an arrest warrant just came through the office and it concerns you."

"DA Belasco has finally decided to lock me up for beating his lawyers in court too often?"

She gave him a look he chose not to describe. "No, it's about this Ossie Coleman business."

"Why would the DA be involved? This is a civil case."

"It was. I mean, it still is, but it's about to be criminal, too. One of that kid's uncles has been murdered."

He felt a hollowness inside his chest. "You're kidding."

"Sorry, no."

"Does the family know?"

"I doubt it. This just broke."

She must be right. They wouldn't be sitting around in the courtroom if they knew a family member had been murdered. "As if this case couldn't get any weirder. Who did it?"

"That's the thing. The police think your client did it. Ossie— or as they say, the man-who-would-be-Ossie. Some officers have already left to pick him up."

"That makes no sense. Why would Ossie want to kill his uncle?"

"Come on, Dan. The only question is why he didn't take out the whole family."

"Motive is not proof of guilt, and that estate has more than enough money to go around. Why do they think it was Ossie?"

Jazlyn tightened her lips. "Apparently, just before he died, the victim ID'd Ossie as his killer. In writing."

CHAPTER TEN

OSSIE HEARD THE SIRENS WELL BEFORE HE SAW THE COP CARS ON the street.

Why? He hadn't done anything. His roommate had a drug problem, but that wouldn't cause a commotion like this. All the other kids in this home were completely non-dangerous. He couldn't imagine them trespassing across an old man's lawn—and he doubted those sirens were about trespassing.

His cell phone buzzed. He pulled it out.

It was that lawyer. He felt an icy chill in his chest. "Yeah?"

"Ossie? Dan. I don't have time to explain, but the police are coming to arrest you."

"Why?"

"I'm on my way, but they'll get to you before I do, so listen up. Do not resist. And do not say a word. No matter what. They will try to provoke you. They will try to get you to say ill-advised things. You ignore them and keep your lips shut tight. I'll do the talking when I get there."

"What's the charge?"

Short pause. "Murder."

"What the hell?"

"It's Harrison, your uncle."

His voice flatlined. "Harrison? *Damn.*"

"That's an example of exactly why you should keep your mouth shut."

"They'll let me hang before they'll let me have a piece of their money." Ossie pulled back the curtain. One cop car was parked outside, blocking the driveway. Another was parked across the street. Two uniformed officers were crossing the lawn.

They had guns.

"Gotta go."

"Ossie!"

He shoved the phone into his pocket. Downstairs, he heard the doorbell ring. He knew Marjorie would let them in.

He listened carefully. Sounded like she was asking for a warrant, but of course they had one. They would be up here in seconds. He had to time this just right.

As soon as he heard the police enter the house, he shoved open his bedroom window and crawled out onto the roof. The angle was sharp. He had to be careful—and be quiet. He didn't want anyone to know he'd skipped out until he was far far away.

Fortunately, it was just a two-story house. The eave of the roof was maybe fourteen feet off the ground. If he swung wide he could avoid the hedges. He got down on his knees and slowly lowered himself off the edge.

A cop appeared in his bedroom window. "Hey, kid! Stop right there!"

He swung his feet out and let go.

He fell hard and didn't quite miss the hedge. His ankle twisted on the rock wall separating the hedge from the lawn. It hurt. He fell on his butt, rolling a bit to avoid the pain. He rolled too far—his head smashed against the trunk of the front-yard elm.

"*Ow!*" He shouted before he thought about it, before he could stop himself. Damn it all, this escape was not going well. He scrambled to his feet, ignored the soreness, and hobbled away as quickly as he could manage.

"Kid, I'm ordering you to stop!"

He kept running.

"You are under arrest. Any attempt to flee will constitute resisting arrest!"

Keep moving, he told himself. You've got a big lead. You can make it.

Across the street, he knew the mismatched fences between two yards left a narrow alley. He could cut through that to get to Glenwood. Once there he could hop a fence—if he could hop a fence—and cross into the Wilcox strip mall. Then he had his choice of shops to disappear into. If kept a low profile, he could wait them out. As soon as the heat was off, he'd figure out what to do next.

What could he possibly do next?

He didn't know, but this was not the time to dwell on it.

Keep moving!

He made it to Glenwood, but he could hear footsteps close behind him. Given the circumstances, he had to assume his pursuers moved faster than he did. He knew better than to look back to check. He couldn't afford to lose time.

He saw the fence and launched himself toward it. He pushed himself upward and grabbed the top of the fence—

He felt a strong pair of hands clutch him around the waist. He tightened his grip but wasn't strong enough to resist. The cop pulled him downward. They both fell onto the grass in a tumble.

Ossie tried to scramble to his feet, but the cop grabbed his foot, holding him back. He twisted and shook but he couldn't get free.

"You're only making this hard on yourself," the cop grunted through clenched teeth.

"I won't let you put me in another cage." He tried to yank his foot loose, but he couldn't do it. Worse, he heard another cop approaching in the distance.

If he was going to do anything, it had to be now.

He pretended to lose balance and fall. Once he was close enough, he grabbed the cop's hand—and bit it.

The cop screamed. His grip loosened just long enough for Ossie to escape. He turned back to the fence—

And the second officer threw him to the ground.

The second cop stood over him, sweating, pinning one arm behind his back. He held a taser pointed downward like a gun.

"You ever been tased, boy? You wanna see what it feels like?"

"Let go of me!"

"You got a hell of a nerve, boy. That nice lady back there trusted you."

"I didn't do anything to her."

His partner snapped a cuff over Ossie's right wrist. Then he pulled the other arm back and cuffed both hands together.

"Lying murdering black trash." He looked at his partner. "Call it in. Suspect apprehended while fleeing arrest."

"You got it." His partner pulled his radio off his shoulder. "We have the suspect. Ossie Cole—"

"Stop."

He looked at his partner. "Problem?"

"Did you read the warrant?"

"Well...no."

"Don't call him by that name."

"Then—what?"

The cop grabbed Ossie by the back of the neck and hauled him to his feet. "Call him John Doe. We don't know who the hell this little thug is."

CHAPTER ELEVEN

DAN RACED INTO THE LOBBY OUTSIDE THE HOLDING CELLS. HE knew Ossie had been arrested and there'd been some kind of altercation. He wanted to get in the middle of it before something worse happened.

He'd been waiting in his car for almost an hour while they completed processing. Jazlyn told him the boy had attempted to escape arrest. Why would Ossie do that? Had the kid not understood his instructions? Where did he think he could go? He just hoped the boy remembered to keep his mouth shut.

What had Mr. K gotten him into this time? He barely knew this kid. He had a hard time believing the boy was a murderer. But if he'd learned anything during his years of practice, it was that people, even good people, could be pushed to actions they would not normally consider. And this kid had been through the worst series of circumstances imaginable.

How would Mr. K feel if the civil case mutated into a murder case? Or did K predict this all along? Did that explain why he asked Dan to get involved in a family dispute over money?

He approached the front desk. During a prior case, Jimmy

had introduced him to Frank, the elderly man who decided who got in and how quickly it happened.

Frank gave him a sad, almost patronizing expression. "You rep the killer kid? Of course you do."

"Innocent until proven guilty."

Frank shook his head. "I saw the cops that brought him in. They looked frazzled. And angry."

"Well, I'm sorry that—"

"Did you know the kid bit one of them?"

"He—what?"

"Like a feral child, that's what Ferguson said."

It seemed there was much more he needed to learn about his client. "Look, can you get me in to see him?"

Frank pushed a few keys on his computer. "Good timing. He's been booked, but they haven't taken him downstairs yet. I'll have them bring him to the holding room."

"How about I just go to his cell?"

Frank laughed softly. "No way. This kid bites."

Dan sat on the other side of the Plexiglas panel, waiting. It was always like this. They should install those little mini-kiosks you saw in restaurants that let you play games while you waited eternally for the guards to bring in your client. He suspected they let him sit around longer than was necessary. He couldn't prove it, but he had a suspicion not all jailhouse personnel thought the world of defense lawyers.

A few moments later, they brought Ossie in. He wore the standard-issue orange coveralls and flip-flops. His face was scratched across the forehead, and one of his eyes was swollen. He appeared to be favoring his right leg.

He picked up the phone receiver and started right in. "Did they hurt you, Ossie?"

"Of course."

"Was it necessary?"

"No."

"Did you hit them?"

Ossie hesitated. "No."

"Did you bite them?"

He tossed his head to one side. "Maybe."

"It's a yes-no question."

"He wouldn't let me go."

"Because he was there to arrest you. What happened to your forehead?"

"I scraped it when I jumped off the edge of the roof."

He pressed his fingers against his temples. "Is that when you hurt your ankle?"

"Yup."

"And the shiner?"

"Cop punched me."

"Why?"

"Because he doesn't like me."

"Why?"

"Because I'm black."

"And...?"

"And escaping. But escaping doesn't explain why he kept calling me 'boy.' Or 'murdering black trash.' And it doesn't explain why he punched me. After I was cuffed."

Dan fell back into the eggshell chair. Sadly, he wasn't surprised. Police racism was reported so often these days it was almost a cliché, in a pathetic way. He couldn't expect St. Pete to be immune from a disease infecting the entire nation.

He opened his backpack and pulled out a legal pad. There would be no kitesurfing or cooking today.

This case just got about a thousand times more complicated.

CHAPTER TWELVE

DAN LEANED CLOSE TO THE PLEXIGLAS DIVIDER. "TELL ME WHAT happened, Ossie. And don't leave anything out. Even if you think it's of no importance. I'll decide what's important."

"There's nothing to tell. Cops showed up at my foster home to arrest me. I got scared and ran. Who wouldn't?"

"That's all it was? You panicked?"

"For years I was trapped in that cabin with Joe. I finally get free and someone wants to lock me up again? Seriously?"

"You freaked."

"Exactly. If that means what I think it means."

He made a note. This kid didn't go to school with everyone else. He apparently had access to lots of books, but he didn't watch television. Some slang might be foreign to him. "Did you kill your uncle?"

"Of course not."

"Look at me this time when you answer the question. Did you kill your uncle?" He had years of experience evaluating witnesses, and had trained in the science of micro-expressions and how to read them. His accuracy rate for reading out liars was excellent.

"No. I did not kill him. Why would I?"

"Look at me when you say that."

"I did not kill my uncle. I barely know him."

Slight twitch behind the right eye. Instead of averting his eyes, he forced eye contact to an unnatural degree.

"He's your uncle. Assuming you are Ossie Coleman."

"Oh great. Now you don't believe I am who I am."

"The police doubt it. They booked you as John Doe."

"They're trying to screw me out of my inheritance. This whole thing is about screwing me out of my inheritance."

A distinct possibility. But the fact that the kid said it didn't make it true. "Why would someone else kill Harrison?"

"Uh, because there's about a billion dollars at stake?"

"Plenty for everyone." When Ossie finally broke his deadlock eye contact, his eyes went up and to the right, which neurologists would say was a sign that he was creating. Inventing.

Ossie seemed earnest, and most of his twitches could be attributed to the stress of being tackled by cops and thrown in jail. No one would be at their best after an experience like that.

Or he could be a lying murderer....

"There was no logical reason for you to run. You have an attorney. You knew I'd represent you."

"Let's see how logical you are when the Gestapo knocks on your door."

"That's no reason—"

"Maybe not to your lily-white skin, but believe me, when someone my shade sees the cops coming, you know your life is in danger."

"You're making a gross—"

"I talk to people, back at the house. I read. I know what's going on in this world today. How many black kids have been killed by cops?"

He fell silent. He didn't have a total at the tip of his tongue—

but he knew it was significant. "Sometimes people put themselves in dangerous situations,"

"Yeah, and sometimes it's an innocent man in his backyard with a cellphone."

He wouldn't bother arguing. Some cops did behave differently when they encountered people of color. "Are you saying that you've been targeted because of your race? Because if I may remind you, everyone in your family is of the same race."

"I don't know what motivates these cops. I know they're bigots, some of them. And I know the only thing they hate more than a black kid is a rich black kid."

Couldn't deny that one, either. "Look, I know the detective in charge, Jake Kakazu, who by the way is mixed-race Asian, educated at Oxford. He didn't come to your house because you're black. He came because he found evidence linking you to the murder. Including, apparently, your name written on a bathroom mirror."

"I don't know anything about that. I didn't put it there."

"No one thinks you did. They think the victim did—to identify his murderer."

"How was Harrison killed?"

"They don't know. The body was completely dissolved in the bathtub."

"And they think I did that?"

It did seem unlikely. "Why would anyone want to frame you?"

"So the money goes to someone else."

"Any particular suspects?"

"I don't know. I don't think the old man trusts me. And what about Benny, the one married to that nightmare woman? Couldn't stand to look at me. What will this murder rap do to our lawsuit?"

"Nothing good. I'll file a motion, try to delay things, but that won't last forever. Judge Fernandez appears to be in a hurry. I can try to exclude evidence relating to the murder charge, but it's already all over town. The judge will know, the jury will know, and no one will let a suspected murderer inherit. We need to get this charge dismissed. Or we need to go to trial as quickly as possible."

"I need that money for college."

"Look, Ossie, beating the murder rap is about a trillion times more important than that money. If you're convicted, you could spend the rest of your life in jail. You could even get the death penalty. Let's save your ass first and worry about tuition later."

"I did not kill my uncle. Or anyone else."

"Were you there? At the theater?"

"No. Never been there in my life."

"Do you know what happened to Harrison?"

"No idea. I'm innocent." His voice rose "I did not kill this man. Someone is trying to set me up!"

Something about the tone of Ossie's voice made the short hairs on the back of his neck rise. He peered deeply into Ossie's eyes.

He was definitely picking up on something, but it was more than the usual micro-expressions, twitches and tics and eye movements. Of course he saw anger and fear, but that was to be expected—innocent or guilty.

He was picking up on...a sense of injustice.

Exactly what he had dedicated his life to preventing.

You could hide and dodge and play the best poker face in the world, but there was still one distinctive look he had learned to perceive with certainty—the look of the innocent man. This kid had the look of someone who has been falsely accused.

The same look his father had. Every time he went to the prison to visit. All those years. Till his dad died, still locked up for a crime he did not commit.

That look was seared into his soul. That look he would never forget.

"I will do everything I can for you, Ossie. But if I find out you lied to me, I'll be gone faster than a heartbeat. Understand?"

"Got it."

He hoped so. And he hoped he hadn't just made a horrible mistake.

CHAPTER THIRTEEN

D<small>AN SAW</small> S<small>ERGEANT</small> E<small>NRIQUEZ</small> <small>POSTED OUTSIDE THE DOOR TO</small> Harrison Coleman's office in the rear of the theater. A sure sign that clue collection was in progress.

He made an imaginary tip of the hat. "Morning, Paul."

Enriquez returned the nod. "Dan."

"Jake okayed me to go inside."

Enriquez held up a hand. "Not to me he didn't."

Could nothing be easy anymore? "Have I ever lied to you?"

Enriquez tilted his head. "I wouldn't exactly use the word 'lied.'"

"Then what?"

The cop pondered a moment. "Stacked the facts to your advantage?"

"That's my job description."

Enriquez almost smiled. "Which is why I can't let you in without—"

Kakazu appeared in the doorway. "It's fine, Paul." He winked. "I'll keep a close eye on the shyster."

Dan stepped forward. "I'm offended by your use of the word 'shyster,' Jake."

"Are you?"

"Yes. It's racist. Against lawyers. I prefer, 'pettifogger.'"

He bowed slightly. "As you wish."

The office buzzed with CSI personnel. He spotted videographers, fingerprint analysts, DNA scrapers. Two people on their hands and knees scrutinizing the carpet. Probably the hair and fiber team. All wore blue booties and matching blue gloves.

Kakazu handed him a pair of booties. He slid them over his black dress shoes. "Are these to protect the crime scene or my snazzy footwear?"

"The crime scene. I could care less about your overpriced shoes. You shouldn't even be in here."

"I appreciate you making an exception."

"I'd rather let you in now than hear you whine at trial that you were excluded from the crime scene so the police could plant evidence."

"I would never do that." Pause. "Unless it was true."

Kakazu escorted him to the center of the room. "I can assure you nothing untoward has occurred. This is completely open and shut. The victim scratched your boy's name in the foggy mirror."

"Or someone did."

"No one else was seen coming in or out."

"But for that matter, no one saw my client coming in or out."

"So far. We're still interviewing potential witnesses."

"The name on the mirror is Ossie. You arrested 'John Doe.'"

"Well, Coleman had to call the kid something."

"Or someone did. The lawsuit will determine whether he inherits in time. This murder was unnecessary."

"Greed makes the calmest of minds impatient."

"Are you quoting Seneca or some Oxford thing?"

"No. I just made that up."

Time to change the subject. "Isn't this theater doing a Shakespeare series?"

"Indeed. The goal is to perform all thirty-eight plays in six years. But I suppose the Bard of Avon isn't really your cup of—"

"Don't you mean thirty-seven?"

"Uh...what?"

"Surely you're aware that current scholarship suggests Shakespeare did not write *Henry VIII*. At least not most of it."

"I...uh..."

"Maybe they didn't cover that at Oxford. What was the play the night of the murder?"

"The Scottish play." He smiled happily. "It's considered bad luck amongst theater folk to say—"

"*Macbeth*. Yes, I know. But I'm not superstitious. Do you think the murder occurred toward the start of the play or the end?"

"Don't know. Why?"

"At the end, Birnam Wood moves to the castle and a huge battle ensues. Lots of noisy sword fighting, I imagine."

"I did see swords backstage..."

"Producing a tremendous racket. I noticed an orchestra pit out front. Did the play have music?"

"Yes."

"Overture?"

"Yes."

"Then that's at least two perfect times to commit a murder. No one would hear anything happening back in this office." He crouched beside the chess table not far from the desk. "Looks like Harrison had a game in progress."

"Yes. The question is, who was he playing. My forensic team only found the victim's prints on the pieces. Both white and black."

It looked like an endgame position. White had a rook and a pawn, in addition to the king. Black had only a rook. "He was playing with himself."

"Uh, excuse me?"

"It's a thing eggheads do. Particularly the ones without many friends. They play both sides of the table. This is going to end up either a white win or a draw, depending upon who plays next and how they play it."

"You can't assume just because there are no fingerprints—"

"You think his opponent played wearing gloves? This is the kind of perfectly balanced game you only get from two equal rank grandmasters—or a guy playing himself."

Kakazu looked annoyed. "I doubt it matters much to the murder. The clues—"

"Show me the mirror."

Kakazu waved him toward the bathroom. "We took lots of pictures while the message was fresh. All the climate controls in the world can't keep a smear on a mirror. We used a powder to set it as we found it, but even that won't last forever."

He could see the letters were fading, but they were still legible. They appeared to have been hastily scrawled—as if by someone in a hurry. Or someone dying. But they definitely spelled OSSIE.

"Look, Dan, I know your job is to find—or create—some kind of defense, but even without all the other evidence, this mirror is proof positive that your guy—"

"Was framed."

"I really wish you wouldn't interrupt—"

"I wasn't sure before, but I am now. All the other evidence is inconclusive. But this mirror makes it clear that the murder was a deliberate attempt to frame Ossie. To cheat him out of his inheritance."

"You think he was likely to inherit? Come on. Your boy's story was thin from the start. An heir to millions suddenly appears out of nowhere after fourteen years?"

"It happens. People escape. Resurface. Amanda Berry. Gina DeJesus. They were teenagers when Ariel Castro abducted them. They were kept in captivity for more than a decade before Berry escaped."

"That's a one-in-a-million."

"So is this one."

"You can't prove that."

"Yet." But he was convinced it was true. "Do you have a cause of death yet?"

Kakazu gave him a long look. "You're joking, right? The body was destroyed."

"I know the medical examiner well enough to know that won't stop him from investigating."

"It might slow him down a step or two."

"Can you give me any details on how the body was destroyed?"

"We're still investigating. But if you want the big picture—bio-cremation."

His lips parted. "That's a real thing?"

"It is. Lye mixed with water, basically. Will destroy a body in about sixteen hours."

"Then how do you know it was Harrison Coleman?"

"DNA traces. In the powder."

He winced. "I know I'll regret asking, but—how does this bio-cremation occur?"

"Not by accident, if that's what you're thinking. Dr. Zanzibar can give you more details, but basically, the killer would have to strip the body naked. Drag the naked body to the tub. Turn on the water, hot as it will go. Toss in several scoops of lye. Cover the tub with something secure—like a rubber sheet. Seal it firmly with duct tape or something similar. Then let science work its magic."

"In sixteen hours?"

"Or less. The bio-cremation would break down skin, tissue, muscle—even the poor man's teeth. At the cellular level. What little is left behind—in liquid form—you eliminate by draining the tub. Bone chunks would be so soft you could mash them into powder with the sole of a shoe. Nothing left but dust."

"Yet you could run DNA tests on that powder?"

"Ask the experts. They can tell you all about it. All I know is it wasn't easy."

He wiped his mouth. This was hideous. Whoever committed this murder seriously wanted to eliminate all traces. Why? Given the location, there was little doubt about who the murder victim was. What was the killer trying to mask?

And worse, what kind of monster would resort to something like this?

And what would he do to anyone who got in his way?

"Despite all this weirdness, you're determined to blame Ossie?"

"Well, given the state of the remains, I think we can rule out suicide."

Very funny. "Let me know when the doc comes up with a cause of death."

"I will. But what makes you think it isn't the obvious?"

"The...obvious."

"The lye. Eating away at his skin."

"I assumed...he was killed first. Then dragged to the tub—"

"And I hope you're right. But maybe not. Maybe he was restrained. Or drugged. And then destroyed. Lye eating away at his skin. Seeping into his internal organs. Cooking him by inches. While he was still alive."

CHAPTER FOURTEEN

DAN COULD HAVE USED HIS PHONE TO TEXT EVERYONE INTO THE kitchen. "Avengers Assemble" or something like that. But texts were easily ignored, even when he leaned in on the exclamation points and added emojis. Experience told him there was a far more effective means of luring his teammates out of their private offices.

"Do I smell food?" Jimmy asked. His cardigan was unbuttoned, which was his way of observing Casual Friday.

"Indeed you do." He lifted his sauté pan off the burner. "Homemade gnocchi with Pomodoro."

Jimmy's eyes widened. "Homemade? Like you made all the little pasta pillows?"

"I did."

"You put the crinkles on the ends?"

"I did."

"That must've taken forever."

"Nah. I made the pasta dough and kneaded it this morning around sunup."

Jimmy took a bite. "I am in heaven. What's in the sauce?"

"Champagne vinegar. Parmesan. Basil sprigs. And a few secret ingredients."

"You added vanilla extract."

"I would never. I scraped the seeds from vanilla beans. Huge difference. The rich complexity and flavor notes of a true vanilla bean become a one-note sweetness when distilled to an abstract."

Maria wandered into the kitchen. "I don't care how you made it. If it tastes as good as it smells, I'm in. Does this have meat in it, Dan?"

"I want you to eat it, not scorn it."

Garrett was the last down the stairs. "Suppertime?"

"Yes, Snoopy. Grab a plate, then let's gather in the living room. We need to talk about what this case has turned into. This may be our last chance to share a meal for a while. So let's make the most of it."

Jimmy covered his mostly full mouth and spoke. "If we're going to make the most of it..."

"Yes, Jimmy. There's dessert. Profiteroles and homemade vanilla toffee crunch ice cream."

Jimmy beamed. "Best law firm ever."

AFTER DAN BRIEFED THEM, GARRETT WAS THE FIRST TO BREAK the silence. "I think we should let Mr. K weigh in on this murder business. He might not like the latest development."

"Mr. K has always told us we can take cases on our own."

"When time permits. But something like this could bring down the whole firm."

"He's the one who brought Ossie to our attention. You think he'll want to abandon the kid now?"

Garrett twisted his neck. His conservative leanings—and his

former prosecutor status—were beginning to show. "I...just don't know."

"As it happens, I've already sent K a text. Hoping for an answer soon. But one way or the other, I'm taking this case."

Maria leaned forward. "You think Ossie's innocent."

"I do."

"You might be wrong," Garrett said.

"I'm not."

"No one is right all the time, Dan. Not even you."

"Granted. But I'm not wrong about this."

"I'm in," Jimmy said, plopping his plate down on the table. "I like the kid. I don't want to see him get railroaded."

Garrett's teeth ground together. "We don't know that he's being—"

"I know the cops are already circling the wagons," Jimmy said, "trying to put him away forever, because he's the obvious suspect. The easy suspect. Or maybe there's another reason we don't know yet. In any case, I don't like it."

"One thing is for certain," Dan said. "We don't know everything there is to know about what happened. We don't even know half what we need to know. We need to start investigating. Garrett—given your obvious reservations, can we count on you for this?"

Garrett drew up his shoulders. "I am a member of a team. If the team takes the case, I'll give it one hundred percent."

"That's what I wanted to hear. Jimmy, I know you're already snooping around—"

Jimmy cut him off. "Why is it you call Garrett's work 'investigating,' and my work 'snooping around?'"

He blinked. "I'm sorry. I know you're already delving into your social contacts—"

"Oh, much better."

"—and now you need to do it even more so. And we need to

talk to those relatives. When so much money is at stake—anything is possible."

"Dan," Maria said, "what about maybe getting a jury consultant?"

"You're the only jury consultant I need."

"Maybe not this time. You can read faces and Jimmy can check people out on social media, but I think there's going to be an onslaught of publicity about this case. We have to make sure no one slips into the jury box who has already decided Ossie is guilty. Or finds the facts so disturbing they vote to convict just to feel like they've done something."

"I still think you're better at it than some alleged jury expert."

"And I think I need help. For that matter—maybe we should run some mock trials. Get people in off the street. See how the facts play out."

"You know I hate all that crap. This has become a cottage industry for so-called experts taking money from defendants foolish and rich enough to pay them."

"We have a young boy's life on the line, Dan. Not to mention a billion dollars."

"Still—"

The doorbell rang.

He turned, annoyed. "Anyone expecting a client? A package?"

All three shook their heads.

"Whatever. I'll go." He opened the front door—

His lips parted wordlessly.

The woman on the other side of the door peered back at him. Tall. Strong. Obviously worked out regularly. Dressed all in black. Red hair in a bun. Asian dragon tattoo on her neck.

"Prudence Hancock."

She smiled. "So pleased you remember me, Mr. Pike. May I come in?"

"We're—in the middle of something."

"This won't take long."

"How can I say no to the Chairman of the Citizens for Responsible Democracy?" He opened the door and ushered her inside.

He didn't need psychic powers to know what was going through the minds of his teammates. He'd let the serpent into the garden. And they did not like it.

He'd met Prudence once before, though he'd seen her in the courtroom several times. She was Conrad Sweeney's top assistant, executing his orders with efficiency, effectiveness—and ruthlessness. Her organization was a charitable front Sweeney used to maintain his public facade.

Garrett rose. "What brings you to our office today, Ms. Hancock?"

"Can't you guess?" She strode across the room with the air of a dominatrix, then seated herself on the sofa beside Maria, who looked distinctly unpleased to have her so close. "I want a powwow. On a matter that concerns us both. You're representing the kid claiming to be Ossie Coleman on murder charges, right?"

Dan's eyes narrowed. "How can you know that? We haven't even entered our appearance yet."

"There's not much I don't know, Mr. Pike. And absolutely nothing my boss doesn't know."

He shouldn't let her get to him, but something about her steely cold manner seriously creeped him out. "Is your boss having me followed? Do you have a spy at the jailhouse?"

More frigid smiles. "That would be telling. And completely irrelevant."

"Okay, I'll bite. Why are you here?"

She spread her hands wide. Maria dodged to avoid making tactile contact. "I've come to offer you my assistance. My help, and Dr. Sweeney's help, of course."

"*Doctor* Sweeney?"

"He has recently received honorary doctorates from three universities."

"That he gave generous donations to," Jimmy grunted.

"Is there something wrong with contributing to higher education?"

No one commented.

"Did you hear the part about me offering to help? Dr. Sweeney is concerned about your client. He thinks your boy is being treated unfairly and wants to help."

Dan took a step closer. "He thinks Ossie is innocent?"

"My employer is not prepared to take a position on that at this time. He wants to wait until more evidence has been uncovered. But he does believe this business with the estate has become complicated. Perhaps dangerous."

"Sweeney knows the family, doesn't he? Especially the patriarch. Zachary Coleman."

"He's known the family for some time. And that is…part of his concern." She reached into her pocket—she did not carry a purse—and withdrew a checkbook. "We are prepared to make a sizeable contribution to your defense fund."

"What's in it for you?"

"Nothing. Can't you believe Dr. Sweeney wants to prevent injustice in his own town?"

"I can believe a huge egotist wants to be perceived as more important than he is."

"You're too cynical. My boss is a generous man."

"When he sees an advantage in generosity. What is it he wants in exchange for this contribution?"

"Nothing, really. He would just want to be informed about and involved in the defense."

"He wants to know our plans? Strategies? So he can undermine them? No thanks. We don't need your money."

"I can assure you there are no strings attached."

"There are always strings attached."

"Couldn't you use some financial aid? A case like this requires—"

"We have all the resources we need, thank you."

"Ah, yes. From the mysterious Mr. K. Is that why you're turning me down? Are you afraid Mr. K might not like it?"

"I *know* he wouldn't like it."

She made a tsking sound. "So sad. A grown man like you, completely dominated—and you don't even know who this K is."

"I know who he is. I just don't know his name. He withholds his identity from everyone to insure—"

"Not from everyone." She grinned.

"What?"

"No secrets from Dr. Sweeney."

"I think it's time for you to leave."

She slapped her knees and rose, peering at him almost nose-to-nose. "Maybe you and I could continue this conversation... somewhere more private."

Behind her, he could see Maria making a gagging face. "That will never happen."

"Never say never."

"Okay. Then how about I say, Go to hell."

She strode toward the door, shaking her head. "None of us knows what the future holds. If you change your mind, just whistle."

She let herself out.

Jimmy shivered. "Man, that woman gives me the heebie-jeebies."

"I know," Maria said. "I feel like I've been lap dancing with Cruella DeVille. What's her game, Dan?"

"No clue."

"It's not impossible that Sweeney genuinely wants to help," Garrett said. "He is a public figure and a major policy maker in this town. Maybe he wants to prevent an injustice. Just as you do, Dan."

"Yeah, maybe." Deep breath. "But no. Sweeney doesn't do anything unless there's something in it for Sweeney. I don't know what that is. But we need to. Because blind spots will doom us." He turned his head abruptly. "Maria? Hire your jury consultant."

Her eyes narrowed. "You're sure?"

He rubbed his hands together, as if trying to fight off a chill. "No stone unturned this time. No stone unturned."

CHAPTER FIFTEEN

In Dan's opinion, arraignments were one of those constitutional requirements that in this day and age were largely a ceremonial waste of time. The idea was that they prevented law enforcement from imprisoning people without bringing charges, but these days, if cops wanted someone out of circulation, they simply arrested them, charged them, and worried about making it stick later. The whole business of informing the defendant of the charges could be handled by a cell phone call. But since the Constitution mandated that they all gather in court, he planned to make the most of it.

He spotted Jazlyn inside the courtroom. "I had a hunch I'd be seeing you here."

"Psychic powers at work again?"

"Common sense. When a case gets a lot of attention, the DA brings in his best prosecutor."

"Best may not be good enough in this instance."

"What do you mean? Aren't you handling this case?"

"For now."

"Who else would do it?"

"That hasn't been decided yet. DA Belasco really wants to

win this one."

"He always says that."

"This time he means it. He's pulling out all the stops."

"Why?" He thought a moment. He knew the DA had his eye on the mayor's seat. "Is he getting campaign funds from Zachary Coleman?"

"I couldn't say. But I have seen the man in the office."

"That's all I need. Big money trying to influence the trial."

"Are you asking for bail?"

"It would be malpractice if I didn't. Will you oppose?"

"It would be malpractice if I didn't. This is a capital offense, Dan. And the details of the body mutilation have leaked to the press. I have to take a firm stand."

"Because you're still thinking about running for the DA's job."

She drew in her breath. "It's more than just thinking. I filed this morning."

His grin spread from ear to ear. "That's fantastic. I'm behind you one hundred percent. Anything you need, just let me know."

"Thank you. But given your rep..."

"I know. I'll stay out of the limelight."

"But still. Thanks."

"You'll be a fantastic DA. Just what this city needs."

Their eyes locked for a moment. They seemed to soften. "Dan—"

"I know Camila feels the same way. And her endorsement is one you can talk about in public."

The marshals brought Ossie into the courtroom. He looked tired. The circles around his eyes suggested he wasn't getting much sleep, which was common for people behind bars. Still it didn't wear on him as badly as some. Youth had its advantages.

"How are you holding up?"

Ossie fell into his chair. "Get me out of there."

"That's probably not going to happen. This is murder, and a

particularly nasty one."

"I didn't do it!"

"I know. But unfortunately, we have to prove that before they let you out."

The bailiff called the court into session, and Judge Smulders entered the courtroom. One button on his button-down shirt was loose. Hair mussed. Bugs Bunny tie. Fingernails needed clipping.

Smulders was reportedly thirty-five, but he looked about eighteen. His robe was ill-fitting, and that was remarkable, given that it was basically a drape. He tugged at his neck, then reached behind himself, as if surreptitiously adjusting his underwear.

The judge cleared his throat. "So...I guess we should do this arraignment thing?"

Jazlyn rose. "The grand jury has convened and we filed our indictment. The defense has received copies."

"That's correct," Dan confirmed. "Waive the reading. Not the rights."

Smulders fumbled with the papers before him. "That means we don't have to read all this stuff out loud to the defendant?"

Out the corner of his eye, he saw the judge's clerk—who he knew had worked here more than twenty years—roll her eyes. Her name was Bertha and he could only imagine how she handled a boss with so much less experience.

"Yes, your honor. That's correct."

"And..." Smulders shrugged. "Anything else we need to do?"

"I've filed a motion for bail, your honor. The defendant has no priors."

"As far as we know," Jazlyn cut in. "The defendant has been off the grid for the past fourteen years—assuming he's Ossie Coleman. No one knows what he did during that time. We're not even sure what his name is."

"His name is Ossie Coleman, and there's a pending civil case that will prove it."

"If I give you what you want..." Smulders' eyes turned downward, staring at the papers. "...this guy gets out of jail."

"Yes, your honor, that would be the point of a bail motion." Stay cool. Don't get snarky. "He can wear a monitoring device so his location can be ascertained at all times."

"Gee, I dunno..."

"Your honor," Jazlyn said, "though not completely unprecedented, I can tell you as someone who has been in the prosecutor's office for more than a decade that granting bail in a capital murder case is highly uncommon. And here we have a crime that is...grotesque in the extreme."

"You're assuming he's guilty. Your honor, please don't be influenced by speculation. My client has no record. He's living in a foster home. He will gladly submit to wearing a tracking device."

Jazlyn frowned. "So we'll know where he is the next time he decides to melt someone in a bathtub."

"So he will be highly unlikely to do anything remotely improper. Not that there's any proof he ever did. He's a victim who was abducted as a child and—"

"Stop. You're talking too fast. I can't follow it." Smulders' eyes were like balloons. He thought he detected beads of sweat running down the left side of the judge's face. "This is all so serious..."

"Your honor, I will personally vouch for my client's behavior."

"Which won't stop him from doing anything," Jazlyn rejoined.

Judge Smulders squirmed. "This is very hard. Do I have to make a decision?"

Technically no, the judge could delay ruling forever. But that wouldn't help Ossie. "My client has already been behind bars, subject to the cruelty of the system and the barbaric behavior of some of the inmates. He's extremely high profile—practically a public figure. Incarceration poses a threat. In the name of mercy and common decency, please grant our bail motion."

Smulders fumbled with his papers. His eyes darted to the left —toward Bertha, the court clerk seated below him. The older woman offered a tiny shake of the head. "I think I'm going to have to say no to this one."

Jazlyn allowed a small smile. "Thank you, your honor."

"Sorry about that, Mr. Pike. I owe you one."

That was something he'd never heard from a judge before. Of course, most judges didn't act as if they were still on training wheels, or let their nanny make their decisions. He texted Jimmy, asking him to dig up anything he could on this new judge. And his clerk.

But since the man apparently thought he owed him something... "Your honor, I'd like to ask for the earliest possible trial setting."

Smulders pressed a hand against his forehead. "Oh, man. Like you want to go to trial today? I'm totally not ready..." He glanced at his clerk. "Am I?"

"I'm not asking for today, your honor. But as soon as you can fit it in. As I mentioned, there's a concurrent civil trial that I can't get postponed. We need to get these criminal charges out of the way before that proceeds. And frankly, I'm concerned about the possibility of...outside influences tainting the judicial process."

Smulders looked tongue-tied. "You—You—" He took a deep breath. "You're not accusing...our pretty lady prosecutor of being a crook, are you?"

Jazlyn looked as if she were about to explode.

"No," he said hastily. "She's as clean as they come. And I'm hoping she'll soon be elected DA so she can give the office the clean sweep it needs."

Jazlyn arched an eyebrow. "May I consider that an official

endorsement? For the pretty lady prosecutor?"

The judge cleared his throat. "Does the prosecution object to this early setting?"

"As long as it's within reason, no."

"Okay, swell. I'll have my clerk set it down as soon as we can get our act together and throw a good trial. Probably need to call juries and all that stuff."

"Yes, probably so, your honor." Where did they find this guy? Gymboree?

The judge tugged at his collar. "Well then. If there's nothing else…"

They rose. His clerk followed behind him, still shaking her head. It was almost as if Bertha was embarrassed to be in the same courtroom with him.

But this Andy Hardy in a black robe would be making critical decisions affecting Ossie's future. Or his clerk would.

"Sorry about that," he told Ossie. "But it was almost inevitable. We'll get to trial soon."

"How soon?"

"Not as fast as you'd like. But we still have much investigating to do."

"I don't think the judge likes me."

"I don't think the judge likes making decisions. Which is sad, since that's like the whole description of what judges do."

"Any chance of getting a different judge?"

"Unless he commits gross malpractice or displays gross incompetence—no."

"Have you ever seen a judge removed from a case?"

"No."

"Does this mean we're sunk?"

He thought for a long moment before answering. "No. It just means we have to make this case as easy as possible for the judge. And the jury." He smiled. "I know you're innocent. Now we have to convince everyone else."

CHAPTER SIXTEEN

OUTSIDE THE COURTROOM, DAN SPOTTED AN ELDERLY MAN IN A wheelchair. He approached slowly, extending his hand. "Sir."

The elderly man raised a weak arm. Bolo tie. Patches of gray hair on a mostly bald head. Missed a button on his shirt. Blanket over knees. Tremble in his voice. "Mr. Pike, I'm Zachary Coleman. Hoped to catch you here. Could I have a word?"

"Of course. Do your attorneys know we're talking? I'm not supposed to interact with—"

"They know all about it. They didn't like it and frankly I don't care." He wheeled to the far end of the corridor where they might have a tiny bit of privacy.

"I'm sorry for your loss, Mr. Coleman. Losing a son—"

The elderly man waved a dismissive hand. "Not the first time I've had to deal with that. This family has been cursed, and it's probably my fault."

"I don't know what you—"

"I'm concerned about this boy you're representing."

"How so?"

"I want him to have the best possible defense."

"You don't think he's guilty?"

"I—" His head drooped. "I hope not. But I want to make sure he isn't railroaded. Cops don't like people who come in our color."

"I'm sure that's not true of all police officers."

"No." He made a grumbling sound. "But a hell of a lot of them. And probably the DA as well."

"Have you been in contact with DA Belasco?"

"Tried. Offered a campaign contribution. He turned me down. Can you believe it? Turned me down flat."

No, actually, he couldn't believe it. A candidate turning down money? "You have no need to worry, sir. My team is one hundred percent behind Ossie, and we will do everything imaginable to make sure he isn't railroaded. I don't believe he committed this grisly murder. I don't think he has that kind of cruelty in him."

"That's good to know." Coleman's voice cracked.

"Forgive me for saying so, sir, but I had the impression your family had...mixed feelings about Ossie. The way he suddenly appeared and staked a claim to the family fortune."

He wasn't sure if Coleman was nodding his head trembling. "We had our doubts, sure. The way it happened, appearing out of nowhere. Damned irregular. But...I always loved Ossie. Broke my heart when he disappeared. This kid doesn't look exactly the way I remember my grandson, but—I'm old and what the hell do I know? If this is Ossie, come back to us by some miracle, I want him to take his proper place in the family."

His eyes watered as he spoke. He seemed genuinely moved. Dan supposed this could all be an act. This man could be a master thespian—but he doubted it.

"Does the rest of your family share your feelings?"

He laughed bitterly. "No."

"Do you have any insights about what happened?"

"You mean who killed Harrison? No idea."

"Any enemies?"

"Harrison? I doubt it. Mild-mannered to a fault. A little too nice, if you take my meaning. Preferred to read plays and hang out with swishy theater folk. Didn't want to be involved in the family business. He removed himself from all positions of influence."

"There's a lot of money at stake here."

"Don't I know that. I made every penny of it. By working like the devil every single day of my life." He fussed with his hands, tugged at his blanket. "I never believed Ossie was dead. Even when the cops told me he must be. I never believed it."

"You had faith. That's a good thing."

"That is what matters most." Zachary inhaled deeply. His breath seemed forced, labored. "You know I loved Ossie's daddy. Carl. My oldest son. Didn't approve of his marriage but —how could I? No one was good enough for my boy. Cheap uneducated thing from the poor part of town, no family, no sense—but that's all water under the bridge now. Carl died and she died and Ossie disappeared and my whole world shattered. Just burst apart like a big piñata. I went from king of the world to a broken man."

"You have a keenly successful business."

"Yeah. And you know what that's worth? Not a damn thing. All this money, and what did it get me? Did it heal the family? No. We split apart. They all hate me. They're just sitting around hoping I'll die so they can get their hands on my money."

"I'm sure that isn't true." Against all odds, Dan felt himself actually feeling sorry for the man.

"It is. And you know what? I deserve every bit of it."

"You're being too hard on yourself. If nothing else, you've ensured no one in your family will ever have to worry about paying the bills, and that's no small thing."

"Money. That's where losers always go, because they have nothing of actual value to brag about. It's true, I amassed a fortune. Not for me. I never spent much. Didn't need much.

Preferred to invest in the future. Watch the money grow. I did all this for them, not me."

"I'm sure they understand that."

He laughed, so abruptly it was startling. "They understand nothing. Why should they? They'll get what they want soon enough. I'm sick, Mr. Pike. Very sick. Payback for all those cigarettes I inhaled when I was younger. I'll be gone, and they'll be rich. And I—" His voice choked. "I don't want my legacy to be... wrong. I don't want anyone cheated."

"I'll make sure Ossie is treated fairly."

"Just make sure he isn't locked away for a crime he didn't commit. He seems like he has a decent heart, whether he's Ossie or not." He reached out and grabbed Dan's hand. "Don't let the bastards lock him away. Or execute him. We've had enough pain in this family. We don't need any more."

CHAPTER SEVENTEEN

CONRAD SWEENEY SAT BEHIND HIS LARGE ANTIQUE MAHOGANY desk, hands folded calmly before him. His executive officer would arrive soon. She had many fine qualities—strength, determination, fierce loyalty. But the greatest of them might be punctuality.

Prudence Hancock strode into the office and glanced at the painting hanging on the wall behind him, illuminated by a spot lamp. "New Van Gogh?"

He raised a finger to his lips.

"Sorry. Acquired through the usual channels?"

He nodded, smiling slightly.

"Does it seem a pity that so few people have the opportunity to admire the vast array of art you've acquired? Seriously, this is the best collection of Impressionist and Post-Impressionist paintings in the United States. MOMA looks thin and spotty compared to what you have."

"When the time comes," he replied placidly, "when the trails are cold and my museum is built, I will share my beauties with the public. But that will come later. Much later. When the trivial questions of provenance are far less problematic."

"Because you're constantly covering and re-covering your tracks."

"Indeed. Do you have a report on the Harrison Coleman matter?"

She did not sit, though there were two chairs opposite his desk. Instead, she stood at his side, hands behind her back, like a dutiful lieutenant in the presence of a commanding officer. "As you predicted, Pike turned us down."

"Pious fool."

"May I ask what the point was? You knew he would refuse."

"One goal was to tell Pike he's on my radar. You see, he thinks he's winning. With the Valdéz woman. With the mayor, who he saved first and bedded second. He can't see the big picture. Yet. I wanted him to know that the chess game is still in progress. And I will be watching every move he makes."

"He probably already knew that."

"Perhaps. But you know, Prudence—no one is completely predictable. Especially a loose cannon like Pike. There was always a remote possibility he would agree to our proposition and accept our assistance."

"And then?"

"Then he would work for me. But it will work out, in the end. You'll see. The bounty of the mysterious Mr. K has made Pike somewhat immune to the usual inducements. If money is not the best persuader...then we'll go in a different direction."

"You have enough dirt to lock Pike away. Revoke his license. Put him completely out of commission."

"Perhaps. But he and his team are not amateurs. Mr. K would spare no expense to defend Pike. No, better to keep weaving the web and wait for the proper moment."

"You heard about the comments Pike made at the court-house today? Practically accused the DA of being corrupt. That's not going to help Belasco's mayoral run."

"Yes, my little spies reported it almost immediately. And there were reporters in that room."

"I think you need to be...more aggressive with Pike."

"And you'd like to be in charge of that, wouldn't you?" He smiled. "I will. When the time is right."

"Belasco has been a good friend to you. And he's likely to be the next mayor, if Pérez goes for the Senate seat."

"And she will."

"Because you're filling her campaign coffers. In secret. Through your holding companies."

"How well you know me."

"And once she's out of the mayor's office?"

"Then we destroy her."

"Jazlyn Prentice will go after the DA spot."

"I have no problem with her, beyond her inexplicable fondness for a certain defense lawyer. I predict she'll shake that off in time. And if not...well, we can take her out of office as easily as we put her predecessor in."

Prudence removed a manila envelope from her briefcase. She pulled several black and white photos out of it. "I have a man surveilling Pike at all times."

"Because...?"

"Because I know how much you hate him. And I know eventually you'll make your move. I will make sure we're ready."

For once a bit of softness crept into his face. "You are a very good soldier, Prudence. A very good...person."

"I try to be."

"You make my work so much simpler. I appreciate it."

"It's a pleasure to work for you, sir. Forgive me for saying so, but there are a lot of people running around patting themselves on the back, preening about their good works. Politicians like Pérez. Blowhards like Pike. But you do your work in the shadows. Fame finds you, not the other way around. What you do matters. What you do lasts."

"You flatter me, Prudence."

"You deserve it, sir." She turned again to peer at the Van Gogh. "Am I the only one who thinks this Dutch master is overrated?"

He pursed his lips. "Thick lines. Globs of paint. You can tell he never had much formal training. Draws like a kindergartner."

"And yet..."

"The alleged drama of his life overwhelms artistic judgment. As far as I'm concerned, he only managed one good painting in his understandably troubled life. And now I have that painting, thanks to Octave Durham. Even the Van Gogh Museum in Amsterdam couldn't find this one. Because I have it. And now that Durham is safely in Dubai where he can't be extradited— they never will."

"You get everything you want, don't you, Dr. Sweeney?"

"In time." He smiled and reached for her hand. "Yes. In time."

CHAPTER EIGHTEEN

DAN PULLED THE "COMPANY CAR"—THE JAG—IN FRONT OF THE "office"—the mansion. Maria slid into the passenger seat, gripping her cellphone tightly in her right hand.

"I assume you've had a horrible accident and just haven't mentioned it," he said, as he pulled away from the curb.

She looked stricken. "Why? Do I look bad?"

"No. But you're letting me drive."

"Oh, that. I need to do some work on my phone. But I look okay?"

"You look fabulous, as always."

"Thanks. You look sharp too, if massively overdressed."

Now it was his turn to look stricken. "You don't like my outfit?"

"Correct me if I'm wrong. That's a bespoke Zegna suit, refined wool fiber, probably around 2500 bucks."

"You don't like it."

"It's terrific. But you might stand out in a strip joint."

"In the first place, it's not a strip joint. It's an adult dancing parlor."

"Where we're going to meet a stripper."

"Exotic dancer. And in the second place, I don't want to blend in." He could see her attention had already diverted to her phone. She was using a forefinger to swipe. "Are you on some dating app?"

She tilted the phone so he couldn't see. "Stop creeping. Eyes on the road."

"Right, right." But his peripheral vision still creeped. "Why are you doing that?"

"Well…" She sighed. "It's been a long dry spell."

"Maria—you're a gorgeous young woman. Stylish, smart. With a great job."

"That takes up way too much of my time."

"You don't need dating apps. Dating apps are for women who don't have your resources."

"Stop Dansplaining. I'm an adult. I can make my own decisions."

"This is beneath you. Look in the mirror. You're—you're—"

"A complete smokeshow? Yes, I am. And you're being a complete munch."

"No one who uses a dating app is worthy of you."

"Get with the brave new world, Grandpa. Everyone with a busy life is on dating apps. We don't have time to troll singles bars. Not that I think that would be in any way superior."

"You're choosing men based on profiles and pics."

"Nah. Most everything in the profiles and pics is bogus. The Net is full of catfishers. Dogfishers."

"Dogfishers?"

"Guys who post pics of themselves with other people's dogs. Because they think women are drawn to guys who love their dogs."

"Does that work?"

"Actually, yes. But now I demand to see rescue-dog adoption papers."

"And you agree to meet men based upon this information?"

"And the restaurant they suggest for a first date."

"Seriously?"

"A girl needs to have standards."

"What if you don't know the restaurant?"

"I research. Post around. See what other women in town think of the place. Losers like loser restaurants."

"So if the restaurant doesn't measure up, it's death by Yelp for your hapless suitors. Do you post online often?"

"Well, I'm not a Kardashian or anything. But I like to stay out there."

"I think this is unbecoming to a young upwardly mobile professional."

She looked up at him and winked. "Maybe that's what I like about it."

———

DAN THOUGHT IT HAD BEEN AT LEAST A DECADE SINCE HE'D entered a place like this, and time had not improved the concept. Calling Ebb Tide an "adult dancing parlor" did not upgrade the environment. It was poorly lit, smoky, alcoholic, and without any redeeming entertainment value—unless you enjoyed watching women wearing next to nothing shimmer and gyrate around a pole. In an age when porn was only a click away, he was somewhat surprised places like this still survived. Perhaps he should be encouraged to know there was still an audience for live theater.

Maria leaned toward him. The music and noise levels were so high she had to shout. "Can you believe how many women are in here?"

He was surprised not only by the single women but the couples sitting around the stage. Did they find this fun? Erotic? "Of course, you're here."

"On business. No choice about it. Jimmy's gay and Garrett's

way too conservative for this sin palace. And I couldn't let you come alone."

"No, I wouldn't know how to handle myself."

"Why couldn't we meet her at her home?"

"She told Jimmy she preferred to meet at work. I get it. She doesn't know us. She's probably been grilled repeatedly by the police. She prefers to be in a crowded place. Feels safer."

"Any idea which one she is?"

He pointed center stage. "Up front."

"The cowgirl?"

"I assume she prefers to be called an erotic dancing animal handler." On the stage, the person in question wore nothing but glittering G-string and pasties—plus a holster with two strategically arranged plastic six-guns, which she occasionally twirled and pointed in imaginative ways.

"I wouldn't have thought this bit would play so well in Florida. We're a long way from Texas."

"Maybe that's the point. Maybe in Texas strippers dress like beachcombers."

"Don't you mean, *undress* like beachcombers?"

———

TWENTY MINUTES LATER THEY WERE BACKSTAGE IN A CROWDED green room that apparently serviced all the dancers, which meant there was a constant flow of women wearing next to nothing. Dan ignored them, as if this was a normal thing to have going on around you. He couldn't help but be impressed by the level of professionalism. These women were not overtly trashy, nor did they resemble the caricatures from *Gypsy*. They were working women getting the job done. The room was brightly lit and a gruesome pop song played much too loudly. Maria informed him it was by someone called Krewella.

"I've been stripping for almost three years," Vanessa Collins said. Light brown skin. Short hair. Purple fingernail polish. The kind of abs that only arise in gyms. She was still dressed in her cowgirl outfit, which was to say, she was barely dressed at all. "Harrison didn't approve. Which is one of many reasons why we're not still together."

"And the other reasons?" Dan asked.

"Well, I think he's gay. Was gay. Sorry. No disrespect intended."

"None taken. I hope you'll be honest about him, despite the tragedy." He thought Maria might take the lead on this interview, but she seemed more distracted by all the women in various states of undress than he was. "I understand you and Harrison dated for some time. What makes you think he was gay?"

"Or bi. Something. A girl gets hints. You know."

He did not know. "Did Harrison have…performance issues?"

"No, he could manage an adequate, if uninspired bedroom encounter. I just sometimes got the impression it wasn't his main jam."

"What was?"

"He liked a little kink. You know, the black leather and handcuffs, that sort of thing. But at the end of the day, I just don't think women were his *raison d'etre*."

"He was quite a bit older than you, wasn't he? Maybe that was a factor."

"Perhaps. But I like to think a man doesn't have to be eighteen to get interested when a woman with a body like mine starts undressing. I've got moves."

"I saw." All fascinating, in a way, but not what he came to talk about. "My partner tells me you used to be a teacher."

"True. Loved teaching. Pity you can't make a living doing it."

"Stripping pays better?"

"Are you kidding? Two years of this and I paid off my house. But there's more to it than money. This helps me stay fit. I'm not as young as most of the girls here, so I have to work harder at it. This job forces me to get off my butt and do the work. And I find it artistically fulfilling. You want to heap on the scorn because this is a little naughty, suit yourself. I'm a big girl and I make decisions to please myself. I love to dance. Hell, I think pole dancing should be an Olympic sport."

"And kitesurfing," Dan added.

"You know, they have pole-dancing competitions. The Miss Sexy pageant. Miss Trixter. Men's and women's divisions."

Maria appeared amazed. "There are male pole dancers?"

He made a tsking sound. "Maria, please. Don't be so sexist."

Vanessa grinned. "You should join the US Pole Dance Federation, Dan. The fastest-growing section is the men's division. Lots of contorting and propelling and thrusting." She gave him a smile. "I'll bet you're good at that, aren't you?"

He dodged the question. "In the competitions, do contestants wear G-strings?"

"No. Normal athletic wear. And you can use your real name, not Candy or Bambi or whatever. Competition is not so much about the whips and the sparkly lollipops. It's about interpreting the music through your body, evoking the mood of the song. But strip club work is good practice. If you can do a complex routine in high heels, doing it in gym shoes is a breeze."

"No doubt."

"I'm saving up to open my own studio. Can you believe St. Pete doesn't have a dedicated pole-dance studio yet? We are so behind the times."

"Shocking. Would you teach students your cowgirl routine?"

"Surely you see that I'm interrogating the whole Western Americana trope. Why aren't there more cowgirls in Westerns? Why are the women always back at the ranch waiting for the macho hero to come home? Or captured by Indians? Or prostitutes? I'm giving women a role in the narrative. A woman doesn't have to be sexually neutered to have a voice."

"A #MeToo pole dance?"

"Exactly."

Perhaps it was time to change the subject. "You've met Ossie, right?"

"The kid who's calling himself Ossie? Yeah. Not a fan. Not convinced."

"You don't think he's the real deal?"

"Definitely not."

"Did you ever meet the real deal? Before he disappeared?"

"No. That was long before I came into the picture. But I thought the whole situation was fishy. Everyone knows Old Man Coleman is sick. Time's winged chariot is closing in and the relatives are circling like vultures. And at the last critical juncture, Ossie suddenly appears to collect a massive inheritance. I mean, that's just not the way life works, right? I didn't buy it."

"But you had no objective reason to disbelieve him. No evidence."

"I didn't take a DNA sample, if that's what you mean. Do you mind if I get dressed? That was my last dance for the evening."

"Please do." And he meant it. Having a convo with a nearly naked woman was supremely distracting. "Do you know of anyone who had a grudge against Harrison?"

"Other than every one of the other potential heirs? Sure." Apparently he wasn't supposed to notice as she peeled off the pasties and slid into a bra. Quality frilly number, probably Victoria's Secret. "But mostly theater people, you know? The kind who think the worst burn is a Shakespearean insult. 'Thy head is full of stuff and nonsense.' That sort of thing."

"Not anyone you'd expect to commit murder."

"No. Maybe a nasty tweet, if they were truly angry. But murder? Like this one? No way. Did they really...dissolve his body?"

"That's what the cops say. Any particular enemies? Among those theater folk?"

"I guess you could look into Margaret Tully. She and Harrison clashed constantly. And since she controlled the funds that kept that theater afloat, he had to listen."

"What did they clash about?"

"Programming, mostly. She thought all this old stuff, Shakespeare and the like, was boring. And you know, she wasn't wrong. I taught English, but come on. That's not how you get bodies into the seats. Margaret wanted more accessible, sexy, contemporary programming. And I suppose now that Harrison is out of the way, she'll get what she wanted."

"No one else will stand up to her?"

"No one else cares enough. Harrison felt strongly about standards. He thought they had a responsibility to the arts, a sacred calling. If people want crap, he said, let them stay home and binge-watch television crap. The theater should be better. Uplifting. Enlightening. He was a special person, Harrison. Even if you disagreed with him, you couldn't help admiring his strength of purpose. He was the rare man who had the courage of his convictions."

"I know someone else like that," Maria said. "It's fun to be with someone who has a strong sense of purpose."

"Agreed. But it wasn't enough to keep our relationship together. I needed more excitement in my life. I broke it off with him."

"When was the last time you saw him?"

"Just before he disappeared. And was killed, I guess. Now I feel gigantically guilty about it. One of his last experiences was me showing up to tell him I was calling it quits. I was planning to go back the next day but—too late." She pointed at the overhead speakers. "Like the song says. He was Dead AF."

"Guess I'd better look into Margaret Tully. I assume she's wealthy."

"Oh no."

"But you said—she controlled the funds—"

"True. But it isn't her money. She represents some wealthy donor guy."

His eyebrow rose. "Who?"

"I can't think of the name. Big guy. Bald."

"Conrad Sweeney?"

"Yeah. That's the one. You know him?"

He and Maria exchanged a look. "Yeah, we know him. And worse—he knows us."

CHAPTER NINETEEN

DAN WOKE ALL AT ONCE, EYES WIDE OPEN, BEFORE SUNRISE, AS usual. Sleeping on his boat gave him the most tranquil rest he'd ever had. Something about the combination of waves and wind and the smell of the sea and the sounds of the gulls—worked. He loved it. He normally slapped on his suit and hit the water by dawn. Perfect way to start a day. But this morning, he thought he might allow himself to linger in bed a bit.

Camila lay beside him, slightly snoring, cute as could be.

He'd stayed over at her place several times, but it took some doing to get her to stay here. His boat was large by sailboat standards, but tiny compared to her apartment. Even harder than convincing her to stay was convincing her security detail, which tended to follow her everywhere. She had received death threats, so he encouraged her to be careful. Just so the security guy wasn't in the tiny alcove he called a bedroom.

He must've fidgeted too much. Her eyes opened. "Is it morning?"

"Not quite."

"Are you leaving?"

"Only if you want me too."

She reached out and pulled him close. "Then stay."

"Your wish is my command." He kissed her lightly on the neck. "Big day today?"

"Like every day. Boring political stuff." She sighed. "My new Chief-of-Staff wants me to make a statement about the murders. And Ossie Coleman."

"It would be better if you stayed out of it."

"Not my style."

"Make an exception. Everyone knows I'm repping Ossie, and many people know we're dating."

"Is that what you call it?"

"Point being, any statement from you could be taken the wrong way. Like you're trying to help your boyfriend."

"What's wrong with that?"

"Caesar's wife must be above suspicion."

"And the mayor has to be a virgin?" She sat up. "What are you doing today?"

"More interviews. After my morning workout."

"I've got an idea for your morning workout." She pulled him closer till he was completely on top of her.

"Madame Mayor, what are you suggesting?"

"For someone who supposedly excels at reading people, sometimes you are seriously dense."

———

DAN GOT ANOTHER CHANCE TO DRIVE THE JAG SINCE HE WAS travelling with Jimmy, who felt that driving interfered with his constant conversation.

"How's everything at home?" he asked, knowing this could well lead to a lengthy diatribe on the travails of living with an ER doc. Or perhaps he would segue into a discussion of *Star Wars* or DC Comics. He wasn't sure how that could be possible, but Jimmy always found a way.

"Fine. Hank gripes about my long hours, but his are just as bad and he's not looking for a new job, so why should I?"

"I think you two make a terrific couple."

"True." He paused. "But would it hurt him to help out with the laundry on occasion? I finally gave in and hired a house-keeper. The dust was destroying my comics."

"The housekeeper might be willing to do the laundry."

"That's too decadent even for me." Pause. "Do you think the housekeeper would cook dinner?"

"You could ask."

"I don't want to be frivolous with money. But we are doing well financially. Maybe I could afford Hello Fresh."

"Might as well enjoy the salary Mr. K provides."

"I suppose. I just keep coming back to the same ethical question."

"Which is?"

"What would Clark Kent do?"

DAN SURVEYED THE MEMBERS OF THE COLEMAN FAMILY, ALL assembled in one room. A motley crew, to be sure, and none of them particularly friendly. Most had nothing kind to say about Ossie, either—or the "Ossie-pretender."

Any potential suspects in the room? he asked himself.

All of them.

Jimmy started snapping his fingers rhythmically.

"What are you doing?"

"*Addams Family* theme song."

"Why?"

"How can you not? Look at this crew. Zachary Coleman's eldest surviving son, Benny, could be Gomez, and his wife is the spitting image of Morticia. The youngest brother, Phil, is a born Pugsley. Benny's daughter could be Wednesday. And her kid, the toddler who won't shut up? Definitely Cousin Itt."

"Who's Uncle Fester?"

"I don't know. Probably me."

The family gathered in the living room of their mansion on and around a sofa, as if positioning themselves for battle. Zachary Coleman rolled his wheelchair beside the left arm.

Dan wasn't sure where to begin. This assemblage was about as far from a typical African-American family as it was possible to be. He suspected he was more likely to hear about trust-fund portfolios than Black Lives Matter. "Thank you for speaking to me."

"We didn't do it for you," Benny said. Puffed-out chest. Gold wedding band. Conservative haircut. "We came for Papa. He wanted us to see you. That's all it is."

"Since we have a civil suit on file, I could have taken formal depositions. But that's expensive and largely unproductive, so with the consent of your attorneys at Friedman and Collins, I opted for a more informal chat. Seems less burdensome for everyone." And more productive. He'd never gotten much out of depositions, with lawyers posturing and every word being taken down by a court reporter. This couldn't be used as evidence, but what he wanted most was insight into the characters. Once he understood who he was dealing with, he'd have a better idea how to put the pieces together.

Zachary Coleman—Papa to them, apparently—made a grumbling growling sound that called them to attention. He didn't have to raise his voice. When his lips parted, they all closed their mouths and listened. "This is not an endorsement of anything Mr. Pike is doing or saying. I just want to get this mess over with, and cooperating seemed like the best way to do it. I spoke to Mr. Pike earlier and I don't believe he's trying to cheat anyone. Just doing his job."

"That job has changed a lot in the past few days," Phil said, teeth clenched. Ironically, the baby of the family was the largest of them, and it looked like he was still very much grieving for his lost sibling. Muscular. Buzzcut. Apple AirPods Pro. "It's one thing to humor a con man. Much different to harbor a murderer."

Zachary shook his head. "He hasn't been convicted. Yet."

"The police wouldn't bring charges if they weren't certain. Wouldn't you agree, Mr. Pike?"

"Absolutely not. Sadly, the number of wrongful convictions in this country is horrifying. That's why people like Jimmy and me exist."

The furnishings, though adequate, were far from plush. Apparently the billionaire did not feel the need to squander his fortune on creature comforts. "I don't like it, Papa," Benny said. "There's more to this than the declaratory judgment suit. This man is helping that upstart kid who killed Harrison."

"We don't know that," his wife Dolly said, clutching her large bag. Practical shoes, Old Navy suit. Big Mary Poppins purse. Direct, no-nonsense, aggressive. "Not with absolute certainty."

"I'm pretty damn certain," Benny mumbled.

He needed to get in control of this conversation somehow, or it was not going to be useful. "I understand you've all suffered a terrible loss," he said, raising his hands, as if to metaphorically hold back the teeming hordes. "And I understand people sometimes become angry when they're grieving."

"Are we grieving?" Dolly looked both ways at once. "How about you, Sabrina? Grieving?"

The daughter glanced up from her phone. T-shirt. Shorts. Flip-flops. "Not me. Couldn't stand Harrison. Creepy. Always quoting Shakespeare, like that proved he was smarter than everyone else. Half the time I think he just made crap up. And when he talked about chess, it was worse. If he was so great, why did he only play himself? And he was always staring at my breasts."

"Really?" Dolly said. "That surprises me. I don't think women were his principal point of interest."

Zachary raised his hand. "Dolly, I won't have that kind of talk."

"Fine, fine." She paced a bit, then positioned herself behind the sofa.

The little boy darted around the room, screaming with arms outstretched, pretending to be an airplane. Everyone ignored him, as if this was commonplace. Sabrina, who he believed was the boy's mother, didn't even look up from her phone.

He wasn't sure whether to direct the discussion with a question or to just let the suspects riff. "Did you know Vanessa Collins?"

"Oh yes," Benny said. "How could we not? She and Harrison dated forever."

"If you could call it dating," Dolly added.

"Wouldn't you?"

"Well, I don't think women were—" She glanced at Zachary. "Anyway."

"They were together a long time."

"Too long," Zachary groused. "Now she's claiming she was his common-law wife. Says she should get his share of my inheritance, since he has no heirs."

Hadn't read that in the pleadings. "Does she have a case?"

Zachary shrugged. "They did live together for a good long time. But he never married her. I think it was just about sex."

Which would be the perfect claim for a palimony suit, though those had fallen out of favor with the courts. "I've talked to her. She spoke well of Harrison."

"Like a wife about her husband?" Dolly asked. "Or a hooker about her john?"

"Like someone who genuinely cared about him. Even though he had...eccentricities."

"Oh, you mean the kink." Dolly waved a hand, purse flapping

before her. "Whatever. Everyone has something. But his wasn't women."

Jimmy looked at her with astonishment. "You—knew about his...kink?"

"You think you're the one who has his ear to the pavement? I don't miss anything of interest. That was how they met, you know. In her...what's the term?"

Benny cut in. "Adult toy shop."

"There you go. Sounds much better than Discount Dominatrix Dildo Mall."

"*Strip* mall," Benny added, winking.

Dan wondered if he should start taking notes. Vanessa hadn't said anything about this. "Vanessa Collins has an adult toy shop?"

"Didn't mention that during your talk?" Dolly said. "Not much of an interviewer, are you? Do you cross-examine witnesses in court? Or just let them talk and assume it's all true?"

"Now wait a minute—"

"She sold the shop a while back," Benny interjected. "She needed a side hustle to support herself. You know what teaching pays these days. But it was apparently not as profitable as she'd hoped, and worse, her middle school principal found out and sacked her. That's when she started stripping."

He felt his teeth clench. Vanessa hadn't mentioned that, either. Could just be gossip—or maybe he did need to push a little harder. "But the relationship lasted a long time."

"Yes," Dolly said, "but at the end of the day, a leopard can't change its spots, and boys will be boys."

Impressive. Three clichés in one sentence. "You think he broke it off...because he wasn't into women."

"I don't think she would've done it. She was a gold-digger."

"And by that you mean...?"

"Like a prostitute. Only smarter."

The little boy raced around the room, screaming at the top of his lungs. Everyone ignored him. Phil rolled his eyes but said nothing.

Jimmy picked up the thread. "Wasn't Harrison dating someone else? At the time of his death?"

"Sure," Dolly said. "Margaret Tully. The theater woman."

"The woman who controlled the theater purse strings? The woman who was trying to steer Harrison away from Shakespeare?"

"I didn't know that part," Dolly said, "but God bless her if it's true. What is this obsession some people have with 400-year-old plays? Maybe try something where people don't talk in archaic riddles?"

"I had the idea that Harrison and Margaret were...antagonistic," Dan said. "That she was using her financial power to control his work." He didn't mention the possible connection to Conrad Sweeney. Or the fact that Vanessa said she broke up with Harrison.

"Is that what the little stripper told you?" Dolly batted her eyelids. "You are gullible, aren't you?"

"I had no reason to question—"

"They were shacking up," Sabrina said, her tone suggesting she was weary beyond measure. "I saw them at the Sackler Gallery one afternoon. They were close. Holding hands and all that BS. I think she had her tongue in his ear. Gross."

Most of the people in the room winced.

"Of course, that doesn't mean Margaret wasn't also trying to take charge of the theater," Dolly opined. "She is a bit of a puppet master."

"And by that you mean...?"

"Like a prostitute. Only smarter."

Phil cut in. "I'm not going to be uppity about strip joints. Men do that stuff. Everyone did it, back when I was in Afghanistan."

He did a double take. "You were in Afghanistan?"

"Two tours of duty. Officer. Bomb squad."

Not the typical rich-kid resume. "You did this by choice?"

"I think we all have an obligation to serve."

"He was on track for med school," Zachary said. "Already got through the first year—the hardest one. But instead of finishing, he decided to run off and play hero."

"Papa tried to get us all in med school," Benny said. "Seems to be an obsession with him."

"Ossie was the one who could've done it," Zachary said. "He was a smart boy. He could've been anything he wanted to be."

Zachary's interest in schooling explained a great deal. Despite his humble origins, everyone in this family spoke like well-educated, well-read, articulate scholars. The upper crust. Zachary clearly wanted to eradicate all traces of his poor black background—and succeeded.

The toddler darted out from behind Sabrina's legs. "Mama! How much longer?"

Sabrina didn't look at him. "I don't know. Not much longer. I hope."

"I'm bored."

"We're all bored, Allen. Being bored is what you have to endure when you're part of this family."

Dolly scowled. "Sabrina!"

"It's true. None of you wants to be here. You're just doing it because—" She glanced at the elderly man in the wheelchair. "Never mind."

Zachary swiveled around. "This is a meeting, not a kidnapping. No one has to be here if they'd rather be somewhere else."

"Yeah. Right." She returned her attention to her phone.

He thought this might be a good time to discuss the civil suit. And break the awkward silence. "May I ask you about Ossie's claim?"

"None of us thought he was a member of this family," Phil

explained. "Everything the kid said sounded defensive, as if he were overcompensating for something. Or guilt-ridden. Like he wanted the money but felt bad about the deception. We'd love to think that boy had been returned to us. But he wasn't."

"For once, you're right, baby brother," Benny said. "None of us."

"Not one," Dolly added.

He noticed that Zachary remained silent. "Did you investigate his claim?"

They all looked at one another silently and somewhat guiltily. He already knew they'd hired Bradley Ellison. What was the big secret? "Come on. You have the resources. What did you do? What did you learn?"

After a long pause, Benny finally spilled. "We did hire someone. Used to work for the local constabulary. Now he specializes in so-called cold cases. He didn't believe the kid's story. And he was an expert on the case."

"Did you agree with the investigator's conclusions?" he asked Zachary.

"I told you already—I didn't know what to think. God knows I wanted him to be my grandson. I missed Ossie so. He loved me, pure and simple. I could see that every time I was with him. Not like—" He stopped himself. "But Ossie disappeared and now I've got—" He gestured around the room.

"A family that loves you," Dolly completed.

"Yes. Offspring hovering for an inheritance."

"Not me," Sabrina said. "I don't care about your money."

"Right."

"I don't. I just want to make sure your only great-grandchild is taken care of."

"I'd like to take care of that kid," Phil muttered, just loud enough that everyone could hear.

"You're all going to be taken care of," Zachary said bitterly. "I don't know what all this backbiting and hostility is about."

"It's about a billion dollars, give or take a few million," Dolly explained, as if there was someone who didn't already know it.

"Which you will all share equally."

"So you say. But I hear you're revising your will constantly."

"Just a few special bequests. Nothing to worry about."

"And you will have to pick a successor. Someone to run the company."

The old man frowned. "It's true. I don't believe in splitting it up. Divide your resources and you end up with nothing."

"The person you anoint as CEO will make out like a bandit."

"It's only fair that the one doing the work profit accordingly."

Dolly gave Dan a knowing look. "So now you understand what the backbiting and hostility is about."

"There's no rush to choose a successor," Zachary insisted.

"Isn't there, though?"

"I'll make a decision when the time comes."

"Yes, and by any logical standard, you would pick your eldest surviving son, my husband. But you don't seem to like him very much."

"That's not true."

She continued as if she hadn't heard. "Mind you, I get it. He is rather a crushing bore. But he's competent, in his own unimaginative way."

"Hey!" Benny said.

She waved him aside. "What we all fear, of course, is that you'll choose Phil, or even worse, someone who is not a member of the family. Worse yet, if Mr. Pike is successful with his civil suit, you might put this ragamuffin imposter in charge of your estate."

"If I were sure that boy was my Ossie..."

"Yes, exactly."

Dan cleared his throat. "All that money aside, do you know of any reason why anyone would want to kill Harrison?"

"Haven't we already given you enough motives to fill a mystery novel?"

"You've suggested Vanessa is a gold-digger. But no one has suggested she's a murderer, and I don't see how Harrison's death strengthens her common-law marriage claim. And Ossie had no reason to kill his uncle."

"Maybe Harrison was just the first," Benny said. "Maybe he's planning to take us all out. One by one. Like that movie. You know. On the island."

"*And Then There Were None?*"

"Yeah, that. Face it, we don't know anything about that kid. He may decide he doesn't want to share the fortune with anyone."

"Personally," Dolly said, "I sleep much more peacefully knowing he's locked up."

"Second that," Phil said.

Now he knew exactly where Ossie stood with this family. "I'm told Margaret Tully works on some of her projects with Conrad Sweeney. Anyone know him?"

They all glanced furtively at one another.

"It's like Voldemort," Jimmy whispered behind his hand. "You're not supposed to say his name out loud."

"Everyone knows Sweeney," Dolly explained. "Isn't that right, Papa?"

Zachary nodded. "Conrad Sweeney and I have worked on a few business deals together, despite the fact that I...wasn't the color I suspect he prefers. And Sweeney has always taken an interest in the community and the arts. I wouldn't be surprised if he was involved with the theater. But if you're suggesting that Sweeney was involved in this murder, forget it. Not his style."

"You're sure?"

The man's voice dropped several notches. "And even if, he'd make sure he didn't get caught."

He thought Zachary was finished, but it turned out he had an addendum.

"If he's involved, Mr. Pike, the smartest thing you could do is stay out of his way. Take it from me. Sweeney does not like obstacles. He eliminates problems with swift and ruthless efficiency. No one stands in his way for long. No one."

CHAPTER TWENTY

Dan saw Garrett in the kitchen noodling on his keyboard. Meditating? Contemplating? Free associating? Brainstorming? Organizing his mental Kanban board?

He wasn't sure what to call it. But he knew whenever Garrett had a particularly sticky problem to work out, he'd wander downstairs to his Casio keyboard and play one of those shapeless jazz tunes only he enjoyed. Shouldn't a song have a beginning, middle, and end? And sound more or less the same each time you play it? What was the point of hearing your favorite song if it was constantly changing?

He tried not to be distracted, though between Maria's Top-40 pop songs and Garrett's jazz, he sometimes thought the office should be soundproofed. But at the moment, he was concerned that his top researcher had a problem so intense it drove him into the throes of Dave Brubeck. This was basically the same as Sherlock Holmes turning to cocaine. Except noisier.

He liked Garrett, but in some respects he was the most inscrutable member of the team. Arch-conservative and typically devil's advocate, he was the one most likely to oppose anything Dan proposed. That made Garrett far more valuable than a think-alike yes man. He wasn't bothered by the fact that Garrett had worked for the government and been a prosecutor. But he always had the sense that Garrett was holding something back, that he didn't totally understand what was going on in the man's brain. With Maria, everything was right up front, and with Jimmy, it was TMI—more up front than you wanted. Garrett tended to keep his thoughts ot himself.

He decided to venture conversation. "How's the research going?"

"It's going."

"Meaning?"

"It's a process. Like all things in life."

Much more philosophical than his norm. "Anything new come in?"

Garrett stopped playing. Had he come to the end of the song? It was so hard to tell with jazz. "Got a prelim tox report from the coroner's office."

He was surprised they could even perform a tox screen, given how little was left of the body. "Anything of interest?"

"A few anomalies. It's hard to draw conclusions."

"And yet, they will." Because the prosecution couldn't possibly convince a jury to convict unless they had some theory of how the murder was committed. Bad enough to not have a body. Impossible without an MO.

"There seems to be a strong feeling that Harrison Coleman was poisoned—but again, difficult to prove, given the scanty remains."

"Maybe that was the whole point of the bio-cremation."

"Or perhaps the police are just pursuing what they want to be the answers. Trying to make that syringe they found in the trash bin significant."

"That could have come from anyone. Or anywhere."

"But when all you've got to work with are crumbs, you make the most of the crumbs."

"Can you get me an interview with the guy who allegedly found the syringe?

"Can and did. But let me warn you—this guy is not your average prosecution witness."

"You think they used him to plant evidence?"

"You tell me. After you've chatted with him."

"Got it." He noticed Garrett's fingers inching slowly back to the keyboard. "Anything else going on? Anything...I should know about?"

"Not particularly."

"Which generally means yes."

Garrett craned his neck, then shrugged slightly. "I just... can't help but wonder if we're taking the correct approach here."

"You think representing Ossie is a mistake."

"You can't always pick your client, right? Mr. K wanted us to represent the kid and we accepted the case. Whatever reservations I might have had are no longer relevant. Once I'm in, I'm all in."

"I appreciate that."

"But. I am concerned about the ramifications of getting on the wrong side of Conrad Sweeney."

"He's vile, Garrett. Manipulative. Evil."

"I don't know that. What I do know is that he's a respected citizen and has probably done more for this city than any other single individual."

"Every charitable act gets him something in return."

"The same could be said for any philanthropist. We all have private motivations that drive us to do what we do."

"This is different. Sweeney has no moral compass. He doesn't mind committing crimes—and letting others take the fall. He manipulates the legal system."

"You have no proof of that. There are no charges pending against him."

"Because he does everything through minions. Makes sure nothing can be traced back to him."

"The fact that nothing can be traced to him could suggest that he hasn't done anything wrong."

"I know better. He's destroyed evidence. Bribed witnesses. Set people up for—"

"Is this about your father?"

That stopped him short. "I—I don't know what you mean."

"Don't you, though? You have some seriously unfinished business going on with respect to your family history, and one of the figures in this case, Bradley Ellison, was involved in it. I can't help but wonder if you're demonizing Sweeney to mentally exonerate your father."

"My father was completely innocent."

"I know you believe that, Dan. But he was convicted by a jury. It was a tragedy for you and your mother. But you can't go on acting as if everyone who played any role—including the entire criminal justice system—is evil and corrupt because your family suffered."

His teeth tightened. "The people who put away my father were corrupt. To the core."

Garrett slowly exhaled. "Are you even listening to me?"

"Of course I'm listening. Just because I don't agree doesn't mean I'm not listening." He wrapped his arms around his chest. "Sounds like you want out of this case."

"No. But I am wondering if you can be completely objective. Maybe this is one you should let someone else handle."

"You don't think I can cut it?"

"That's not what I'm talking about."

"Maybe you want me to throw the case."

"Of course not. I would never."

"Maybe you're on Sweeney's payroll!"

Garrett straightened, silent. They both stared at each other for a long moment.

He knew he shouldn't have said that. "Look—"

"If you seriously believed that, even for a moment, we can't work together."

"I'm sorry. I just—I don't get where you're coming from. This case—"

"You need to get a grip, Dan. Figure out what's going on in your head and deal with it. This is a bad case and it's only going to get worse. Your blind spots will end up losing it. You're no good to Ossie like this. You're no good to anyone."

Garrett switched off the keyboard and walked away.

Well. Damn everything to hell. This was turning into a terrific day, wasn't it? The only thing that could possibly be worse than an impossible case would be an impossible case when one of your partners is seriously pissed off.

He pressed a hand against his throbbing forehead. He'd have to figure all this out later. He had to get ready for the next interview and—

The doorbell rang. Were they expecting someone? Seemed unlikely that Garrett would come out of his office to answer after that big conflagration. He'd better get it himself.

He opened the door. The man on the other side wore a UPS uniform and carried a package.

"Daniel Pike?"

"That's me."

"Need you to sign."

"Okay." Seemed odd, but whatever. "Where?"

"Just a moment." The man fumbled with a scanner clipped to his belt, lost his footing, and in the process of recovering managed to drop the package.

It fell to the porch with a thud. "Damn! I'm so sorry."

"Let's hope it wasn't Waterford crystal."

"It wasn't." The man bent down to pick it up, then lurched forward suddenly...

The blow pounded into his stomach with such swift ferocity

that Dan had no chance to react. He felt the pain, and then the pain became all he could think about. He was thrown sideways against the door. His head slammed back with a sickening thud.

"Wha—" He felt breathless, unable to speak. He should do something. But—

Too late. The next blow arrived with the force of a pile driver, hammering home to the same spot.

His eyes bulged. He didn't want to cry out, but he couldn't help himself. His legs weakened and he tumbled downward.

Get up! He told himself. *Defend yourself!*

But he couldn't find the strength. The next blow pounded him on the side of the head. A sudden shockwave of pain rippled through his body. A mix of drool and blood trickled from his lips.

"Garrett," he mumbled, but so weakly he knew there was no way anyone could possibly hear. "Jimmy…"

This time the man's fist blew the air out of his lungs. He rolled over and started coughing uncontrollably, spitting up blood. In seconds, the man had reduced him to a puddle on the floor. And there was nothing he could do to stop him from doing more.

The man grabbed him by the collar and jerked his head up. "This time I hit you where it won't show. This time I let you off easy. That won't happen again."

He released him, letting his head smash against the porch. Lights erupted before his eyes. Consciousness waned.

"This is a warning. You won't get another one. Drop the case."

The man left him lying on the porch, barely able to move, barely able to think.

What was it Garrett had said? This case was only going to get worse.

It just did.

CHAPTER TWENTY-ONE

TERRY DODGSON LOVED TO HIKE AND THE EVERGLADES WERE HIS favorite place to do it.

He'd wandered into a complete no man's land. Still swampy, but uncharted. No boardwalk, no park signs, no rangers. Just him and the great outdoors. No traces of civilization, no tampering, no people. As far as he could tell, no one had preceded him. He was probably not the first vagabond to ever come this way. But it was a pleasing illusion, just the same, and the natural environment supported his fantasy one hundred and ten percent.

In one day, he had seen swamps and beaches, forests and lakes, butterflies, herons, egrets, ibis, storks, alligators, large turtles, and more birds than he could identify in a lifetime. He had read there were more than a thousand different species birders could spot out here. All that identification seemed like a lot of work though—and for what? He preferred to simply drink it in. Enjoy.

Terry fancied himself a great navigator, but this far from civilization, even he could become lost. He had a compass and, if worst came to worst, a cell phone. He was not at all sure, however, that Google Maps could save his bacon today. He was a good long way from the nearest cell tower.

His father used to hike with him, once upon a time, but his father had been taken much too early. Throat cancer, and the man had never smoked, not even a pipe. Sometimes it seemed like nothing made sense in this world. Losing his father had been the worst experience of his twenty-two years, but he liked to think that every time he took himself outdoors, just him and the world, nothing but a backpack of essentials—he was remembering his father. He was living the life his father wanted for his son.

In a very real way, of course, his father wasn't gone at all, not as long as Terry stayed active, kept moving, kept hiking. Held on to the dream. Didn't let himself get swept up in the all-too-mundane world of day jobs and mortgages and keeping up with the Joneses. His father had given him a strong sense of identity. He knew who he was. He wasn't some cardboard excuse for a man—he was independent, someone who knew what he wanted, who didn't want anything not worth having, and who didn't let others stand in the way of what mattered.

That's what it's all about, isn't it? Knowing who you are? After you've got that down, all the other questions are easy to answer.

He checked his watch. Almost five. He didn't mind being out late. It was going to be an all-day hike, and he had a tarp in his backpack he could use for a lean-to. If he was going to spend the night out here, though, it might be smarter to head back. Exciting as it was to break new ground, it would probably be smarter to camp closer to civilization, where there was some vague notion of law and order and he might be able to find help if he needed it.

Okay, one last look before he turned around. Maybe a few photos. He took out his phone and focused on the horizon.

He zoomed in to bring the faraway wonders of the world close.

Wait a minute.

He looked at the horizon, then glanced back at the phone screen, his handheld binoculars.

There was something strange on the horizon. And unless he was very much mistaken—something manmade.

A house? Cabin? Whatever it was, it was not tall and the colors were muted, as if the shelter was meant to blend into the surroundings.

Was it possible someone lived out here? Literally in the middle of nowhere? He didn't see how anyone could survive here long, in the swamp, so far away from everything. Getting supplies would be so hard it wouldn't be worth the trouble.

Except perhaps for someone who did not want to be found. Ever.

He hesitated in mid-step. The smartest move would be to turn around and make tracks, as quickly as possible. There was something seriously unsettling about this entire situation. If someone wanted this badly to not be found, it was probably best to leave them alone.

And yet...

What would his father do? Turn tail and run?

Hell no. His father would see what in blazes was going on out here.

But slowly, one footstep at a time. Moving cautiously...

A few minutes later he had a clearer view. It was a cabin, slapped together with the cheapest possible building materials. Nothing to brag about, but it probably kept the rain off. Couldn't be more than a room or two in there. Maybe a kitchenette.

Was anyone home?

He took another step closer. Slowly. Quietly...

He was in the cabin's front yard, not that it was much of a

yard. No mowing or edging took place here, which was just as well, because there was no grass. Just brush. Dirt. Mud.

He didn't hear anything. He didn't see a soul.

There was a foul stench though. Even ten feet away he could smell it. Just as well he hadn't eaten much.

Another step closer. Then another...

And that's when he saw it.

The yellow paint on the gable above the front door was the first thing to trigger a memory. He'd read something in the papers. Not recently, maybe a month or two ago. A story about a missing boy...

The number over the front porch cemented it. 1980.

He knew what this place was.

He stepped onto the porch. No windows, but the door was slightly ajar. He stepped toward it. Gently, he pushed the door a little wider...

He turned and ran as fast as his legs could carry him. He felt certain his father would approve of this decision.

He realized what was causing the stench.

Run, Terry, he told himself. Move those legs.

Run!

CHAPTER TWENTY-TWO

"DAN, STOP BEING SO DAMN STUBBORN."

"I'm not being stubborn. I'm being practical."

"There's nothing practical about getting yourself killed."

"That wasn't exactly my plan."

"And yet I found you bleeding on the front porch."

He drew in his breath. And even that hurt.

The last blow from the killer UPS guy must've pushed him into unconsciousness. The attacker had been a pro—not a single blow left a visible mark, and he didn't make much noise, either. He delivered his message without attracting attention. He was lucky the man stopped short of the killing blow—because he had the distinct impression the man could have killed him, just as quickly and just as quietly. His partners upstairs didn't hear a thing. Maria found him on her way back from a run.

He stretched across the sofa in the living room while she hovered protectively overhead. "I appreciate your concern, Maria, but I've got this covered."

"You've got what covered? Your grave? You haven't even been to the doctor."

"Don't need one. I checked myself out. I'm okay."

"You've been spitting up blood."

How did she know that? He wondered if he could make an end run around her and get out the door before she stopped him. Probably not, given his current condition. "It stopped. I'm healing."

"Internal hemorrhaging won't stop itself."

"I don't have—"

"You have no idea what you have. Your brain could be bleeding for all we know."

He leaned forward and laid a hand on her shoulder. "Maria, stop. I truly appreciate your concern. But I'm okay, and we don't have time to mess around. Our trial date is rapidly approaching and we still don't have anything resembling a defense. Garrett worked hard to set up this interview and if we don't do it now there's no telling when or if we'll be able to do it later."

"The whole point of the attack was to get you to quit this case."

He struggled to his feet. "I won't do that."

She blocked his path to the door. "Then I'm coming with you."

"Don't you have an appointment with your jury consultant?"

"Canceled. I'll talk to him later. I'm coming with."

"It's not necessary." But then again, he probably shouldn't drive. At the moment, he could barely walk. "You've got work to do. And this guy looks like major skeeze."

"All the more reason I should be there."

"Exactly why you should not be there."

"Oh stop. I'm coming. Get used to it." She grabbed the keys to the Jag and led the way out the door. "Last time you dragged me to a strip joint, for heaven's sake. This can't possibly be any worse."

AS IT TURNED OUT, SHE WAS WRONG.

Dan tried to give Charlie Quint his usual comprehensive once-over, but it wasn't working. There was simply too much to drink in. He couldn't absorb it all without staring. He didn't like being in this tiny motel room with this man, and he could tell Maria liked it even less. She kept a significant distance between the interview subject and herself, as if at any moment he might throw up on her Dolce & Gabbanas.

"You wanna know about the syringe, right?"

"Right." Mousy little guy. Comb-over of next-to-nothing. Egg-shaped head. Bronx accent. Mid-fifties. Soiled shirt—mustard, if he wasn't mistaken. Barely covered a pot belly. Holes in his tattered sneakers. "You were going through Ossie's trash?"

Quint shrugged. "It's what I do."

"You talk about it like it's a profession."

"It's how I survive."

What series of unfortunate events could possibly lead someone to a life like this? Quint was a former custodial worker who'd lost his job, lost his family, and ended up in St. Pete, rummaging through people's trash for food, clothing, and the occasional object he might be able to sell at a pawn shop for a few pennies.

Maria spoke. "You can support yourself like this?"

"For three years now. Best job I ever had."

She rolled her eyes. "This is not a job."

"Says you, with your snazzy too-tight designer jeans and your law degree. I didn't have the cash to go to law school. And I got tired of pushing a broom around."

"You dig through garbage."

He gave Maria a surreptitious signal. She needed to tone down the hostility. They wanted him to talk, not throw them out of the room.

"More people are doing this than you might imagine. This is a tough world, especially on the homeless, and there are a lot of us these days. I don't normally have a nice place like this."

Maria hid a gagging face.

"You do what you gotta do. I got a routine. I hit the residential areas in the morning. As it turns out, wealthy neighborhoods are the worst, not the best. They never throw out good stuff. More action in the middle-class and lower-class areas."

"I'll remember that."

"I hit businesses in the afternoons. Restaurants at night, when they start throwing out ridiculous amounts of food. It's a full day, but I've never been one to shy away from hard work."

"I can see that," Maria said, without a detectible trace of sarcasm.

"I tried panhandling. Wasn't good at it. Didn't like the hobo life. Too dangerous."

"At least you're not on welfare."

"I have been. Maxed out. Didn't like it much. Case workers are so snooty. They call themselves 'employment advisors' now. Give me a break."

"So how did you happen to be in Ossie's trash?"

"That's been a good neighborhood for me." Dan watched Maria pace awkwardly as Quint spoke. He didn't mind being on the opposite side of the bed, but Maria wasn't coming anywhere close. She wouldn't even take the chair. She just stood, occasionally moving from one side of the room to the other. No doubt her Fitbit approved. "Those foster homes get all kinds of weird crap. Sometimes valuable. Found a whole baggie full of coke in the trash once."

"Why would anyone throw that away?"

"Because they're high. I wouldn't know from experience—I can't afford bad habits like that—but I assume when people are tripping they don't always use the best judgment."

Probably a safe assumption. "And you never get any complaints?"

"Oh, sometimes. You know, every neighborhood has some old lady who spends her day looking out the window, hoping she can catch someone violating the neighborhood association code or something. But there's nothing they can do about me. Once that trash barrel is placed on the street, the law says it's no longer yours. You have no right of privacy and no claim of ownership. Which means I can take whatever I find."

He couldn't argue. Despite not attending law school, Quint did more or less understand the relevant property law. "And that's when you found the syringe?"

"Exactly. Over the years, I've developed a talent for knowing what's valuable. A second sense, you might call it."

He wouldn't. "Why would you keep a syringe? I wouldn't think you'd want to go anywhere near that."

"You'd be wrong. All kinds of possibilities there. Might indicate other drug paraphernalia is about, or the drugs themselves. Might still be something yummy in the syringe. For that matter, the syringe itself is of some value. Junkies are always looking for clean needles. Hard to get good supplies without attracting attention. They reuse syringes out of desperation—and you know how that ends."

Maria looked like she was about to vomit. "If you sell syringes to addicts, you could spread all kinds of diseases."

"They're junkies. They're killing themselves anyway."

Oh, well, that makes it okay. "Drug paraphernalia means lucrative items for resale."

"Or cop money."

"Wait, what?"

"A syringe in the trash means drug users. You give that info to the local cops, you get paid. Usually ten bucks for a solid tip."

"You squeal to the cops for money?"

"I report a possible crime. Ain't that what good citizens are supposed to do?"

Maria tapped the toe of her shoe against the threadbare carpet. He could tell her patience was reaching its limit. "Is that what you were doing when you found the syringe in the trash outside the foster home where Ossie was living?"

"Yup. I thought someone in there was a druggie. I had no idea he was a murderer."

Dan raised his arm—and it hurt. He had to remind himself. No sudden movements. Moving sent shivers of pain radiating through his body. "Ossie isn't guilty. He didn't kill anyone."

"That's not what the cops told me. They said he must've shot that theater guy up with something, maybe to kill him, maybe to paralyze him so he could cremate the body."

"That doesn't even make sense. Why would he kill Harrison Coleman at the theater—and then bring the syringe home, only to throw it away where someone could find it?"

"Just because I don't know all the whys and wherefores doesn't mean it didn't happen. Crooks aren't always geniuses. They get scared, panicky."

"You don't have any reason to believe that syringe was tossed into the trash by Ossie, right?"

"They tell me he lived there."

"But anyone could've done it. Lots of kids lived there. For that matter, a passing stranger could've thrown a syringe into the trash bin."

Quint looked as if he were about to say something—then stopped himself. "I think I've said enough. Maybe you should go now."

"You can't withhold information from the defense."

"I can do any damn thing I want. Maybe the cops have to talk to you, but I don't. Get out."

This conversation was finished. He pushed himself to his

feet—slowly—so the pain was intense but not excruciating. "If you think of anything else important, please give me a call."

"That's not going to happen."

No, he didn't expect it would. "But if something important—"

"Everything's important," Quint said quietly. "If you know the story behind it."

CHAPTER TWENTY-THREE

MARIA DROVE BACK TO THE OFFICE, WHICH FREED HIM TO daydream about stretching his aching body across a nice soft mattress.

"Well, that happened," Maria said.

"Talking about Quint?"

"Yeah. A ten-minute, completely unproductive conversation that left me desperate for a bath." She glanced at him. "Do we need this garbage? Maybe we should ditch the courtrooms and start flipping houses. I hear those guys make tons of money. I'll be St. Pete's Joanna Gaines."

"Only if I can be Chip."

Maria glanced at him. "I will say this, Dan. At least you're consistent. First you took me to a disgusting strip joint. Then to an even more disgusting motel room. What's next, a deposition in the sewer system?"

"I think it's time we confronted Conrad Sweeney face to face."

"That would be even worse."

A jazzy ringtone burst from his phone. "What's up?"

Garrett got straight to the point. "The cops may have found the cabin."

"Ossie's cabin?"

"There's a yellow triangle on the porch gable. Texting you a location pin. Out in the Everglades."

Dan slammed a fist onto the dashboard. "Yes! That's what I'm talking about!"

Maria grinned. "Good news?"

"If it confirms Ossie's story—absolutely." He glanced at the map on his phone. "Truly secluded. No wonder no one found Ossie all those years."

He switched the call to speakerphone so Maria could listen in. "What else do you know?"

"Not much. The cops aren't in the habit of spilling everything they know to defense attorneys. But I did get a call from Kakazu's lieutenant."

That made sense. Kakazu was a straight shooter. "He knows it relates to our case. He's doing his duty to inform us of potentially exculpatory evidence. Does anyone still live there?"

"I don't think so. But I didn't get many details. You need to get out there."

"Course correction as we speak," Maria said. "I'll drop you off."

"You don't want to come with?"

"Tramping through the swamp in these two-thousand-dollar jeans? No thank you."

"Tell Kakazu I'm on my way, Garrett. Do you know what they found inside the cabin?"

Garrett's voice dropped several octaves. "Yeah. Bodies. Lots and lots of dead bodies. Corpses." He took another breath. His voice wavered. "Mummies, actually. Most of them young boys."

Dan couldn't believe...well, most of what he'd learned in the last twenty-four hours. But at least this startling development was a positive one. For the first time ever, the crazy story Ossie told that no one thought had the slightest credibility started to look as if it might be true.

The other massively unbelievable aspect of this journey, of course, was that he was being led by a police guide through largely uncharted and undeveloped stretches of Florida swampland. His Air Jordans did not function all that well in wet, marshy ground, and the less said about what this was doing to his Zenga suit, the better.

He usually liked being outdoors, but this was something else again. Birds dive-bombed with such frequency he felt he was in a war zone. Cranes? Herons? Egret? He really should have spent more time studying the local birds, and he would've too, except he was terribly busy and that sounded terribly boring.

He pulled his jacket tighter around himself. It was cold out here, cold and wet, even though the sun was shining. Maybe it was the power of suggestion. Get your sneakers wet, and you'll be cold for the rest of the day, regardless of the climate. Still, the hike took hours. He should've chartered a helicopter.

"How much longer?" he asked Sergeant Enriquez. Kakazu always seemed to put him in charge of the crime scene, even when it was a million miles off the beaten track.

"At least another hour." Enriquez appeared to be using some combination of cell phone location service and compass app to navigate. He said they had asked the FSBI to loan them a drone to help the forensic teams find their way. "We can't take the most direct route. Too much brush in the way."

"And yet we think someone lived out here?"

"Guess that will be your client's story. I can't imagine." Enriquez looked up. "I'm a homebody. I like to be where I can get Netflix and order a pizza."

He took another step—and felt his foot sink into a pothole, past his ankle. "Blast!" He jerked his foot out.

"Be careful," Enriquez warned. "It's possible to get completely stuck. You might lose your shoe. Or be here a very long time."

Maria was right to stay away. He probably should have followed her lead. But time was ticking. He was already starting to regret his whacked-out idea of asking for the earliest possible trial setting. This eleventh-hour discovery only made it worse. But if there was something in that cabin that might help Ossie, or shed some light on what was going on in this case, he had to know about it. "Any other advice?"

"Give up the lucrative life of the defense attorney and join the forces of good."

"Something more practical."

"Start buying your suits at JCPenney."

DAN WAS GREETED BY KAKAZU AS SOON AS HE AND ENRIQUEZ emerged from the clearing. It was almost as if the homicide detective was waiting for him. Or was so amazed Dan had actually made it that he decided to offer his personal congratulations.

"I must say, I am impressed," Kakazu said.

"You didn't think I'd come?"

"I knew you'd try. I just didn't think you'd make it."

"Ridiculous. I'm an athlete. This was easy." He brushed the mud and grunge from his clothes and wrung out his lower pant legs. "Kitesurfing is hard. This was just…"

"Miserable?"

"Something like that."

"Come inside. There's a lot you're going to want to see. Correction—" He stopped short. "There's a lot here you don't want to see and will never be able forget. You'll probably never forgive me for showing it to you. But you insisted."

"I can handle it. I've seen a lot in my time."

Kakazu almost smirked. "Believe me, you've never encountered this. I should've sent you a trigger warning."

He mounted the porch. The front gable did have a yellow triangle on it. The triangle pointed upward and appeared a bit smudged at the bottom. And the cabin faced west, so Ossie's description proved true on two counts. Of course, the whole place was so filthy it was hard to see anything clearly.

Kakazu opened the front door. The odor sliced him up like a knife. Sharp and inescapable. Putrid. Made his eyes water. Took a death grip on his lungs and wouldn't let him go.

Kakazu handed him a blue face mask, like something a surgeon might wear. He put it on. It didn't help much, but he left it on just the same.

Kakazu led him into the cabin. It appeared to have only one room furnished with standard table and chair, some dishes by a sink, a cot in the corner. A few doors that might lead to other areas. Kakazu pointed toward a gaping hole in the floor. A wooden plank revealed a ladder leading down into what appeared to be some kind of basement.

He drew in his breath. "Were they children?"

Kakazu nodded grimly. "Young boys. Every one of them."

He felt a catch in his throat. "How—" He looked around the tiny room. "In here?"

"There's a cage in the back. Chains."

"And then?"

Kakazu drew in his breath. "When he was done playing with them, he killed them and brought them down here."

"It's...a basement full of rotting child bodies."

"Not rotting." He started down the stairs, apparently assuming Dan would follow. "Mummified."

CHAPTER TWENTY-FOUR

DAN HATED TO ADMIT IT, BUT KAKAZU WAS RIGHT. HE HAD NOT seen anything like this before. The cabin was the most horrific crime scene he had ever witnessed, bar none. Eleven small mummified bodies. Wrapped in cloth bandages like something out of a third-rate horror film.

The human remains were dressed like little dolls. Some were even posed. Some had painted faces. One was dressed like a teddy bear, with a decapitated teddy head over the actual head. Four sat around a small table laid out with decorations. A birthday party for those who would never have another birthday.

"Where did these boys come from?"

"We have no clue. We've barely begun to collect information. But the cabin does appear to some superficial similarities to the one your client described—"

"And none of you believed."

Kakazu tucked in his chin. "I'm still not convinced. But this does match the description, so we're dutifully notifying defense counsel."

"The killer couldn't have found these boys around here."

"We're speculating that the killer made occasional forays into civilization to pick up supplies. Food, sundries—"

"And children." He pinched his nose, trying unsuccessfully to block out the stench. "Couldn't have done it often. Too hard to get back and forth. But he probably didn't need to. Or want to. And once he had them back here—where could they go? Even if they escaped, trying to get from here to anyplace they might be found would be almost impossible."

"Or would require a great deal of good fortune. The angels smiling."

"No kid who was abducted and dragged out here is going to claim the angels were smiling upon him. Do we know who any of the kids were?"

"Not yet. We're going through missing persons reports for the last fifteen years, but that takes time. And if the boys were runaways, there may be no local reports."

"Do we know what...the killer did with these boys? I mean —" He swallowed, then tried again. "Was it just for murdering? Or torture and murder? Or was there...more?"

Kakazu's head lowered. "We don't know. But common sense suggests...more."

"Some kind of pervert."

"More like, pathological sadist."

"Gets off on seeing children tortured?"

"Another grotesque possibility."

"So basically...the worst thing it could possibly be."

"We haven't seen any signs of cannibalism. But other than that...yes. As repulsive as it gets."

"And if Ossie came from here—"

"There's no evidence of that."

"He described the cabin."

"In the vaguest possible way."

"There's nothing vague about a yellow triangle on the gable. Or the number."

"Could be a lucky shot. Something he saw somewhere else."

"I'm not buying it." He turned his head away from the bodies. Was it too soon to leave? He thought he'd done a good job of playing the tough guy and pretending this didn't make him want to hurl. But if they stayed down here much longer, he was going to vomit, tough guy or no. "I think you know Ossie was here."

"Then how did he get away?"

"Presumably he left after his captor—the corpse upstairs —died."

"Then how did he get back to St. Petersburg?"

"That's what we need to find out."

"And how did the heir to a fortune end up in this hellhole in the first place? What happened to his memory?"

He felt a shiver. "If I'd been here, I'd want to block it out of my memory, too."

Dan stared at the body on the stretcher. Since this adult corpse, unlike the others, had not been mummified, the techs from the medical examiner's office were able to deal with it in a more typical fashion. After a preliminary examination and the removal of exemplars, they prepared it for the arduous journey back to the city.

The body was covered with tattoos. Caked blood on the right hand. Bald, wiry, stained flannel shirt. In his fifties or sixties. "Joe."

Kakazu squinted. "What?"

"That's what Ossie called the man who lived with him in the cabin."

"Did he mention the man was a serial killer?"

"No. He probably didn't know about that part."

"It would be hard to keep that hidden."

"Maybe not. Serial killers tend to be careful. Meticulous. And Ossie was young. Innocent." He looked away from the corpse. "What killed him?"

"Believe it or not—natural causes."

"Too bad. I was hoping one of his victims got free and came after him with a chainsaw."

"No signs of that. Looks like his time was up and he stroked out."

"Is it wrong for me to hope it was painful? At least for a little while?"

"No." Kakazu thrust his hands into his coat pockets. "I hope he thrashed on the floor for days in complete misery. But in all likelihood, it was quick. And there was no one around to help him."

"Because he'd killed everyone who might possibly help him."

"I have a hunch the boys he brought to this cabin would not have been that keen to help. Torture has a way of turning people against you."

No doubt. If he saw the fake UPS guy who'd attacked him writhing on the ground, he was relatively sure he'd keep walking.

He bent over to get a closer look, peering over the shoulders of the technicians prepping the body to be moved. Not terribly healthy, even before the stroke, probably. No ring, nor trace of a ring, on his left hand. "Can we be sure this is the man who killed those boys?"

Kakazu moved to the other side of the room, by the window. He guessed the man probably needed some fresh air. He'd been in this death trap most of the day. "I don't see anyone else around. Or traces of another person."

"Ossie was here. I can feel it. It can't just be a coincidence. But something here…damaged him."

"Everything about this place is damage." Kakazu walked toward him. "But you have no proof Ossie was here. And even if he was, it doesn't prove he's the heir to a fortune or that he didn't kill Harrison Coleman. To the contrary, child abuse on this level could easily turn someone dangerous. This discovery doesn't help you and it doesn't explain anything."

"Strong disagree. This could explain everything, if we knew more about it. This dead bastard on the floor was a twisted killer. Probably some kind of sex pervert. Judging by the number of corpses, he's been making runs into town for years, finding vulnerable boys, abducting them, probably drugging them, then hauling them back here. What happened to Ossie Coleman fourteen years ago? This monster got him."

"You're making a huge assumption."

"It explains why the cops never found the kid. When there's a billion dollars floating around, it's only natural to assume that's the motive behind a disappearance. But what if it had nothing to do with that? What if was just damned bad luck? We know Ossie's mother killed herself—"

"Probably."

"So afterward the boy was wandering around alone. Easy prey for a sick sadist."

"I know you're just making this up as you go along," Kakazu said. "But you haven't addressed the elephant in the room."

"Which is?"

"If this serial killer kidnapped your client and brought him back here—why isn't he dead?"

He fell silent. "I just got here. It usually takes me at least forty-five minutes to come up with the complete answer to everything."

Kakazu smirked. "Before you become unbearably smug, let me show you one more unexpected discovery."

Kakazu walked to the north wall, just to the side of the sink that appeared to be all the cabin had in the way of a kitchen. He ran his palm along the wall—then found a slight indentation. He pushed on it.

A disguised door popped open.

"This place is not quite so simple as it seems."

"Far from it. All kinds of hidden cubbyholes and storage places, including a well-stocked drug cabinet. We probably haven't found them all yet. But you need to see this little hideaway."

"What is it?"

"The trophy room."

He felt his heart sink. "I'm going to hate this, aren't I?"

"Depends. You hear all these rumors about defense attorneys. Do you actually have a heart?"

"Strong and functioning."

"Then you're going to hate this."

"It can't be worse than mummified corpses."

Kakazu gave him a look that spoke volumes.

"Oh, damn it to hell." He didn't want to follow—but he had to. Not just because he couldn't bear to show any weakness. This was crucial to unraveling the increasingly complex mystery surrounding Ossie Coleman.

So he stepped inside. And gasped.

He fell backward a step, staggering. "That can't be—That can't—"

"It is," Kakazu said softly.

"T—Trophies?" He felt cold and weak, almost as if he had been transported out of normal time and space.

"That's our preliminary theory. You got a better one?"

"And they were all—alive?"

"Once. He posed the mummies—but left these so he could remember their faces, I guess."

The wall was lined with a series of ashen white face masks. Life masks. Or perhaps death masks. All different. All appeared to be recordings of the face of a different young boy. Made of papier-mâché, or something like it. Hung on the wall. His personal scrapbook.

"There must be—" He stopped and counted. "Twenty-three masks up there. More masks than mummies."

"Yes. We may just be bumbling policemen, but most of us can count to twenty-three."

"You think there are more dead bodies somewhere? A—A body farm or something like that?"

"Distinct possibility."

All at once, he felt a powerful wave of nausea wash over him. Something inside started to give. Probably a combination of the physical strain of getting here combined with the shocks that awaited inside. Plus the realization that this Ossie Coleman case was a thousand times more complicated than he had ever imagined.

"I...think I need to sit down." There were no chairs in the tiny trophy room, so he lowered himself to the floor...

And that's when he spotted it. One of the masks, on the bottom row. Staring at him.

"Is that...Ossie?"

He pointed at the face mask, then took a snap with his phone. Given the primitive nature of the collection, it was hard to say anything with certainty. The hollow openings where eyes should be sucked the soul from the portrait.

But it looked like Ossie. More accurately, it looked like Ossie —but younger.

In that instant, he realized that he understood absolutely nothing about this case, this case with a billion dollars and a young man's life hanging in the balance.

And the trial was just a few days away.

CHAPTER TWENTY-FIVE

DAN CHECKED HIS WATCH BEFORE HE LEFT THE OFFICE. HE REALLY didn't want to do this. But hadn't that been true about virtually everything he'd done since this case began?

Apparently Garrett picked up on his anxiety. "I could handle this interview for you."

"No, I'm fine."

"It...might be best. I know that trip out to the cabin was grueling."

Is that all he was implying? He hoped Garrett wasn't going to reopen that can of worms about his supposed lack of objectivity. He didn't need another fight. "No. I'm doing this. And— by the way. I apologize for what I said before. I lost my head. I didn't mean it."

"I know. No worries."

"I am doing this interview. But I'm glad to have your company."

Maria buzzed past them, phone in one hand, Hermes purse in the other. "I'm going to stop by the jailhouse, time permitting. I haven't seen Ossie recently. Want to see how he's handling the latest breakthroughs. Talk about the trial. How to dress, how to act."

"Thank you," he said, but she was already gone.

"Keep the door open," Jimmy said, chugging right behind her.

"You're going by the medical examiner's office?"

"Yes. Chatting with the CSIs too. When they submit a flurry of reports right before trial, I sniff trouble." Jimmy paused a moment. "And what are you doing this morning, Cragheart?"

A reference to Gloomhaven, the official Last-Chance-Lawyers team sport. "Stirring up trouble, mostly."

He pointed a finger. "Don't stay dry too long. Aquaman needs frequent immersion to maintain his strength."

"I will bear that in mind." He turned his attention back to Garrett. "Ready to do this thing?"

Garrett grabbed the Jag keys from a dish on the table. "One last time. I can do this alone."

"No." He grabbed his backpack and led the way. "This is the bastard whose lies put my father behind bars. We should've talked a long time ago."

ACCORDING TO GARRETT'S REPORT, BRADLEY ELLISON HAD BEEN a member of the St. Pete police force for twenty-two years. He retired a detective captain, one of only six in the department. His reputation was strong and unsullied—not a single complaint or Internal Affairs investigation in all those years. Since he retired, Ellison spent his days investigating cold cases, sometimes for clients, or when he had no clients, on his own initiative.

"He seems to have a strong desire to see justice done," Garrett explained, as they stood on the front porch of Ellison's home waiting. "He doesn't get any compensation for some of his work."

"I guess a man has to do something in retirement. Better than working crosswords all day."

"I don't think you're hearing what I'm saying. He cares about right and wrong. He is not the kind of person who would accept bribes. Or offer false testimony."

He turned slightly. "What are you saying, Garrett?"

"You know exactly what I'm saying."

"You're wrong."

The door opened. Ellison was probably around sixty-five. He'd gained some weight since retirement, but not all that much. Rolled-up sleeves. Faded blue jeans. Muscular biceps.

Ellison dispensed with the usual pleasantries. "You're Sam Pike's boy."

He felt his lower lip tremble. He tried to stop it but couldn't. "I am."

"Thought so." Ellison opened the door wider. "Come in."

They stepped into his living room. Ellison gestured toward a musty and worn sofa. They both seated themselves.

"Just to be clear, I'm not here to talk about my father."

"Glad to hear it," Ellison said. "It was an unpleasant business. Long time ago. Best to leave it alone."

He bit down on his lip. "I will never leave it alone."

"I'm sure any son would feel the same way."

Dan felt as if everything inside him was going to erupt to the surface. "My father was not a murderer."

Ellison pressed his lips together. "I liked your father. Testifying against him was the hardest thing I ever did. But it had to be done."

"Why?"

Ellison raised his head slightly. "Justice."

"My father—"

Garrett cut in. "It would probably be best if we stuck to the Ossie Coleman case."

"Agreed." Ellison walked to his desk and lifted a tall stack of files. "I guess you boys already know that I like to dabble a bit in unsolved mysteries."

"And you've had an astounding rate of success, from what I've read," Garrett said.

Ellison shrugged. "I have a lot of time on my hands, since I left the force. Wife died. Daughter is in California, just as far away from me as she could possibly get. Might as well try to do some good for the community. The Ossie Coleman case always bothered me. So I got obsessive. Turned out all that knowledge was useful. Once someone claiming to be Ossie showed up. You're representing the kid, right?"

"Yes." He was glad Garrett could be congenial. Because he was afraid he couldn't open his mouth without something terrible coming out.

Ellison sat in a recliner, on the opposite side of a battered coffee table. "This case is probably the most famous unsolved mystery in the city. In the history of the city. There have been other claimants, you know."

"But they were all easily disproved. Until now."

Ellison continued. "Most people didn't believe the crime would ever be solved. I mean, realistically, after fourteen years, the chances that a missing child will be found are all but nil. But I held out hope."

"Did you find any of Ossie's missing records?"

"I wish. That would simplify matters considerably."

"Any idea what happened to them?"

"None."

"Care to speculate?"

"No. We do have some old photographs of the real Ossie, before he disappeared. I've worked with them quite a bit. Doesn't look like your client to me."

"Did you know you're on the prosecution witness list?"

"They're hoping to call me as some sort of an expert witness. Thought it might have more credence to have an independent investigator rather than another member of the police department."

Probably true. "What are you going to say?"

"That depends on the questions put to me."

Wiseass. "Are you going to dispute my client's claims?"

"I don't think he's the missing heir, if that's what you mean. I don't know that much about the murder."

"You think Ossie's a con artist."

"I didn't say that. I'm told he claims to have some memory loss, and there is evidence of brain trauma. He may genuinely believe he's Ossie Coleman." Ellison took a deep breath. "But he isn't."

"Have you heard about the cabin in the woods?"

"More than heard. I've seen it."

"You went out there?"

Ellison shrugged. "It wasn't that hard a journey. I used to go out that way quite a bit, once upon a time. Great fishing."

The police gave him a view of the crime scene? "Doesn't that create a plausible explanation of where Ossie has been all these years?"

"Not to me." Ellison put his feet up on the recliner. "To me, it creates far more questions than it answers. Who was behind the abduction? A cipher who spent the occasional weekend torturing, molesting, and killing kids? Why wasn't your client killed? How did he escape? How did he find his way back to civilization?"

"The medical examiner said the corpse on the premises had been dead a long time. Perhaps after he stroked out, Ossie left—"

"I can't rule any theory out or say anything is too outlandish.

No explanation is going to be commonplace. This is an extraordinary case. Has been from the start."

"And what do you think is the correct explanation?"

"I don't know. Insufficient data."

"The sparsity of evidence doesn't prove my client isn't Ossie. Just like it doesn't prove he's a murderer."

"But he does have the strongest motive to eliminate Harrison Coleman. Harrison was the oldest surviving son and the one the old man was closest to. They were tight. If the old man were going to leave his fortune, or an extra-generous share of it, to anyone—"

"Or put someone in charge of his business—"

"Exactly. It was going to be Harrison. Would you like to see my files? I'm more than happy to share my research."

"That's a ton of work to do without getting paid."

"It fills the time."

"You sure you're not on anyone's payroll?"

Ellison turned slowly. "What exactly do you mean?"

"I've already talked to one witness I'm certain the police are paying to cooperate. And you have a history of saying...exactly what the police need someone to say."

Garrett winced and tried to speak, but Ellison cut him off. "What exactly are you suggesting, Mr. Pike?"

"Your history of lying goes way back."

Ellison rose. "I have never given false testimony in my entire life, Mr. Pike. And that includes when I testified against your papa."

He could feel his fists clench. He told himself to stay cool, but it wasn't working. "I will not rest until I see you and whoever put you up to your lies behind bars."

"You'd rather believe some big conspiracy theory than accept the simple truth."

"You don't get it."

"I do. I loved my pa too. Broke my heart when I lost him. But at some point, a man has to grow up and realize no one is perfect."

"My father was not a murderer! And I won't let you—"

Garrett stepped between them. "Okay, we're getting off topic."

He shoved Garrett away. "I'm watching you, Ellison. Now and always."

"I'm not hiding," Ellison shot back. "You want to take a shot at me? Go for it."

"We don't need any of that." Garrett grabbed Dan's arm and pulled him toward the front door. "I get the distinct impression this conversation is concluded. Thank you for your time, Mr. Ellison. We truly appreciate it."

"You're right about one thing," Ellison said, as Garrett dragged Dan away. "There are people in this town who don't want Ossie Coleman to reappear. And if you have any sense, you'll stop obsessing on me and start worrying about them."

"Who? Conrad Sweeney? Is that who you're talking about?"

"This broken-down old ex-cop is never going to do you any harm. But Sweeney could shoot you in front of a dozen witnesses and there'd be no arrest, no repercussions."

"I think you're exaggerating."

"I'm not. He'll kill you dead. Or hurt you so bad you'll wish you were dead. Whichever he thinks will be most effective."

CHAPTER TWENTY-SIX

"I WANT TO SEE SWEENEY. I WANT TO SEE HIM RIGHT NOW."

Garrett continued driving back to the office. "That would be incredibly stupid."

"Would it? How many people have mentioned this man? He's got his fingers in every pie. He's got everyone in town either loving him—if they don't know the truth—or scared to death of him—if they do."

"No good can possibly come from a face-to-face."

"I should've confronted the big bastard a long time ago." He pulled out his phone and punched a few buttons. "I'm going to rectify that mistake right now."

"Dan, for once, think before you act." Garrett made a hard right and drove up a ramp onto the highway. "All you would do is give away what little you know. Sweeney isn't going to tell you anything."

"Not intentionally." He stared out the window. "But I'm a careful observer. Sometimes I get information people don't know they've given."

"Sweeney is way too smart to give anything away."

"Let's just find out."

"Plus, you have no time. This trial is breathing down your neck."

He heard a ping and glanced at his phone. "Jimmy set it up." He paused, reading more. "Seems it was no trouble at all. Conrad Sweeney is just as anxious to speak to me as I am to speak to him."

"Which means there's something he wants. It's a trap."

"Doesn't matter." His teeth clenched. "I'm tired of being on the outside, reacting instead of acting. Piddling around on the outskirts while the real action is happening somewhere else." He gave Garrett a hard look. "Turn this car around. I'm going straight to the belly of the beast."

PRUDENCE MET THEM BOTH OUTSIDE SWEENEY'S DOWNTOWN skyscraper. He wasn't surprised.

"So glad to see you again, Mr. Pike." Her swagger only reinforced the dominatrix vibe he'd had before—and he didn't think that was an accident. "I hope this means you've reconsidered Dr. Sweeney's offer."

"I just thought it was time we had a talk."

"By all means. Did you bring your swimming trunks?"

His head cocked to one side. "Uh, no. Why would I?"

"This is the time of day when Dr. Sweeney takes his regularly scheduled exercise. For a busy man like him, if it isn't on the schedule, it doesn't happen. He was happy to accommodate your last-minute request—but the schedule is sacrosanct." She turned her attention to Garrett. "I've been instructed to show you some documents I think you'll find of great interest."

"Documents pertaining to what?"

"The Ossie Coleman case. Dr. Sweeney understands you obtained little from Bradley Ellison."

"Well, we left before—wait. How would he—"

"Privilege prevents Ellison from revealing much. But as the client, Dr. Sweeney can reveal anything he wants."

"You're saying Ellison has been working for Sweeney?"

"Was it a secret?"

"Ellison said he was just indulging his own curiosity."

"Well, investigators often won't disclose their clients' identities."

"And you're going to share what you got?"

Prudence stepped closer to Dan, practically nose to nose. If that was meant to be intimidating, it almost worked. "Surely you realize Dr. Sweeney only wants to help."

"I didn't get that, no."

"And I feel the same way." She inched even closer. Her eyes widened. "I think maybe we could help each other."

Even though he desperately wanted to step back, he didn't. "If this is meant to be sexy, it isn't working."

She leaned in, lips parted. "My only interest is in being of service."

"To...?"

"To whomever I find worthy."

"Meaning Sweeney." He stepped back and winked at Garrett. "But I didn't bring swim trunks."

"As it happens, I have some in precisely your size."

"How would you know my size?"

She gave him a long look. "The pool is outside. I'll show you to your cabana. Mr. Wainwright, my associate will show you to the reading room."

Garrett shook his head. "I'd rather stay with Dan."

"Not an option, I'm afraid. This is a private meeting."

"We're a team. Wherever he goes—"

"Dr. Sweeney contemplated the possibility of this discussion expanding to matters other than the pending case. Private matters." She gave Dan a penetrating look. "Family matters."

He pursed his lips. "It's okay, Garrett. I can handle this."

"You're sure?"

"I'm sure."

Prudence gently pushed Garrett aside. "Ready to see the pool, Mr. Pike?"

"I am."

"That's what I like," she replied, as she led the way. "Someone who's always ready to jump off the deep end. Come what may."

WHAT PRUDENCE HAD NOT MENTIONED WAS THAT SWEENEY WAS not yet in the pool. He was in his own custom-built cedar steam room, not far from his private pool, private Jacuzzi, and private juice and coffee bar, with its own barista on call whenever Sweeney was on the premises. Dan passed on the blood-orange spinach cocktail, changed clothes, and got ready to take the heat.

He'd seen people in movies sitting round in steam rooms, but he'd never understood the point in real life. He'd rather plunge into the ocean and stay cool than plunge into a steam room and be uncomfortable. Matter of taste, he supposed.

Or perhaps the whole point was to make him uncomfortable. Dress in next to nothing, go someplace vision was limited and sweat was certain to pour down your face. They were clearly on Sweeney's home turf, even more so than if they'd met in his office.

He stepped inside. A strong eucalyptus scent cleared his sinuses. A gush of steam hit him, blinding him. There were probably benches along the walls, but he couldn't see them.

He wasn't sure what to do. Maria would strut into the fog. Jimmy would try to use the Force.

"Ride the wave." The voice came from somewhere in the steamy haze, low-pitched with a bit of gravel in it.

"I'm...not sure what that means."

"You're a surfer, aren't you?"

Of course, Sweeney would know that. And it probably gave him pleasure to show that he knew all about someone he'd never met before. "Sometimes."

"Major wave jockey, from what I hear. Conventional. Corkscrew. Kite. You love the water, don't you, Mr. Pike?"

He tried to get a fix on the source of the voice, but it was impossible. He steered away, assuming that he would eventually collide with one of the benches but not end up in Sweeney's lap. "Always have."

"I love the water myself." Was he joking? Impossible to know, since he couldn't see the man's face. "Just not so crazy about people."

"Unless you can control them?"

Sweeney ignored the jab. "I hate crowds. All those people jostling around. Beaches, malls. Even parks. Not my métier."

Seriously? He couldn't—

And that's when it hit him. The real reason they were meeting for the first time in a steam-filled room. Sweeney had undoubtedly learned about his gift for reading people. For collecting small observations. In here, that skill would be almost completely negated. If he couldn't see or even hear clearly, the playing field was level.

He bumped into a bench, found the seat with his hand, and slowly lowered himself onto it.

"It's a pleasure to finally meet you, Mr. Pike. I've heard so much about you."

"Likewise." A general outline of his companion started to emerge. Of course, he knew Sweeney was a big man. But he didn't come off as obese. More like strong. Formidable. "Your name keeps coming up."

"You mean in your current case."

"And my previous case. And I think you had something to do with one before that."

"I do try to stay involved. Help out when I can."

He tried not to smirk. "Is that what drives your quest for power and control? Your desire to help others? That would certainly explain these palatial digs."

If he'd expected some kind of denial, he was disappointed. "You can't do much for others if you don't take care of yourself. Fortunately, I've been able to build SweeTech into one of the most prosperous firms in the state. And I've used that money to make life better for a lot of people."

"Judging from this spread, you've spent a little money making life better for yourself, too."

"True. And my workers. I employ over a thousand Floridians. I grow the economy. But I also believe in self-care."

"And the art collection?"

Even through the fog, he could hear the smile in the man's voice. "I do love paintings. Is it wrong to indulge my passions?"

"Depends on which passions you're talking about."

"You love your boat, right?"

"True."

"And water sports. And our beautiful mayor."

All at once, he felt distinctly uncomfortable. "You were part of the conspiracy to get rid of her. Lock her up on a trumped-up murder charge."

"You have no proof of that."

"I'm not the only one who believes it. Someone wanted Camila put away."

"I've tried to help the woman."

"I know you contributed to her campaign. But that's just something you do, right? Spread money around, call in favors later."

"As I said, I like to stay involved."

"But some people think you aren't too keen on inclusion. You liked the world better when it was dominated by rich white males like you. You've consistently opposed immigration policies that—"

"I do think we have a completely irrational approach to immigration, both in this state and this nation. But please don't try to turn me into some petty redneck in a white sheet. I'm nothing like that."

He wondered. Men who crave power are always driven by something. And every time he tumbled across the government railroading someone, every time he discovered some gross inequity in the system, Sweeney seemed to be involved. "Can we talk about the Ossie Coleman case? Do you know anything about this cabin the woods? The dead man? The mummies?"

"Nothing whatsoever. Disgusting matter. All those boys, alone and taken advantage of. Sickens me."

He heard a flapping sound, wet and heavy. Apparently Sweeney had removed his towel.

Was he doing this just to put him off guard? Was he sitting there naked?

"I've known Zachary Coleman for decades," Sweeney continued. "We both started in business about the same time. I went into tech. He's more old-fashioned. Prefers to invest in simple things he understands, like hotels. That man was devastated when his grandson disappeared."

"He has a granddaughter now. And a great-grandson."

"Not the same. That whole mess with the boy's mother, running off, killing herself. So unfortunate. I hired investigators then and I've hired investigators now. But we've never gotten any solid information about what happened to the boy."

"You mean—until now?"

"Are you referring to that young man you represent? He's an imposter."

"How do you know?"

"Common sense, for starters. A boy suddenly appears out of nowhere. Can't be quizzed because he's lost his memory. Can't be ID'd because someone disappeared the prints and dental and DNA records. Can't account for the missing years. Only a fool would believe this fairy tale."

"Stranger things have happened."

"Maybe. But when a billion dollars is ripe for the taking, I have a tendency to be skeptical." He slowly rose to his feet. Was he going to walk around in here?

"Ossie tells a convincing story."

"I thought he didn't remember anything."

"I mean, he himself is very convincing."

"I'll have to take your word for it." Sweeney paced back and forth in the sauna. "I know Zachary isn't convinced the boy is the real thing."

"But given how much time has passed, how could he possibly know?"

"He's Ossie's grandfather. He would know."

"He's elderly. His memory is imperfect."

"That would make him more likely to accept the imposter. Zachary's skepticism shows he still has a grip on himself."

"How do you explain the cabin? Quite a coincidence, don't you think? Ossie describes a cabin with a yellow triangle, and not too long thereafter, someone finds one. Isn't that proof?"

"Not to me. And not to my investigator."

"He found what you paid him to find."

"Mr. Pike, is it possible that in your quest to demonize me and blame me for all your problems, you've missed the much more obvious explanations?"

That slowed him down.

"As we speak," Sweeney continued, "Prudence is showing your partner all our files on the case. Everything. Regardless of where it came from."

"Thank you." But would you please stop sashaying your big naked body around the sauna? "Maybe we could talk again after I've had a chance to review the files."

"You're not running off, are you? We haven't even made it to the pool yet."

"I need to prep for—"

All at once, Sweeney plopped his considerable girth down beside him. The bench shuddered. "Aren't you going to ask for what you really came here for?"

"I came here because I represent Ossie Coleman."

"Bull. You came here because your father died in prison. You know Ellison had something to do with it and you think maybe I did, too."

His throat felt extremely dry. "Did you?"

"No. I knew your father. Good man, if a bit naïve. I wasn't completely surprised when he ended up getting a raw deal."

"You're saying he was framed?"

A long pause ensued. "I can't say that. Bradley says he killed a man."

"Bradley lied."

"Why would he do that?"

"The obvious answer would be, for money. From someone with a lot of money to throw around."

Sweeney leaned forward. Good God, he wasn't going to put his arm around him, was he? "If by that you mean me, you're wrong. I have no interest in causing miscarriages of justice."

"Even if they benefit you?"

"Why would putting your father behind bars benefit me?"

"I don't know." This time, he stood. "But I intend to find out."

Sweeney wasn't ready to let him go. "Is this some crazy notion Mr. K put into your head?"

His eyebrows knitted. "What do you know about Mr. K?"

"More than you, I'll wager."

"I've been working for him—"

"But you have no idea who he is. Or why he finances these quixotic quests of yours."

"He does it because, like me, he can't stand to see innocent people get railroaded."

"Is that it? Or is that you projecting your own motivations on someone you don't know. Someone you can't even see."

He was becoming uncomfortable, and not just because of the heat. "I think this conversation is over."

"I could help you, Mr. Pike."

"I don't need or want your help."

Sweeney wiped sweat from his brow. "Such exuberance. Or arrogance, perhaps. But still, I admire your verve. You know, I'm subject to a constant stream of lawsuits. Happens to everyone in business today. I could use a firebrand like you."

"I don't think so."

"Would it be so bad? To work for someone you can actually look in the eye?"

"Forget it. I can't be bought."

Sweeney chuckled. "You've already been bought, son. Mr. K gives you a ton of money and you come when he calls."

"I only take cases—"

"You're his little toy solider. Give the boy a sports car and he'll believe anything you want him to believe."

"You don't know what you're talking about."

For the first time, Sweeney's voice took on an edge. "He's using you, and you're going along with it because he pays well and bloats your Zorro self-image. Let me tell you something. The true crusaders aren't showboats. They're people like me who work quietly behind the scenes, doing what is necessary to make the nation strong, to quell the forces that want to destroy our way of life."

"Codewords for racism and old-school smoke-filled-room politics."

"You're being childish."

"You're trying to bribe me out of the courtroom."

"The truth is—I already have enough information to keep you out of the courtroom. Permanently."

"Then why don't you use it?"

"Because that's not in my best interests. At this time." Sweeney slowly rose to his feet. He was naked. And extremely imposing. "You don't want to mess with me, son."

"Is that a threat?"

"I don't make threats. Why warn? When it's time to act, I act."

"Were you behind the delivery guy who came to my office and tried to kill me?"

"Obviously not."

"Not so obvious to me."

Sweeney leaned forward, towering over him. "If I had wanted to kill you, Mr. Pike—you'd be dead."

CHAPTER TWENTY-SEVEN

DAN RUSHED INTO THE COURTROOM. HE DIDN'T LIKE BEING LATE. Since Judge Smulders was new, he had no idea how the jurist handled tardy lawyers.

He spotted Jazlyn at the prosecution table. "Thank goodness," he said, smiling. "After what you said last time, I was afraid you might not be here."

She arched an eyebrow. "And you're more comfortable with someone you know you can beat?"

"I'm more comfortable with someone I know I can trust."

"Now you're just buttering me up." Pause. "But don't stop."

"I don't trust your boss at all. I'm convinced Belasco is in deep with Sweeney. And I definitely don't trust anyone associated with Sweeney."

"Are you sure? That Prudence is a looker."

He pulled a face. "Not my type."

"Gorgeous. Athletic. Smart. Sure, nothing there you'd be interested in."

"She works for the devil."

"No one's perfect." She passed him a pile of paper. "Here's our brief. Sorry I didn't get it finished sooner."

"I'm just glad you're still here."

"Don't get used to it." She glanced over her shoulder. "My suspicions were correct. I'm being replaced."

"You're kidding me."

"Nope. Belasco is bringing in a hired gun. He's supposed to arrive tomorrow."

His eyes narrowed. "The DA's idea? Or Sweeney's?"

She shrugged. "How would I know? Belasco really wants to win this case."

"But why?"

"Because he's the DA. Because he's about to run for higher office and he doesn't need to lose a highly publicized case."

He shook his head. "Camila's case was just as high profile. But he didn't bring in a hitman prosecutor. Something's different this time."

"When you figure it out, let me know."

"Will do. I suppose this frees you up to focus on your campaign."

"Maybe. Belasco has dumped lots of other cases in my lap. Busy work, mostly. I don't think he's going to be offering me his endorsement."

"You don't need it."

She laughed. "I can tell you've never run for office. Rule Number One, Dan—you need all the help you can get."

DAN ROSE WHEN JUDGE SMULDERS ENTERED THE COURTROOM.

"Okay," the judge said, jerking his robe around as he sat. It appeared to be too long and too big for him. He looked like a kid in a Christmas pageant struggling with his angel smock. "We've got some kind of motion to keep out evidence or something?"

He cleared his throat. "It's a motion in limine, your honor.

The defense wishes to suppress any mention of the syringe allegedly found in an unattended trash bin outside the foster home where my client lived prior to his arrest."

"Okay. All right." Smulders shuffled through the papers on his desk. "Got it. You want to keep out the syringe." He glanced up at Jazlyn. "You ok with that?"

She pursed her lips. "The prosecution is most definitely not ok with that, your honor. We oppose the motion. The syringe is keenly relevant. It has the defendant's prints on it—"

"Possibly," he interjected.

"—and contains traces of a deadly poison."

"Possibly."

"We believe it was the murder weapon."

"Even though," he added, "the corpse was dissolved virtually without a trace and thus could not be tested for cause of death."

"But the tox screens indicate that the victim might well have been poisoned before he was...dissolved."

"And then again, he might not have been." He knew this was not the strongest motion he'd ever made, but given the judge's lack of experience, he might get away with it. No judge likes the thought of being reversed on appeal, and a judge so inexperienced, saddled with a big case, his first-ever death penalty case, might be particularly nervous about screwing the whole thing up. "Listen to what she's saying, your honor. Possible. Virtually. Believe. Might well have been. Everything she says is equivocating and uncertain. Evidence of this nature will only confuse the jury."

Jazlyn didn't let that pass. "The jury is always free to disregard evidence they find unconvincing."

"But will they?" He took his voice up a notch. "We all know the prosecution has a massive advantage, particularly in high-profile cases like this one."

"I don't know that at all," Jazlyn murmured.

"Evidence like this confuses jurors, most of whom already

have problems dealing with complex forensic matters. The prosecution goes on and on about prints and trace elements and before long you've got an incorrect verdict based upon next to nothing."

The judge shifted his weight uncomfortably. His eyes darted to his clerk. "Well, I certainly don't want the jurors to be confused..."

"But the prosecution does, your honor. Even if people don't believe the syringe was the murder weapon, introducing it could suggest some kind of illegal drug use. That could be defamatory and prejudicial, though not relevant to the question of who committed the murder."

"Drug addicts have been known to commit crimes," Jazlyn said dryly.

"Not a crime as complicated as this one. Are you now shifting to a crazed druggie theory?"

"No, just pointing out how relevant this evidence is."

"If you want to bring drug charges, go for it. But you won't, because you're not even sure Ossie put the syringe in the trash can. My point is, your honor, the only evidence that should be admitted is evidence of who committed this murder."

"The syringe is far from the only evidence we have against the defendant," Jazlyn said. "I could recite a long list—"

"But please don't. If you have so much evidence, you don't need this keenly disreputable syringe. If I may explain further, your honor, this syringe was found by a so-called Dumpster diver, basically a homeless person living off the trash of others."

"Which does not in any way impugn his testimony," Jazlyn insisted. "We can't all live on a yacht and drive a Bentley."

Ooh, nice burn. "My sailboat is not a yacht, but that's beside the point. The witness says he found the syringe in the trash bin outside the home where my client was staying, but we have only his word for that. And many people lived in that house. And the prints are sketchy and uncertain. And the prosecution isn't even sure about the cause of death. Bottom line, your honor, this evidence is far more likely to confuse than to assist. The court should apply a balancing test, and the balance will come down against this evidence."

Judge Smulders raised a finger. "Balancing test. I remember hearing that phrase in law school."

Which apparently was about ten minutes ago. "Furthermore, there is the matter of payment. The prosecution paid this man for his testimony."

"Now wait just a minute," Jazlyn said. "I explained the situation in detail in my brief. The witness was in a bad way when he came to the police and he requested assistance. We provided food and clothing and a motel room where he could stay temporarily. We did not give him money."

"No, you gave him something far more valuable. But the point is, he was compensated for his testimony. More to the point, he came looking for compensation, knowing he'd have to give you something good to get it. He's basically a jailhouse snitch, except he's on the streets rather than behind bars."

"All we did was give the man clean clothes and a place to sleep."

"Which for someone in his situation, was manna from heaven."

Judge Smulders raised his hands. "Please slow down. This is getting confusing." He frowned, deep lines creasing his forehead. "Can't you just...bring all this up during the trial, Mr. Pike? Let the jury decide?"

"Exactly," Jazlyn said. "Trust the citizens of this county. Let them decide whether the evidence is credible or not."

"That's not the best approach, your honor. The jury will have enough to deal with. Let's make this a little simpler." He paused, then played his trump card. "After all, a man's life is on the line here."

Judge Smulders' face turned pale white. "Well, gosh. I just—I'm not sure—" Again his eyes drifted.

To his right, at her desk, his clerk Bertha raised her hand to cover her mouth, then muttered—quietly, but not so imperceptibly that everyone didn't hear it. "More probative than prejudicial."

Judge Smulders snapped to attention. "Yes, that's it. This evidence may not be perfect, but it's more probative than prejudicial."

Bertha's hand didn't move, but her lips did. "Cross-examine."

The judge nodded his head furiously. "And you'll have a chance to cross-examine at trial, right? You can bring out any problems you have with the evidence then."

He'd never seen anything like this in his life. Mortimer Snerd as death-penalty judge.

More rumbling from the clerk's desk. "Renew motion."

The judge smiled enthusiastically. "And you can renew this motion at trial, if it appears that the evidence is more prejudicial or not so probative."

But by that point, the irreparable damage will already be done. "There's no point asking the jury to disregard something they've heard, your honor. It only reinforces it in their brains."

"Still, I think this the way to go. So, sorry Charlie, but I think this means your motion is overruled. Right? You lose. She wins. No hard feelings, ok?"

He literally did not know what to say.

"Thank you, your honor," Jazlyn said.

The judge wiped his brow. "Whew. Glad that's over. Okay, if there's, like, anything else we need to deal with, then—wait." He reached under his robe and withdrew his cell phone. "Oh gosh. People are yakking about this case online. Should I do a gag order or something?"

He thought for a moment. That would certainly create confusion. But it would also create delay, and he wanted this trial to stay on track. "I don't think you can halt a Twitterstorm, your honor."

"Probably right." He tapped his phone a few more times. "Wow. Maria Morales. Isn't she a member of your firm, Mr. Pike?"

"Ye-ess…"

Judge Smulders smiled. "We're Facebook friends."

Did that mean they would win the trial, or lose it?

Jazlyn spoke. "Is that…completely appropriate, your honor?"

He shook his head. "Oh, don't fuss. I have 420 Facebook friends."

"Still…"

"And I'll accept you too, Ms. Prentice, if you care to follow me. Boost my numbers. Yay." He looked away from his phone. "Anything else, lawyers?"

"Not at this time, your honor."

"We're going to start the trial on Monday morning, right? You'll be ready, Mr. Pike?"

"I will be, your honor." And be sure to bring your clerk, so you can get past the first objection.

CHAPTER TWENTY-EIGHT

DAN HUDDLED AROUND THE KITCHEN TABLE WITH GARRETT AND Jimmy. The mood was dark and their expressions were grim. Garrett was not noodling on his keyboard and Jimmy was not playing with his action figures, so he knew they felt the ominous mood just as profoundly as he did. "I don't think I've ever gone into a trial feeling less sure of myself. Or of my case."

"Don't beat yourself up," Garrett said. "I know the hours you've been pulling. You've left no stone unturned."

"And yet, there are still so many unturned stones. I've been over all the evidence provided by the prosecution, but I can't shake the feeling that there's something more. Something important we don't know."

"The prosecution has to produce all exculpatory evidence," Jimmy reminded him. "I've talked to Shawna and my other pals at the courthouse. She doesn't think the DA is up to anything sneaky."

"And yet we know he's bringing in a ringer to prosecute. That's another problem. I don't even know who my opponent is yet."

"The word on the street is that Belasco is tired of being

beaten in the courtroom by you. I think there was some concern that...you and Jazlyn are getting too chummy. When the prosecutor and the defense counsel start attending the same birthday parties..."

"We don't have to pretend to be hostile to do our jobs properly."

Jimmy raised his hands defensively. "Hey, don't kill the messenger. I'm just suggesting a possible reason for hiring an outside prosecutor. Belasco wants to win."

"Have you had a chance to review my witness outlines?" Garrett asked.

"Repeatedly. You did the usual fantastic job I've come to depend upon."

"I predict the prosecution will come on strong. They almost have to, given the circumstances. They don't have a body. They're only guessing about how the murder was committed."

"When witnesses come on strong, when they stick to their guns despite all evidence to the contrary, jurors stop believing them." A light bulb flashed in his brain. "Oh hell. Judge Smulders asked for trial briefs. Why would he do that?"

Jimmy shrugged. "Because he has no idea what he's doing."

"Probably heard the phrase 'trial brief' and thought it sounded cool. Has no idea what a waste of time they are."

"Only a waste of time if you have to write them. In his case, anything might help."

"That babe-in-the-woods is not remotely ready to preside over a death case."

"Have you considered filing a complaint?" Garrett asked. "Ask the chief judge to appoint someone else?"

"And make an enemy for life? Possibly several?"

"Better than letting our client be executed because the judge is incompetent."

"I think that's a bad idea," Jimmy said. "In the first place, I don't think it would work. You'd just end up with a trial judge who thinks you don't like him, so he constantly rules against you. In the second place, it looks like you're running scared."

"We are running scared."

"But we don't want it to show, right?"

He frowned but acquiesced. "I suppose I can carve out some time tonight to write the brief."

Jimmy plopped a tall stack of papers in front of him. "Don't bother. Already did it."

"Why didn't you—" His eyes widened. "Bless you. That is such a relief. One less thing to worry about."

They heard a slamming door. Maria raced inside. "Sorry, everyone. Got tied up at the jailhouse."

Jimmy arched an eyebrow. "I assume you mean that metaphorically."

She dropped some notebooks on the table and collapsed into a chair. "I think that old guy at the front desk might enjoy tying me up. He seems the type." She passed the notebooks around. "This is our final-draft trial strategy. I made a copy for everyone."

Dan took his and opened it, scanning the first page. "You think the prosecution will say it's all about the money."

She nodded. "That does seem like the most persuasive path to take, doesn't it? I know people who have been killed in a fight over fifty bucks. When there's a billion dollars on the line—it would almost be more surprising if no one got murdered. But we can use that, too. After all, Ossie isn't the only relative involved."

"Are we naming an alternate suspect?"

"I don't think we have to. Benny, Dolly, Phil, Sabrina. That obnoxious kid. Even Zachary isn't above suspicion. I don't think you even have to put them on the stand, and it might be better if you didn't, given how much they despise Ossie. Just make sure the jury knows they're out there lurking."

"So our strategy is, Pin the Tail on the Relative."

"No, that's how we spin the prosecution strategy. Our strategy is, the police are in cahoots with powerful forces trying to frame our client."

He rifled through the pages of the notebook. "You think this could work?"

Maria pulled some reports out of her briefcase. "We've tried it several different ways in our mock trials, and this seems to work best."

"When you employed this strategy, Ossie was acquitted?"

Maria craned her neck. "Well…the mock jury thought about it longer, anyway."

He gave her a stern look. "How often did this actually succeed?"

"Success is a relative term….'"

"How often did your mock juries acquit Ossie? Fifty percent? Forty?"

"Actually…" Her eyes wandered off. "None of them did."

"None? Not one?"

"Sorry. It's in the report. But there's been so much pretrial publicity—"

"How many mock trials did you run?"

"Fourteen."

"And not a single jury voted to acquit?" His eyes moved from one partner to the next. "We're doomed."

Jimmy sniffed. "I don't put that much stock in mock juries."

"Neither do I. But—none? Zero acquittals out of fourteen?"

"Bear in mind," Garrett said, "there's one very important difference between all those mock trials and the real deal."

He tried not to look completely despondent. "And the difference is?"

"Those mock trials didn't have you, Dan."

He pressed his hand against his brow. He knew his teammates were trying to stay positive. But the future looked bleak.

He'd never heard of a mock trial run that didn't have at least one positive result.

"What about the jury consultant?" He still hadn't met the man. And now he didn't want to meet him. "Does he have any brilliant advice?"

"He thinks we have a tough job. The prosecution holds all the cards. We have lots of bad forensic evidence, plus a damning name written in steam on a mirror. And with so much money in the balance, it's easy for people to become cynical." Maria reached out and squeezed his wrist. "I've seen you produce miracles before, Dan."

"Not like this."

"I visited with Ossie at the jailhouse. That's why I was late. He didn't want me to leave. He's so sad. But he hasn't given up. He still has hope." She leaned forward. "Because of you. He believes in you. Or more accurately—he thinks you believe in him."

"I do believe in him. I'm convinced he did not commit this crime." His voice broke. He felt despair welling up in his throat. "But I have no idea how to convince a jury."

DAN WALKED DOWN THE LONELY SIDEWALK THAT LED TO THE marina where *The Defender* was docked. No one else was around, which tended to be the case well past midnight. He'd worked as long as he could keep his eyes open, trying to cover every contingency, every possible turn of events. He wasn't sure he'd accomplished a thing. He just wanted to assure himself he'd done all he could—so he wouldn't blame himself if it all went bad.

Except he knew he would.

Maria said as long as he was in the picture, Ossie still had a chance.

She believed it. He didn't.

Camila was at her own place, wisely assuming he wouldn't want company on the eve of trial. So he would be left alone with his thoughts—which wasn't necessarily a great thing.

He walked down the lonely boardwalk and unlocked the gate leading to his beloved boat.

Three men waited for him on the other side of the gate.

The one in the middle was the tallest, half a head taller than Dan and a lot thicker. The one to the left had small dark eyes. The one on the right smiled.

He'd seen that man before. But on the previous occasion, he was wearing a UPS uniform.

"Did Sweeney send you?"

None of them answered. The man in the middle stepped forward silently.

"Is this supposed to intimidate me? It won't work. I won't betray my client."

No response.

"You know, I have a lot of friends and—"

The tall man's eyes shrunk. His lips contorted into a smirk, then a snarl.

The other two stood on either side, watching.

The man in the middle bent his knees and swung his fist around toward Dan's face.

He didn't wait for the punch to land. If he was going to survive this, he had to take the initiative. Last time, he'd been a punching bag. He wouldn't be that helpless this time around. He led with his best right punch, fast as he could, right into the solar plexus. The man might outweigh him, but if he lost his breath he'd be incapacitated, at least for a moment or two.

The punch landed. The tall man staggered backward. His two companions looked surprised and not pleased.

Turning toward the man on the left, he threw a left uppercut into the smaller man's ribs. He tried to put as much weight into it as he could. The man grunted and bent over, clutching his stomach.

He whirled around to face the third man, Mr. UPS—

But too late. The tire iron clubbed him on the side of his head. The dock rose up to greet his face. He attempted to break his fall, but he was too slow. Another blow to the head followed. Flashes of light erupted before his eyes.

He tried to roll over, but before he could, he felt a heavy boot in his ribs. Something broke, he was certain of it.

He needed to do something fast or he was dead. But he couldn't move, couldn't even roll over on his side. He should call out for help. But that seemed too hard, too impossible. If this were a movie, the cavalry would come running to his rescue about now.

But no one came.

Two more kicks followed, another to the ribs, then another between the legs. He cried out, high-pitched and tortured. He was completely paralyzed, helpless, unable to do anything but take the punishment.

The three men surrounded him, brutal, angry, raining their fists and boots down upon him, punching and kicking all at once. They were doing more than just completing an assignment. They were doing it with pleasure. They were angry. And they weren't worried about leaving a mark.

Someone's fist collided with his face. His lower lip split. He tasted blood.

He saw the tire iron coming down again. He could register it, but he couldn't raise a hand to stop it. The last thing he remembered was the sight of that deadly metal baton headed for his brain.

And then, nothing at all.

THE TROUBLE WITH KNOWING

CHAPTER TWENTY-NINE

CAMILA SAT BOLT UPRIGHT IN HER BED. SOMETHING WAS WRONG. She knew it. She couldn't explain how she knew. But she did.

She caught a glimpse of herself in the mirror hanging on the wall beside her bed. She looked a mess. Good thing tv cameras couldn't get in here. She'd been sleeping hard.

And yet, something awakened her. Something...not right.

Or maybe, girl, you just don't like sleeping alone. Maybe you've become accustomed to that warm male body snuffling and snorting and snuggled up close.

A horrifying thought. What would her #MeToo pals think about that?

An even worse thought—maybe her feelings were hurt because it appeared Dan was capable of getting through the night without her.

No, that wasn't it. She understood. He had to focus on the case. He would stay up late and get up early. He didn't need distractions. She would feel the same way if this were the night before an election...

Except that wasn't even true. If this were the night before an election, she'd want him close. They be watching the returns roll in, probably hand in hand...

She pounded a fist against the mattress. She shouldn't feel like this! But she did.

Men. Why couldn't she make do with a dog?

And why couldn't she shake this feeling that something was wrong? Was her subconscious sending her a message? To be fair, Dan was constantly threatened (as was she) and they'd learned to live with it. Then again, he had been attacked recently...

She checked the clock on the end table. Almost four in the morning. Heck, Dan was probably awake, wondering if he could squeeze in some kitesurfing before he dressed for court.

But still...

She grabbed her cell and punched the buttons.

She needed to hear his voice, that was all. Then she'd put her head back on the pillow and sleep much better...

He didn't answer.

That was weird. She knew he slept with his phone nearby, and that he left the sound on, and that he'd given her a distinct ringtone—the main theme from *Wonder Woman*. Given how small the bedroom on that boat was, he couldn't miss it. Even if he decided to turn the ringer off, he'd probably feel the vibration.

The call switched to his voicemail. "Talk is cheap. Leave your name at the beep."

That was her Dan. So full of social grace...

But no answer.

Ok, now she was officially worried. She called again and he still didn't pick up.

She glanced at the clock. Even if she threw on some clothes and left, it would take her almost half an hour to get to the marina. But Maria's apartment was only a few blocks away.

Count on a girlfriend. Despite the early hour, Maria picked up on the second ring.

Her instincts were good, too. "What's wrong?"

"I can't get Dan on the phone. Maybe he's screening his calls—"

"From you?"

"Maybe he lost his phone."

"No chance." She could hear movement on the other end of the line. "Already half-dressed. I can be at the marina in five."

"Thank you so much, Maria. It's probably no big deal."

"If it were no big deal, you wouldn't have called. I'll get back to you as soon as I know something."

MARIA LOVED ST. PETERSBURG, BUT SHE WAS NOT A FAN OF ANY city in the pre-dawn hours of the morning. Something about darkness left her feeling vulnerable. Sure, she was a modern independent woman and she could handle herself...but still. Unidentified noises. Sparse light. Staggering drunks. Creeptastic.

She left her car and jogged across the street. If she had to be up this time of the morning, she might as well get in a little exercise. She could skip the workout that probably would've gotten pushed aside anyway to make more time for fretting uselessly about the trial.

Truth was, she'd been worried about Dan ever since the incident with the fake UPS man. That sort of thing wasn't supposed to happen to lawyers. Maybe to criminals and Mafioso. Maybe in cop shows or John Wick movies. But not to lawyers. Not to someone who isn't guilty of anything other than doing his job. Well.

Dan was impossible and quirky and full of himself—or pretended to be. But he was also whip-smart and dedicated and at times, when they sat quietly at the table working, she saw traces of the little boy who lost his father so tragically at far too young an age. She liked that boy, and she liked what he had become. Instead of letting it destroy him, he used it to turn himself into something important, something that mattered. He made himself one of the strongest, most courageous people she knew.

She liked working with him. She liked having him on her team.

She couldn't bear the thought of anything happening to him.

She remembered that first time she'd gone to Beachcomber's to recruit him and he, predictably, tried to pick her up. She had to put him down hard, but at the same time...she was a little tempted. He was older and had wildly different tastes. But still. Smart is sexy.

Whatever. That ship sailed a long time ago. They were best pals and partners and she even thought of him as the brother she never had. She thought her late father would approve of that appointment. He saw far too many of his immigrant friends abused and mistreated by government officials. He would've admired Dan just as much as she did.

Maybe the reason she liked Dan was that, in a way, they had so much in common. Dan lost his father—which changed the direction of his entire life—and she worshipped her father who worked so hard to give her everything she could want—which changed the direction of her entire life.

Please God. Let Dan be out for a run or surfing or picking up chicks at that strip joint. Anything. Anything safe.

She rounded the corner and raced up the boardwalk. She knew where *The Defender* was docked well enough to find it with her eyes closed. The gate was locked—so what? A child could get over that. She leapt the gate without even slowing down. She turned toward the sailboat—

And stopped cold.

Oh my God. Oh no. Oh my God no.

Dan!

JIMMY RACED DOWN THE HOSPITAL CORRIDOR. HE KNEW HIS BELLY
was swaying back and forth like a Tupperware bowl of Jell-O—
and he didn't care.

He ran to the administrator's station in the center of the
corridor. "Which room?"

He didn't have to explain. Everyone knew Jimmy. "412."

"Thanks." He raced down the hall. As soon as his husband
Luke called to tell him Dan had been admitted, he jumped into
the car and hadn't stopped moving since. Only once had he
glanced at his phone—

And saw that it was filled with text messages and voicemail
from Maria. He listened to the first one while he drove.

"They tried to kill Dan. He's in Kindred Hospital. He's alive,
just barely. Come as soon as you can."

He didn't need to hear anything more. He rounded the
corner, then slowed and gently pushed open the door.

Maria, Garrett, and Camila all stood on the far side.

Dan lay on the bed, a tube in his mouth and all kinds of
wires connected to his body. His eyes were shut and covered by
black circles. His neck and arms were bruised. His mouth
looked wrong, lopsided. His abdomen was bandaged. His face
was pale.

He looked like a corpse.

"Is he—Is he—?"

"He was barely alive when I called 911," Maria said quietly.
"He was concussed and losing blood. If I hadn't found him when
I did…"

"And that wasn't soon enough," Camila said. "I should've
called earlier."

"You couldn't possibly know."

"I should've been with him. I never should've left him alone."

"If you'd been with him," Garrett said somberly, "you'd probably be in the hospital now too."

"When did this happen?" Jimmy asked.

"After Dan left the office," Garrett explained. "And that was after midnight. I saw him leave because—"

"I know. You never sleep. What happened?"

"Apparently someone met him at the boat," Maria explained. "They didn't leave a calling card. He's been unconscious since I found him, lying in a pool of his own blood and broken in about a dozen places."

Jimmy's lips trembled. "Who—Who's looking after him and—"

"I have the best doctors in the city on this," Camila explained.

"What do they say?"

"Three severe blows to the head. They used some kind of metal weapon. He probably has a concussion, which may be why he doesn't wake up. Two broken ribs. Bruising all over his body. Someone knocked out a tooth, which he almost choked on."

Jimmy closed his eyes tightly. "Why?"

Maria shook her head. "We assume it was related to the case. Someone did not want him to appear in the courtroom today."

"I think they wanted him dead," Garrett said. "And if you hadn't shown up when you did, he would be."

"I should've known this would happen," Jimmy said, wiping tears from his eyes. "Especially after that fake UPS guy attacked him. I should've seen this coming. I should've hired security. Should've had him watched night and day."

"Dan would never have agreed to that."

"I should've done it anyway."

Maria walked around the bed and placed her hand on his

shoulder. "There's no point in blaming yourself, Jimmy. We all could've done more. But we didn't. We've had threats before. We had no way of knowing that...it would escalate so dramatically."

"It's our business to know." He pounded a fist into his hand. "This is Sweeney's work. He's the one who needs a pounding. I'm gonna burn that bastard's palace to the ground."

"We don't know Sweeney's behind this," Garrett said.

"Don't we?"

"No. Sadly, there are many possibilities. Don't do anything rash that makes the situation worse."

"He's right." Maria hugged Jimmy tight. "That won't make it better."

"Then what do we do?"

"Wait. Hope. Pray."

"We can't lose Dan. He's our team leader. He's our Crag-heart. He's—He's—" Jimmy wiped more tears away. "He's our Aquaman."

"I know," Maria said, dabbing at her own red eyes. "I know."

CHAPTER THIRTY

THE FIRST THING HE REGISTERED WAS THE LIGHT. BRIGHT WHITE hot harsh light. Bearing down on him, unrelentingly.

Stop. Make that go away. He was fine where he was.

The darkness had been more comfortable. Calm, reassuring. Even pleasant, in a way. Drifting in the void. No stress. Perpetual calm.

Emptiness.

He and his father were having a chat. *Everything I did, I did for a reason.* No conflict. Acceptance. Only smiles, no regrets. *At some point in everyone's life, they decide who they want to be. They make a choice.*

But that light wouldn't let him go. And there was more. Something else intruded on his reverie.

Pain. All over his body, but especially in the center. His stomach. Hurt like hell. And his head. Throbbed. Pulsed like a rhythm instrument.

He tried to move, but even trying hurt, and he didn't get anywhere. Maybe that could wait.

The light grew brighter, and all at once, he realized that he had opened his eyes.

"Dan? Are you awake? Dan?"

He found it required effort to speak. Each syllable grated. Enunciation was almost impossible with swollen lips. Something was wrong with his mouth. It felt as if...something was missing. "Would someone...turn off the damn lights?"

"He's awake!" He heard someone clap hands together. "Say something."

"I just did."

"I think you're awake. Are you awake?"

"My eyes are open."

"You've done that before. The docs said it was an autonomic response. Didn't mean you'd regained consciousness. But now you're speaking!"

"And asking you...to turn off the damn lights."

"Now you're speaking and complaining! You *are* back!"

He could barely turn his head, just enough to see Camila and Maria embracing.

"What happened?"

"You don't remember?" Camila said. "The docs warned us you might suffer some memory loss."

He paused for a moment, drew in his breath, and tried to focus. "We were prepping for trial. Oh my God." He tried to sit up, but couldn't. "The trial. I need to get to the courthouse."

He felt a firm hand on his chest. Jimmy. "Slow down, cowboy. You're not going anywhere."

"But the trial—"

"Has been postponed."

"Fine." He did feel stiff and wasn't anxious to get out of bed. "But first thing Tuesday morning."

A silence filled the room.

Garrett was the first to speak. "Dan—it's Thursday."

"What?"

"You've been unconscious for more than three days," Garrett said. "Do you remember what happened to you?"

He closed his eyes and thought as hard as he could. "I finished working. Really more worrying than working. Left the office. After midnight. Walked home. Got to the boat." His eyes opened. "Three men. There were three men waiting for me."

"Did you recognize them?" Camila asked.

"One was the fake UPS man. The other two were new."

"Would you recognize them if you saw them again?" Maria asked.

"Definitely." He sighed. "But I won't. Probably in another county by now. I tried to fight back, but it was dark and I was outnumbered..." He frowned.

"No shame, dude," Jimmy said. "It was a sneak attack. And they apparently had a weapon. Pummeled you on the head. What was that—a baseball bat?"

"Tire iron. I distinctly remember the tire iron." Just thinking about it made the pain intensify.

Maria pushed a button beside his bed. "The docs told us to alert them if you woke."

"If?" He tried to sit up again. "Who are these docs?"

Camila cut in. "That is a complicated story. As soon as I heard you were hurt, I contacted the people I know to be the best physicians in the city." She chuckled. "But when Mr. K found out what happened, he called my bet and raised it. Flew in some of the best physicians in the nation."

"Really?"

"Mayo Clinic. Cleveland Clinic. The President of the United States doesn't have better doctors."

He thought for a moment. "Then why do I hurt so damn much?"

"You've got two broken ribs," Maria explained. "They're wrapped, but apparently there's not much the docs can do except keep it all aligned and wait for them to knit naturally. They'll give you something for the pain if you want but...it's still gonna hurt."

"And you lost a tooth," Jimmy added. "And you have two black eyes, head injuries that bled like crazy, and severe contusions and lacerations all over your body."

"Apparently they didn't want me to forget the beating," he muttered.

"I think they wanted you dead," Garrett said. "You just got lucky. These two wonderful women saved your bacon."

"Not for the first time." He smiled as much as he could muster. "Thanks, wonderful women."

"Don't worry," Camila said, "I'll be expecting some payback in the near future. When you're...you know. Hardy again."

Jimmy covered his ears. "Ick. Please stop."

Camila laughed. "What?"

"It's like hearing Mom and Dad talk about getting it on. Please."

Dan laughed—then regretted it. He turned his head as far as he could manage. He found a mirror on the right, just over a cabinet.

He did look like hell. And he hurt like hell too.

And then it came back to him, in one terrifying, horrifying wash of painful memory. Every moment. Every blow. As if it were happening all over again. The sadist in the center with the ham-sized fists. The tire iron. The way they kept kicking him even after he was down, after the misery was so intense he couldn't even scream any more. He was completely helpless, more a baby than a man.

He felt tears wash into his eye sockets. Stop, he told himself. Not with all these people around. He visited his father a hundred times while he was in prison, and did his father ever cry? The man never even complained.

His father. Something triggered inside his head. It was almost as if they'd just been chatting. But that was completely impossible...

"Do the police have any idea who did this or why?"

"No. Kakazu came by one afternoon and paid his respects. Jazlyn has visited too. But they're clueless. We're all assuming someone didn't want to see you in court."

And it would be so easy to grant their wish. He could bail on medical grounds. Or mental. Let Maria take over, or let it be assigned to another firm.

"When does the trial resume?"

"It's on indefinite stay."

"And the civil case?"

"The relatives are pushing for it to resume. They actually opposed the continuance, believe it or not. We won't be able to hold them off forever." Garrett paused. "I've talked to Mr. K about this. We think we should let someone else take over the cases. We'll advise, of course. But let someone else take the lead."

"Do you know anyone who could do that?"

"We'll find someone. Someone who will do right by Ossie."

"It's for the best, Dan," Camila said. "You need to rest. Get your strength back. It won't happen overnight."

"I agree," Maria said. "You don't need to be taking any risks right now."

Was she talking about risks to his recuperation? Or the risk that those brutes, or others like them, might return? And this time, finish the job.

He didn't know which was worse—the thought of dying, or the thought of being beaten senseless, one painful blow after another. On and on, never ending, unrelenting...

He couldn't bear that. Again he felt tears welling up. He had felt so helpless, so useless. Like a rag doll those men could brutalize. He had never experienced anything like that before. No one had ever—

Except that wasn't true, was it? Was his beating worse than what his father endured, day after day after day? Better a beating than the mental torture of being locked away forever, imprisoned, defamed for a crime you didn't commit.

What was it his father was trying to tell him?

"Call the judge's clerk. We want to start as soon as she can schedule us. Monday morning, if possible."

Maria's eyes bulged. "Monday? Dan, you can't—"

"I'll be ready. We've already done the work. And I'll have all of you there to help."

"Dan, it's too soon."

"We can do it."

"No!" Maria's voice peaked. "I'm sorry, Dan, I almost always let you have your way, but this time I'm putting my foot down. I won't stand around and watch you kill yourself. Or get yourself murdered. You are not the only lawyer in this town. We'll let someone else take the case. And that's final."

He drew in his breath. He knew she was speaking out of love, but he still needed to make her see it from his perspective. "Maria, think for a minute. What was the point of the beating? Truly? Beating me up—or even killing me—wouldn't prevent the trial from happening. The prosecution isn't going to drop the charges. The court isn't going to let Ossie be tried without a lawyer. So what's the point? *Delay.* That's the only thing attacking me might accomplish. That's what someone wants. I don't know why, but I'm damned certain I'm not going to cooperate. If the judge is agreeable, we start Monday morning."

A nurse appeared at the door. "The doctors are on their way. I'm going to have to ask the visitors to leave for a bit. We need more room."

Most of them nodded and moved toward the door, but Maria held back. "Dan, this is a mistake. You were seriously injured. You can't rush your recovery."

"I'll be fine. Promise."

"At least wait and see what the docs say."

"Nothing they could say is going to change my mind."

"No one will think ill of you because you quit the case. You were attacked. Almost killed."

"And that's where they screwed up," he said, a thin smile crossing his swollen face.

"What do you mean?"

"If they wanted this trial delayed, they should've killed me. But as long as I'm breathing, I will not concede. I don't quit." He pushed himself up. "We're going to trial, Maria. And we're going to win."

CHAPTER THIRTY-ONE

MONDAY MORNING, DAN LIMPED INTO THE COURTROOM, BRACING himself with a cane in his right hand. He hated using a support prop, but he would hate falling on his face worse. It was a compromise. Maria wanted him to use something more reliable, like a walker, but every time he tried, he felt like the old guy in *Up*. The cane was a compromise.

He could tell every eye in the courtroom darted his way as he entered the room. They all knew who he was and what had happened to him. Did they admire him for showing up? Did they think he was a fool? Or did they worry that he might bring his problems their way?

He scanned the courtroom for Jazlyn—then stopped himself. She wasn't going to be here. What was that man's name? Something Irish with a lot of K sounds...

A tall man in a shiny blue suit strode up and thrust out his hand. "Paul Kilpatrick. Pleased to finally meet you, Mr. Pike."

That was it. Kilpatrick. He was the hired gun. Tall, lean, a mouthful of teeth. Cheap suit, off-the-rack. About fifty. Full head of hair. Toupee? Southern accent. Alabama?

Jazlyn had told him all about this guy. He specialized in

WILLIAM BERNHARDT

prosecuting murder cases. That was all he handled, and according to the word on the street, he was extremely good at it. Insanely good at it. Pundits said Dan had the best win-loss record in this courthouse—but not while this man was on the premises. Kilpatrick had a perfect record—he always won.

"Very glad to see you back on your feet. I was horrified when I heard what happened. Can I call you Dan?"

"Of course."

"I want you to know the DA's office is taking the assault on you seriously. They've got detectives rustling the bushes, trying to see if they can learn what happened. Shake enough snitches and eventually something's going to fall out."

"I appreciate that." It was complete bull, but nice of the man to say. DA Belasco didn't care what happened to him. For all he knew, Belasco was behind the attack. Even if he wasn't, he'd be more likely to give the attackers a gold medal than a prison sentence. "I assume you're ready to proceed?"

"That's what I do. Life is much easier when you only have one case to manage."

That was, of course, part of the point of bringing in a ringer. Normally, lawyers in the DA's office had to juggle many cases at once, given the terrific overload of work and pitiful under-staffing. Kilpatrick had been hired to handle a single case, so he could focus all his time and energy here and leave people like Jazlyn free to concentrate on their other, lower-profile but still important cases. It was much like the deal Mr. K offered him when he was recruited for the Last Chance Lawyers. One case at a time—the catch being that Mr. K would choose the case.

"You know," Kilpatrick said, "no one would care if you wanted to wait a little longer before we start this trial."

"No. My client is anxious to get it done."

Kilpatrick tilted his head. "You know, this will be a long case."

"No worries. I'm up to it."

"You're sure about that?"

"Positive." And stop with the professional courtesy overkill already. It only made him more suspicious. "Anything we need to discuss?"

"Not that I know of."

"Are you licensed to practice in Florida? I'd consent to a *pro hac vice* motion if—"

Kilpatrick smiled. "I'm licensed to practice in every state."

"That's not possible."

"You mean, that's not easy. But it is possible and I've done it."

"You've passed the bar in every single state."

"I love taking those damn essay exams. Turns me on."

"I pity your wife."

"Some states practice comity so I don't have to take the tests. Point is, I'm ready to go wherever the job takes me, and I don't need a babysitter holding my hand during the trial. For me, it was worth the trouble."

Probably true. Jazlyn didn't know the specifics, but she thought Kilpatrick was getting paid an exorbitant amount of money to handle this case. "Do you have an offer?"

"Sorry. I have no authority to settle. The DA wants this to go to trial. He thinks the public would feel cheated if it didn't receive a full and fair hearing."

That didn't make sense. Why would the DA turn down a chance to avoid trial with a no-risk settlement that might not give up much? "And you're going for the death penalty. Despite my client's youth?"

"Your client claims he's Ossie Coleman, which means he's eighteen, which means he can be tried as an adult."

"Barely."

He shrugged. "The DA insists."

"Then I guess we have nothing more to say." He nodded curtly and headed for the defendant's table. Despite Kilpatrick's effusive courtesy, he didn't like or trust the man.

And it was more than just that he was on the opposite side of a lawsuit.

Ossie waited for him decked out in a lovely charcoal suit Maria provided. The tension must be killing him. His life was on the line. His attorney had been attacked. But he seemed to be holding it together. At the far end of the table, keeping to himself, was Maria's jury consultant, a man named Cooper Fisk.

One more courtroom professional to dislike.

"How you holding up?"

He raised a hand to give Ossie a high five, but to his surprise, Ossie rushed forward and embraced him. "Dan! It's so good to see you!"

"Um...you too."

"I was so worried about you. Maria told me what happened."

"Well, I'm fine. And you're looking good, too."

"Like these fabulous threads Maria picked out for me?"

It was an excellent suit. Made him look respectable, but it wasn't showy.

Wait—was that why Kilpatrick was wearing such an obviously ordinary suit? To create a contrast between the lawyers? Between the slick defense attorney in his expensive Italian threads, and the regular guy man-of-the-people?

He would have to watch Kilpatrick carefully. "Maria spent a lot of time picking out your suit."

Ossie appeared flattered. "You did?"

She explained. "This isn't a sexist women-fuss-over-clothes thing. It's about making the right first impression with the jury. First impressions can be of critical importance in any arena, but with people who have the power to decide how you spend the rest of your life—you want to look your best."

"And so," he said, "the courtroom becomes, not a forum for finding the truth, but a fashion show."

"It isn't quite that bad," Maria explained, "but clothes do matter. Especially in this social media era. You've seen the memes. A celeb shows up in court and people comment on their dress or accessories more than their guilt or innocence. It's absurd, but it happens. That's why I hired a courtroom image consultant. Hope that's ok, Dan."

His eyes bugged. "You did what?"

"Sorry. You were in the hospital. I ran it by Mr. K and he approved it. Studies have shown that juries are influenced by attire. It may all be subconscious, but that doesn't mean it isn't important." She smiled at Ossie. "We dressed you in a suit that's attractive, but conservative. No jewelry. No name-brand nonsense. That okay, Dan?"

He tucked in his chin. "Maybe you should dress me, too."

"I have tried. You don't listen." She continued talking to Ossie. "I've got suits for you to wear the rest of the week. I don't mind if you personalize them, but remember—no logos, no brash colors, no jewelry. No visible tattoos. Nothing that distracts from your message: I didn't commit this crime. I dressed you like this is a job interview, because in a way, it is. The most important job interview of your life. Gray is safe. It may not be anyone's favorite color, but no one actively dislikes it."

The bailiff emerged from chambers and told everyone to rise. A few moments later, Judge Smulders stumbled into the courtroom, looking very much as if he wished he were anywhere but here. The judge took a look at the gallery—saw that the room was almost full—and blanched.

He took his seat at the bench. "So, I guess people want to see what happens next, huh?" He smiled lopsidedly, then erased it when he realized no one else was smiling. He straightened some papers, then tapped them against the bench. "So...how do we get this thing started?" He glanced at his clerk.

Bertha cleared her throat. "Would your honor like to call the case?"

"Oh right. You can do it."

She looked mortified. "Well then. The Honorable Judge Smulders calls this court into session. The case on the docket today is the State of Florida vs John Doe, a.k.a. Ossie Coleman."

"Waive the reading," Dan said. "The defendant reiterates his plea of not guilty."

Kilpatrick also rose. "No amendments, your honor. The State is ready to proceed."

The judge cocked his head to one side. "Well then. I guess we should just...move along." He glanced down. "I don't see anything we have to handle first. No motions or any of that stuff. Maybe we should just..."

He decided to give Bertha a break. He could steer the marionette judge for a while. "Would your honor like to impanel a jury?"

He pointed at Dan. "Bingo. Yes. Let's do that. How do we..."

"Perhaps the bailiff could draw eighteen names at random. And then we could start the *voir dire* process."

"Fantastic. Great idea." Smulders let out a high-pitch laugh, almost a giggle. "This should be interesting. Let's get this show on the road."

Ossie leaned close. "Why does our judge look...my age?"

"He's just baby-faced. He has in fact been to law school, been to judge school, and has even spent a few years on the bench. You just...can't tell."

"He seems nervous."

"This is his first death-penalty case."

"Mine too," Ossie replied.

He had to smile. "No worries. I'll keep the judge on track. This might even work to our advantage."

"How?"

The first phalanx of potential jurors entered the room. "I'm not sure. But I prefer to remain optimistic."

CHAPTER THIRTY-TWO

DAN KNEW JURY INTERROGATION WOULD TAKE HOURS, POSSIBLY all day. He'd seen cases in which it took several days, but he hoped this wouldn't be one of those. He could help this proceed expediently—as long as no one tried to game the system. Take advantage of the judge's inexperience. Resort to trickery.

Unfortunately, he had a hunch Kilpatrick was likely to attempt all three.

While the bailiff read some preliminary instructions to the potential jurors, he had a chance to talk with his associates.

"You need to be more realistic about your situation." Cooper Fisk had been hired to consult on jury issues. Portly, ill-fitting suit, corner square that matched his tie. A New England manner of speaking that almost approached a British accent. Exactly the kind of egghead he couldn't stand. Technically, Fisk worked for them, but you couldn't tell that from his attitude. "Kilpatrick has been hired for a reason."

"I get that. The DA wants to win."

"It's more than that." Fisk held up a finger. If he pointed, Dan was going to slap him. "The DA wants to play dirty. But he doesn't want any blowback, so he hires a ringer. 'Gosh, we didn't know he was going to do that. He's a loose cannon.' Etcetera."

"You don't know that."

"I've dealt with Kilpatrick before." He supposed that made sense. There could only be so many trials big enough to command the fees these guys charged. "His reputation is built upon two things. Always winning. And making his DAs happy. He'll be trying hard to do both."

Maria inched forward. "Maybe you should explain to Dan what you told me earlier. Your strategy for jury selection."

Fisk shrugged. "Some of it is obvious. We have an African-American defendant. So we want African-American jurors."

"You can't assume jurors will always vote along racial lines."

"No. Just 93% of the time."

He frowned. "Age is also a factor. And prosperity. Wealthy African-Americans may not empathize with someone they perceive as an upstart. Or a criminal."

"But realistically," Fisk said, "rich people can get themselves excused from jury duty. You won't see any African-American CEOs on this panel. You'll see housewives and blue-collar employees, primarily. And that's good—those are the jurors you want." He paused. "And those are the jurors Kilpatrick will rigorously remove."

"You're aware that the Supreme Court has barred juror dismissal based upon race."

"I'm sure Kilpatrick can assert some other reason. But he'll get as much color off the jury as he can. Probably will remove Hispanics as well."

"Actually," Maria said, "in some neighborhoods, there's a lot of tension between Hispanic and African-American communities."

"I'm aware of that. But at the end of the day, color will be the driving force. You follow me, Mr. Pike?"

"Is it impossible to imagine that some jurors will listen to the evidence and try to render a fair verdict?"

Fisk smiled, almost patronizingly, as if he were speaking to a naïve child. "Your last two capital defendant clients were both Hispanic, right?"

Why was their jury consultant investigating him? "True."

"Did you consider race when you questioned the jurors?"

"Of course, but—"

"This community saw a major gangland shootout not long ago. Got huge publicity."

"True."

"And many people felt the cops went after their targets based on race."

"Also true."

"They may be looking for payback."

"You can't assume that."

"You're familiar with the OJ case?"

He almost rolled his eyes. Here it came. Everyone's go-to trial. "Of course, but—"

"At least two of the OJ jurors have admitted that they acquitted, not based upon the evidence, but because they saw this as payback for the Rodney King incident. Not just the initial beating, but the fact that the LA court exonerated the cops involved."

In the legal world, there was a saying—tough cases make for bad law. Similarly, ridiculously high-profile incidents like the OJ case made for bad examples. They were too atypical be instructive for any remotely normal case. "You think these jurors will want to punish the prosecutors because law enforcement has harassed people of color?"

"We can hope. Does your client feel he has been harassed by cops based upon his color?"

"Yes. To be fair, he was fleeing arrest."

Fisk raised a hand to stop him. "Never mind that. Use it."

"I don't want to play the race card unless I think race actually has something to do with it."

"Do you want to win the case?"

"Well, of course I want to—"

"Use it."

"The jury should make its decision based upon the evidence, not—"

"You hired me to help, so I will. If the jury makes a decision based on the evidence, you're toast. You need to muddy the water with everything you can. Like race. Like hostility toward law enforcement. Make them believe this is a massive frame. The cops can't stand the thought of a black punk getting rich, so they tried to make sure he wouldn't inherit. And that should be your go-to theory for jury selection. Keep everyone of color. Keep everyone who appears to suspect cops, or prosecutors, or the justice system."

"People who don't believe in the justice system are routinely removed."

"Only if they admit it. You need to find the people who don't admit it because they're hoping to throw a wrench in the works. And while you're at it, keep everyone who hates rich people."

"I'm not sure that's even a thing."

"Are you joking? Have you not seen the t-shirts around town? 'Kill the rich.' Have you not noticed the growing trend toward socialism? Some people deeply resent anyone who has more than they do—even people like Zachary Coleman, who worked his way up from nothing. In fact, sometimes that's worse—because theoretically anyone could have done it. Rather than admit they didn't have the right stuff or do the work, some prefer to blame the system and resent successful people."

"I don't see how this helps us."

"We live in the era of the greatest wealth disparity in history. The upper 1% have more wealth than the lower 90%. When you're struggling to pay the bills, there's nothing worse than hearing about some tech billionaire who just bought an island."

"I still don't see—"

"The prosecution is planning to tell the jury it's all about the money, right? I read Maria's strategy notebook. It's all relatives squabbling over a huge inheritance?"

"Sort of..."

"Great. That plays well into the 'kill the rich' sentiment. Make your client the underdog. He suffered in poverty and degradation for fourteen years, and then when he's finally about to come into his own, the family tries to stop him, aided by the bigoted white law enforcement community. Make the other relatives your super-villains."

"Wait," Ossie said. "I don't like that."

He turned his head. He didn't even realize Ossie was listening to this.

"My grandfather is sick and fragile. He doesn't need—"

Fisk completely ignored him, as if his opinion were of no import, or worse, as if he weren't even there. "You also want to remove any self-made successes, not that you'll get many, and anyone with money, not that you'll get many. You might see some doctors' wives. Society matrons."

"So basically, we want an all-poor, all-black jury."

"You won't get anything that perfect. But if you get a majority of desirable jurors, or even a plurality, you'll be in good shape. For that matter"—he tilted his head to one side—"it only takes one determined juror to hang the jury."

"I don't want a hung jury," Ossie said. "I don't want to do this all over again a year later."

"A hung jury is better than a conviction."

Dan spotted the bailiff holding a bowl full of names. They needed to wrap this up. He didn't like being the old fogey who objected to new ideas, but he thought this jury consultant was a waste of time. He was far more likely to trust his own observations and instincts than to listen to this amalgamation of clichés.

And his back was killing him. Sitting in one place too long reminded him that he had two broken ribs that hadn't healed. But he didn't say anything. Let them think his discomfort was just because he didn't agree with Fisk.

He noticed Maria watching him closely. He thought she was about to speak, but Fisk cut her off.

"What is your theory of jury selection, Mr. Pike?"

He shrugged. "The prosecution wants soldiers. People who will overlook the flaws in the case and do their patriotic duty. The defense wants thinkers. Because if you take seriously the requirement of finding guilt beyond a reasonable doubt, almost no prosecution case meets the standard."

Fisk made a tsking sound. "I think you may have made the tragic error of starting to believe your own BS."

His back stiffened.

"Listen to me, Pike. The defense does not want thinkers. You get a jury full of thinkers and you're dead in the water. Maybe you haven't read the forensic reports and witness affidavits, but I have." He glanced at Ossie. "No disrespect intended. But ninety-nine juries out of a hundred would convict on this evidence. And this jury will too unless you start getting way smarter about the process. Jury selection may be the most important thing you do."

"Of course, you would say that, since you're getting paid a small fortune to advise on jury selection."

"Yes, I advise," Fisk said, folding his arms across his chest. "But I do not, unfortunately, have the power to make people listen."

CHAPTER THIRTY-THREE

TYPICALLY, THE JUDGE ASKED THE JURORS A FEW PRELIMINARY questions before turning them over to the lawyers. But it became readily apparent that Judge Smulders had no questions other than those written out for him on a piece of paper he clutched in his hands. Bertha to the rescue again? This forced Kilpatrick, because the prosecutor went first, to kill a lot of time asking the obvious. Do you know any of the people involved? Have you already formed an opinion on the case? Do you believe in the justice system? Are you capable of delivering a death sentence, if you feel the evidence warrants it?

Kilpatrick worked through the obvious dutifully, and Dan didn't want to make it any slower or more tedious than it already was, so he made no objections. At Fisk's recommendation, he removed a few jurors early, and neither Kilpatrick nor the judge posed an objection. He was impressed by what an even-handed job Kilpatrick did, never taking advantage of his lead. Until one of the man's questions made him feel distinctly uncomfortable.

"Does anyone have problems with defense attorneys?" Kilpatrick looked at them with a wide-eyed smile, as if they were all in on the same joke. "I know you said you were okay with the justice system. But that doesn't always extend to lawyers. You know the clichés. They're all crooked. Will say or do anything for a buck. Put crooks back on the street. Anyone feel like that?"

Kilpatrick hadn't said anything quite meriting an objection —yet. Was he trying to suggest that he wasn't a nasty old lawyer —but Dan was?

A well-dressed, middle-aged white woman in the middle of the back row raised her hand. "Are you talking about that man back there? The one in the fancy suit? I think I know him."

Kilpatrick gave her a straight-faced reply. "That's Daniel Pike. He represents the man accused of murder. How do you know him?"

"I've seen him on tv. He represented the mayor when she was accused of murder."

"How did you feel about that?"

She seemed hesitant. "Well...I never voted for the woman."

Dan made a mental note. He didn't need Fisk to tell him that woman got his next peremptory removal.

"Did you have an opinion as to her innocence or guilt?"

The woman shrugged. "Looked guilty to me. Rich people can always buy their way out of trouble."

Ok, this was irritating, if only because it reinforced what Fisk had been saying.

"Do you have negative thoughts toward Mr. Pike because he represented the mayor?"

"I'm...sure he was just doing his job. And making lots of money in the process."

The worst possible answer. If she had answered the question in the affirmative, he could remove her immediately for cause. But instead, she denied having a grudge—which meant he'd have to use one of his limited peremptory challenges.

Kilpatrick continued. "We shouldn't resent Mr. Pike because

he makes a lot of money and can afford fancy suits." This was why Kilpatrick wore a lame suit. He anticipated how Dan would dress—and countered it. He was the regular guy. Dan was the slick shyster.

It was never pleasant, realizing you were wrong. But Maria had been correct about the importance of courtroom attire. And Fisk had been right about the threat posed by this prosecutor.

"For that matter," Kilpatrick continued, "they've dressed the defendant up in fancy duds that I'm sure he doesn't own, but don't hold that against the man. Your decision must be based upon the evidence. Ma'am, can you set aside your feelings about the attorneys and make a decision based upon the evidence?"

"Sure," she said. "I just wanted to be honest."

"And we appreciate that. New question. There's some controversy about exactly who the defendant is. Does anyone feel they won't be able to treat him fairly because the court is calling him John Doe?"

Dan didn't get his shot at the jury until well in the afternoon, and by that time, they were tired. He knew if he went on too long it would only result in irritation, and he didn't need to get on their wrong side before the trial began. He had chatted with not only Fisk but Maria and Jimmy, so he felt like he had the consensus opinion on which jurors needed to be removed.

There were a few more questions to ask before they ended the examinations. For the most part they went smoothly and without difficulty. Until they didn't.

"As you may already know, this case involves a great deal of money. Almost a billion dollars. More money than most people are ever going to see. More moolah than most of us can even conceive of. Some of the players in this drama are extremely rich. Will you hold that against them?"

At first, no one took the bait. Finally, a small man on the left side of the back row raised his hand. Mr. Bailey, he recalled.

"I wouldn't hold it against them exactly." He thought a moment. "But I know whenever there's money to be had, some people do crazy things."

"And…what exactly do you mean by that?"

"I had a stepsister. Used to be nice. But when my mother died, she went off the deep end. Started saying all kinds of ugly things about me. Claiming I…did stuff. Course it was all because she wanted the money. I ended up giving her half my inheritance just to shut her up. And Mother didn't leave that much money. Imagine if it had been a billion dollars. Some people would do anything for that kind of cash."

"Your stepsister may have lied about you…but she didn't try to kill you, right?"

Bailey looked supremely uncomfortable. "I wouldn't put it past her. If she thought she could get away with it."

"What about the rest of you? Do you agree?"

Another woman, Mrs. Kravitz, spoke. "Depends on the people. But when the circumstances are sketchy and you don't really know who someone is anyway…it's easy to think the worst."

Like when a claimant appears out of nowhere after fourteen years? He was starting to worry that just hearing these theories spoken aloud would influence others. He was tempted to shut this down, but he needed to make sure there was no more serious prejudice lurking beneath the surface. "You wouldn't criticize someone for fighting for what's theirs. Would you?"

Back to Mr. Bailey. "When someone like my stepsister wants something badly enough, they start lying. Thinking they deserve more than they're getting. Once they've convinced themselves they're a wronged party, they can justify anything in their minds. Lying, cheating, scheming. Maybe even murder."

"Agreed," Mrs. Kravitz said.

"Anyone else feel the same way?"

No one admitted it. But they probably did. He would have to address both the civil and criminal claims in this trial. Because if they believe Ossie was lying—about his identity or anything else—it would be all too easy to believe he was a murderer.

CHAPTER THIRTY-FOUR

DAN WAS RELIEVED THAT THEY MANAGED TO COMPLETE THE JUROR selection, but since it took most of the day, the judge postponed opening statements to the following morning. He was grateful for the additional chance to strategize, incorporating what he learned about the jurors during the quizzing. He even practiced his opening a few times for his teammates.

As he entered the courtroom the next day, he spotted Zachary Coleman in the gallery, rolling about in his wheelchair. Benny and his wife Dolly were present, though he didn't spot the other son, Phil. Why were they here? Sure, they didn't think Ossie was really Ossie. But even if they didn't want him to inherit, did that mean they wanted to see him executed?

Today, he wore a cheaper suit to court. Not as cheap as Kilpatrick's. He didn't want it to be obvious that he was reacting to what Kilpatrick said. And in truth, he didn't own anything that cheap. But he toned it down a bit. From Zenga to Brooks Brothers.

He still used the cane, but the aching in his back had subsided somewhat. He thought about choosing a tie that matched the cane but decided that was taking coordination too far.

Prudence Hancock was in the courtroom. Scouting for Sweeney, no doubt.

While he contemplated where to go first, Prudence strode right up to him. "Good to see you again, Pike. Hate the suit."

"Well…you know. Juries."

"If you think you're going to convince them you're a man of the people, forget it. They've already got you pegged."

"Meaning what?"

"Meaning you're a highly compensated showboat and they know it. Might as well be who you are. At least that's honest. Juries respect honesty. And they turn on anyone they think is putting on a show."

He'd be more irritated if he didn't know she was right.

"Dr. Sweeney instructed me to ask if you were okay."

He tried not to sneer. "Tell him I'm fine."

"You're limping."

"I'm fine."

"And he wanted me to say that his offer still stands."

"So does my complete disinterest."

"Your funeral. I personally have my heart set on engaging in some extreme sports with you. I want to see what you're really made of."

Was this going where he thought it was going? "Maybe after the trial."

"I understand you need time. But when you're ready—I know a great place for heliskiing."

One of the most dangerous extreme sports. But he didn't doubt her. "I'll keep that in mind. Excuse me—I need to get to work. Please give Sweeney my worst."

He headed to the defense table. Ossie sat with Maria—and both looked worried.

"Top of the morning, Ossie."

"Looks like you're walking a little easier."

"Yeah. Practically back to normal again. Hey, I'm sorry about that business with the consultant."

"He thinks I'm guilty."

True. "He's concerned the jury will think you're guilty. And he wants to make sure we do whatever we can to avoid that."

"Everyone thinks I'm guilty. Do you see how my relatives glare at me?"

He did. "You're probably imagining that."

"I'm not. They hate me. My own family hates me."

"Families are complicated. Once all legalities are smoothed out, things will change."

"They will never accept me. Even if I win. I might get the money. But what's the point of money when you don't have family?"

Maria tried to comfort him. "They'll come around, Ossie. It just takes time. But right now, we need your head in the game. Focus on the trial."

He didn't appear any happier, but he didn't argue. "If you say so."

A few minutes later, Judge Smulders called the court into session and asked for opening statements. Kilpatrick went first. He scrutinized the prosecutor carefully. He sensed that every move Kilpatrick made, every syllable he uttered, was carefully calibrated, possibly pre-tested, for maximum impact. He appeared to be wearing the same suit, with a different shirt and tie, and a rather potent aftershave. Not unpleasant, but noticeable.

"Ladies and gentlemen of the jury. Thank you for allowing me to speak to you this morning. I wish we were meeting under happier circumstances. My mother used to bring me out to St Pete during the summer when I was young. She was a teacher, so she always made the most of summer months. She loved to get out in the boat, ski and swim. Wonderful woman. This is sort of a homecoming for me."

All completely irrelevant, of course, but he knew why Kilpatrick was saying it. He was acting more like a pal than a lawyer, trying to get the jury to warm up to him. His Southern accent helped. Seemed smooth and pretty, like a glass of bourbon, neat. Was it his imagination, or was Kilpatrick's accent thicker when he spoke to the jury?

"Course I don't know much about boats and watersports. I can't afford to live on a boat and spend my money on daredevil sports like my worthy opponent." He gestured toward the defense table. "Only thing I ever did with a kite was fly one at the park. But I do love this area. My momma taught me to love the water, and she's always been the biggest influence on my life."

Okay, if the man didn't get to the case soon, he was objecting. The unsubtle digs were bad enough, but this ingratiating talk about his mother—to a jury that was predominantly female —was offensive.

"But I'm afraid there won't be much swimming this week. We have a serious matter before us—the most serious kind there is—so I'm going to have to ask you all to be patient, to remain attentive, and to give this difficult matter the respect and consideration it deserves."

He bobbed a little from one foot to the other. "Here's my promise. I will not waste your time. No showboating, no tricks, nothing that isn't important. I'm not a slick high-flyer. I'm a worker bee. I get the job done, no theatrics, no messing around. I'm a straight shooter, so if I say something, you can darn well believe it's true. My momma taught me to tell the truth, and that lesson has stuck with me ever since."

This was more than a little improper, but Judge Smulders didn't say a word. If anything, he appeared to be mesmerized.

"This case is quite simple, ladies and gentlemen. My oppo-

nent will try to complicate matters, but there's nothing complicated about it. It all comes down to three facts, each of which
we will prove beyond a reasonable doubt."

Of course it would be a list of three. That was the mathematical key to success in public speaking, and an old lawyer trick.
People called it the 'rule of threes,' or 'mathematical truth.' Every
story should have three parts. Every list should be a list of three.
Lists of threes seemed to have an almost magical resonance. You
saw them everywhere—poetry, literature, the Bible. Jokes often
had three people going into a bar or something happening three
times—the last time resulting in the punchline. Contract
lawyers frequently used lists of threes—even though the three
words were redundant synonyms. Goods, chattel, and personal
effects. Right, title, and interest. Give, bequeath, and bestow.
Somehow, in the human brain, a list of three equaled truth.

"First, the young man who pretends to be Ossie Coleman
committed this murder for the same reason he pretends to be
Ossie Coleman. A billion dollars waiting to be claimed. That
amount of money might be a sore temptation to the gentlest of
people—but as the evidence will show, this defendant is not the
gentlest of people.

"Second, though the entire family opposed this young
upstart's claims, the victim, Harrison Coleman, posed a particular problem, because had known the real Ossie well. So he had
to be eliminated. The evidence will show that the defendant met
with the victim and, after an unsuccessful bargaining attempt,
killed him.

"Third." Kilpatrick raised three fingers, just in case someone
was having trouble keeping count. "We have a veritable
avalanche of scientific and forensic evidence showing that the
defendant was at the scene of the crime, met the victim, hid the
murder weapon, and had the ability to perform a...frankly terrifying means of disposing of the body. We can argue all night
about eyewitnesses and memory—but science doesn't lie. And

in this case, science points in one direction. If that weren't enough, in his dying moments"—he whirled around and pointed at Ossie—"the victim wrote *his* name at the scene of the crime."

He took another step even closer to the jury. "I will show you the plain, unvarnished truth. It may disturb you. May even shock you. But these are shocking circumstances. I am confident that once you have seen this irrefutable evidence, seen the world for what it is and acknowledged that science does not lie —you will find the defendant guilty of murder in the first degree."

With that, Kilpatrick pivoted and took his seat.

He exchanged a glance with Maria. They didn't speak, but he knew what she was thinking. He liked to believe that he was the best courtroom orator in town.

But Kilpatrick was better. Way better. Perhaps all these years of doing essentially the same thing had allowed him to hone his skills. But that opening was a masterpiece. Short, succinct, effective—even a little entertaining. Most importantly, it got the jury thinking the way he wanted them to think. Yes, it was stagey, calculated, manipulative—but it was also persuasive. The trial hadn't even begun, and Kilpatrick already had the jurors leaning in his direction.

Good thing he'd spent the night practicing. This needed to be the best opening he'd ever delivered.

"Mr. Pike. Would you like to open at this time?"

"Yes, you honor." He walked to the right side of the jury rail —if only to create some contrast. "My compliments to Mr. Kilpatrick on that fine opening. He's a pro. That's why they brought him in from New York City, where he lives, to try this case in St. Petersburg." Complete dirty pool, but what the hell. Kilpatrick started it. "I know you will take your job as jurors seriously, so you're not going to be as interested in lawyering as you are in the facts."

He paused, smiled, then continued. "My name is Daniel Pike and I represent the defendant, Ossie Coleman. Yes, I live on a boat—it's cheaper than property tax around here—and I love water sports, but that's not relevant, so let's talk about the case. This may surprise you but—I actually agree with much of what Mr. Kilpatrick said. In fact, I agree with most of it." Seem reasonable, not antagonistic. Find common ground. Act as if you're only helping them see the truth. "For instance, I agree that when this kind of money is in the mix, some people will be driven to extreme actions. I also agree that this crime was horrific. It was planned and calculated with a cold-blooded efficiency and maturity that only someone in complete control could master. And I also agree that science can provide reliable evidence—if it's interpreted reliably."

He walked slowly toward the other end of the rail, trying to create visual interest to keep the jurors alert. "But that's where Mr. Kilpatrick and I part company. Everything else he said is bogus and unsubstantiated, part of a concerted effort by powerful forces to frame my client for a crime he did not commit. There are a host of potential heirs to the Coleman family fortune—so why single out my client? Ossie is still tied up in lawsuits—filed by the family, not by him—intended to determine inheritance rights. Surely he would wait to see how that comes out before he started executing the other relatives. On the other hand." He turned and cast an eye toward the many Coleman relatives in the gallery. "If you're a relative concerned about how the civil trial might come out, framing Ossie for murder might seem like a smart move. Because if he's found guilty of murder, even if he wins the civil trial, he won't be permitted to collect the dough. As you view all the evidence in this case, keep asking yourself a single question: How can I know who is guilty when there are other people with the exact same motive, same opportunity, but more maturity, more resources, and a far greater ability to commit the murder?

"The scientific evidence is important, but most of these technical matters—DNA and tox screens and such—require interpretation. The forensic experts Mr. Kilpatrick intends to call to the witness stand are all people who work for the police department, people who have repeatedly come to court to say what the DA needs them to say. I will point out the flaws in their testimony and the holes in their so-called science to demonstrate that the evidence is not only questionable—it isn't even very good science. The prosecution even plans to call a homeless person, a Dumpster diver, to testify about what he allegedly found in the trash. Now ask yourself—if the prosecution had airtight scientific evidence, why would it resort to a witness like that?"

He placed his hands on the rail. "I am concerned that some of you may be so repulsed by this crime that you want to vote to convict just to feel that someone has been punished. You must resist that instinct. Your verdict should be based upon evidence, not emotion. Don't be manipulated. Be logical. Use your brains. Be critical thinkers. To convict you must find that this mastermind murder and chemically complex body disintegration was executed by one young boy, who so far as anyone knows, has never hurt anyone in his entire life. Does that make sense? Or is it more likely that someone older, wiser, with more wherewithal, is responsible?

"Unlike Mr. Kilpatrick, I'm not going to make any promises. I'm just going to remember that you have already made a promise. You promised to faithfully execute your duties as jurors. That's a heavy responsibility. And an important one. I trust you to fulfill it."

He looked up and smiled. "At the end of the day, just remember one thing. To convict, you must find that Mr. Kilpatrick has proven his case against Ossie beyond a reasonable doubt. That's a high standard. It's meant to be. If you feel the prosecution's case is anything less, regardless of what you privately or secretly think, you must find Ossie not guilty. That is your sworn duty. And I know I can count on you to execute it faithfully."

He turned and walked back to the defendant's table, but as he passed, he gave Mr. Kilpatrick a raised eyebrow. Okay, Mr. Hired Gun.

Game on.

CHAPTER THIRTY-FIVE

JUDGE SMULDERS CALLED FOR A SHORT BREAK BEFORE THE prosecution launched its case. Just as well. The jury probably needed time to unpack and consolidate. They'd heard a lot of information in succinct packets from lawyers—and probably didn't understand the significance of much of it. In opening, lawyers were technically not supposed to argue. They did, of course, but less overtly. Opening was a time for planting seeds, a theme, an idea, a skepticism, that would become important later.

Although the judge gave them ten minutes, he noticed that Kilpatrick did not leave the courtroom. No bathroom or snack break. He also noticed that Kilpatrick did not chat much with his colleagues. Belasco had sent two assistant DAs to sit at the table with him. Probably more gofers than colleagues, or perhaps planted to give the table a local connection. But Kilpatrick was clearly an island unto himself, a man who kept his own counsel. And apparently didn't need food or bathroom breaks.

He spotted Bradley Ellison entering the courtroom and taking a seat on the back row of the gallery. He supposed he shouldn't be surprised. Ellison had been investigating the Ossie Coleman case for years. It was only natural that he'd be interested in the trial.

Kilpatrick's first witness was the medical examiner, Dr. Zanzibar. Dan had crossed Zanzibar many times and knew him to be an essentially reliable medical witness. He might lean in a little to help the prosecutor, but he wasn't going to flat out lie or make claims broader than the evidence allowed.

Zanzibar was called to establish that a death had occurred. In most cases, this was a pro forma exercise in the obvious, but unless there was proof of death, no murder prosecution could succeed. This case, however, was more complicated than most. Given the virtual destruction of the body, someone could theoretically question whether Harrison Coleman was dead. So Dr. Zanzibar had to discuss trace calcium particles and lye residue. He did it with admirable aplomb, staying scientific while dumbing it down enough to communicate to the jurors. After he finished explaining about amino acid particulate in the drain, no one would be expecting to see Harrison walk through the courtroom doors unexpectedly.

The next witness was Jake Kakazu, one of the first officers to arrive at the crime scene and easily the best courtroom witness on the force. Maybe it was the tony British accent, but Kakazu seemed so relaxed and convincing that sometimes he just wanted to lay down his cards and fold. Kakazu's hand wasn't that strong this time around, but he still made an excellent impression.

Kakazu described how, long after Harrison disappeared, someone called the cops. He described Harrison's office and of course, how he found OSSIE written in the foggy mirror. He established that he immediately taped off the room, including the bathroom, to prevent anyone from contaminating the crime scene. His testimony backed the coroner and would support the evidence later admitted by the forensic experts, but it did nothing to incriminate Ossie.

That part of the prosecution case was yet to come.

After Kilpatrick finished the direct examination, Dan rose to cross. "Was this name written in steam apparent when you first entered the bathroom?"

"No."

"You had to make it appear."

"Sort of. I turned on the hot water in the shower. I didn't write the name."

"But you could've."

"But I didn't."

"How did you know there was a name written in the fog if it wasn't visible?"

"I didn't. I just had a hunch."

"You had a hunch that there was a currently invisible name that would identify the killer? That's one heck of a hunch."

"I could see there was something on the mirror. It looked dirty. Of course, it was the oil naturally secreted by human fingers."

"And you could see that by looking?"

Kakazu was not ruffled in the slightest. "I've been working this job a long time."

"What a happy coincidence that the mysterious message you could see even though it was invisible also identified the killer for you."

Kilpatrick rose. "Your honor. Mr. Pike is being disrespectful."

And that's unusual on cross? "I'm demonstrating how far-fetched this story is, your honor. That's not disrespect. That's doing my job."

Judge Smulders' brow creased. His cheeks flushed. "Umm... is this an objection thing?"

"Yes," Kilpatrick said. "I made an objection."

"Actually," Dan corrected, "you never said the magic word."

"Abracadabra?"

"Objection."

"Oh." Kilpatrick cleared his throat. "Objection."

"Grounds?"

"Disrespect to a fifteen-year veteran of the St. Pete police force."

"Your honor, I cannot effectively cross anyone if he's going to start complaining about my manners. Cross is meant to be confrontational."

"It doesn't have to be rude," Kilpatrick shot back.

"I hope you remember that when it's your turn to cross."

The judge swatted the air. "I don't think I can go along with this objection. The defense is supposed to cross. Just...you know. Be nicer about it."

And how exactly did that work? "Thank you, you honor." He turned back to Kakazu. "I will submit that it is an amazing coincidence that you saw the invisible, made it reappear, and it was exactly what you needed."

Kakazu smiled. "And I would submit that this is the natural result of experience, training, and a thorough investigation." He paused. "Just to be clear, I did not write the name on the mirror. I had a sergeant with me at all times. He saw it appear just as I did, when I did."

"Why would anyone write a name on a mirror like this?"

"I assume the victim did it before he was killed."

"When did he have time?"

Kakazu shrugged. "After he saw your client enter his office. But before he was murdered."

"You're still not telling me why he would do this."

"To identify his killer."

"But the killer hadn't killed him yet."

"Presumably he could see that the defendant was about to

kill him. Or perhaps the defendant said he was about to kill him."

"So they'd already seen one another. The killer laid eyes on him—then stood there quietly while Harrison wrote his name on the mirror?"

"I don't know exactly how it happened."

"Or why. Or when. Detective, isn't it far more likely that someone else wrote that name on the mirror to incriminate Ossie? Like, the true murderer."

"I see no reason to assume—"

"The medical examiner testified that the process of decomposing the body with lye required lots of hot water."

"Yes."

"Which would create steam. Making it possible to write a name on the mirror."

"Yes."

"Why would there be steam before that?"

"I don't know, but there are many—"

"The one time we know there was steam was when the body was being destroyed. The true killer wouldn't write his own name." Pause. "But he might write someone else's. Don't you think?"

"Objection," Kilpatrick said. "Calls for speculation."

"I agree with that," the judge said. "So, you know...sustained."

Dan smiled. "It's okay. I think the jury got the point."

CHAPTER THIRTY-SIX

KILPATRICK'S NEXT WITNESS WAS MARGARET TULLY, THE THEATER board member who allegedly clashed with Harrison on many occasions and urged him to forego Shakespeare in favor of more crowd-pleasing productions. Kilpatrick wasted little time establishing who she was, her credentials, or the fact that Harrison worked under her direction.

What surprised him was how little talk there was about the conflicts between the two. Perhaps Kilpatrick thought that might make her testimony seem suspect. But as far as you could tell from her direct testimony, she and Harrison got on like bandits, and she was grief-stricken by his death.

"I noticed that Harrison hadn't come backstage during or after the performance, as was his custom," she said. Late fifties. Thick black glasses. Hair in a bun. "I assumed he had a reason. He had seemed stressed lately. If I had only taken the time to knock on his door..." She shook her head. "Maybe this would have turned out differently. Maybe I could have saved him."

More likely, she would've ended up dead herself. "Did you notice anything of interest that night?" Kilpatrick asked.

"Yes. I saw the defendant at the theater. Earlier. Backstage."

That caused some of the jurors to lean forward with interest. "Did you mention it to anyone?"

"No. I had no reason to think anything was wrong."

"But you recognized the defendant."

"Yes. I'd seen his picture in the paper. I knew he was the imposter claim—"

"Objection," Dan said.

The judge shrugged haplessly. "Maybe you could use a different word..."

"I knew he was the boy claiming to be Ossie Coleman," Tully continued. "And I knew Harrison didn't believe it."

"Did you talk to the defendant?"

"No. Wish I had."

"Did he do anything suspicious? Say anything?"

"No. And he wasn't around long." She snapped her fingers. "But he was wearing a backpack. Dark green, I think. I looked away for a moment to watch the show, and the next thing I knew, he'd disappeared."

"Thank you. Pass the witness."

Presumably Kilpatrick wanted to establish that Ossie was on the premises before he called the forensic witnesses to explain what he supposedly did while he was there.

He stood between the witness and the defense table, blocking her view. "Ma'am, when you were backstage that night, was it lighted or dark?"

"I—I'm not sure what you mean."

"Were the lights on backstage?"

"No. But there was a lot of light coming from the stage."

"A lot, or a little?"

She shifted uncomfortably. "Enough to see by."

"Enough to see by a little, right? But not all that clearly."

"Clearly enough." She obviously did not like being questioned.

"Did you tell anyone about this at the time?"

"No. I had no reason to."

"But you told people after."

"Starting with the police. Are you suggesting that I shouldn't've?"

"I'm suggesting there wasn't enough light for you to identify a stranger."

"It was your client."

"Did you decide that when you saw him—or after you heard the police wanted him for murder?"

"It was...at the time. When I saw him."

"Are you sure?"

She hesitated just an instant before answering. "Yes."

"Did you talk to any members of the Coleman family about it?"

"Did I—what?"

"Harrison Coleman wasn't the only member of the family you know, was he?"

"No."

"And you're aware that they'd all like my client to disappear?"

"I—only—I've heard Dolly mention a few—"

"But you maintain that you knew the figure in the darkness was my client, even though you'd never seen him in person and the lighting was low, because...what? His height? His build?"

"His face."

"Which you could make out in the darkness."

"Yes."

"Think hard about this. Is it possible—even remotely possible—that you saw someone else backstage?"

"No."

"Listen to my words. Is it even remotely possible?"

"No." She pointed toward defendant's table. "It was him. I saw him."

"But you didn't say so at the time. Only after the police

arrived, and Detective Kakazu saw the name in the fog and issued a warrant for his arrest. Then you connected the name with the shadowy figure you saw backstage. But not before."

"It was him."

"Let me ask you another question. Is Harrison's office backstage?"

"Not exactly. It's in the rear of the theater. Near the back door."

"Which is presumably how a killer would enter, right?"

"I'm sure I don't know."

"A person wanting to keep a low profile wouldn't come through the front door, would he? He'd be spotted by dozens of people."

"True."

"And if you're traveling from the back door to Harrison's office, which is right next to the back door, and you're carrying a bunch of diabolical chemicals to eradicate the body, you're not going to stroll backstage for no reason, are you?"

"He had a reason," she said, her back stiffening. "I just don't know what it was. He was probably looking for Harrison. When he didn't find him backstage, he went to the office."

"Ms. Tully, please don't speculate. Just tell the jury what you actually know. You saw someone backstage. You're not sure who it was. The killer had no reason to wander backstage. You clashed constantly with Harrison and probably didn't like him very much."

"I didn't dislike him."

"This identification is a guess you're making after the fact. If the police hadn't suggested Ossie was there, you never would've thought you saw him."

"I'm telling you, I saw him." She pointed again. "Him. *Him!*"

He smiled and turned toward the jury. "Well, that's funny, ma'am. Because as I expect most of the jurors have already noticed, during the break, I asked my client to step out and brought in another man to sit at the table with me. He's a young kid who works downstairs at the coffee shop. He's about the same size and age as Ossie, but hardly an identical twin. And you just identified him as the man you saw backstage. Even though he tells me that on the night of the murder, he was vacationing at Disney World."

He nodded toward the judge. "No more questions."

CHAPTER THIRTY-SEVEN

DAN TRIED TO TAKE STOCK BEFORE THE NEXT PHASE OF THE TRIAL began. That had been a decent trick, but would it have much impact on the jury? He couldn't be sure. Yes, the woman had gotten worked up and defensive and said something she shouldn't—but that didn't prove she didn't see Ossie backstage. He would have to keep his eye on the jurors and continue trying to read their minds.

He was surprised that Kilpatrick didn't follow with someone from the CSI department. He started with probably the sketchiest witness on his list—the Dumpster diver. But maybe that made sense. First establish how you got the syringe, then let an expert explain why it was important.

To give Kilpatrick credit where due, he didn't try to sugar-coat the reality of the situation. Quint had been groomed and dressed for trial—cheap gray suit—but in the first minute, the witness acknowledged that he had been homeless and searched trash bins for food and items he might sell for petty cash. He also revealed a minor record for theft—which was disappointing, because Dan had planned to reveal that during his cross-examination.

"Where did you find the syringe?" Kilpatrick asked.

Charlie Quint tugged at his collar. He looked uncomfortable, like he'd never worn a suit before in his entire life. Coupled with his natural nervousness, he came off as edgy and somewhat defensive. "In the trash bin outside the foster home."

"Why were you there?"

"It was a good neighborhood for me. You'd be amazed what some people put out, especially in a house that's feeding a lot of kids. You could live a week on it."

Out the corner of his eye, he saw Maria's face curl. Eating out of trash cans was not for her. How likely were you to find kale?

"Why did the syringe attract your attention?"

Quint squirmed a bit. "You see a syringe in the trash, you immediately think—druggie."

"And why is that good?"

"Because there might be heroin in the syringe. Or elsewhere in the trash. And you can get big money for street drugs."

"If they're so valuable, why would anyone throw them out?"

"Messed-up people do messed-up stuff."

Not elegant, but he made his point. "Did the syringe contain anything?"

"Not enough that I could sell."

"Then why keep it?"

"I thought the police might be interested."

"Did you contact the police?"

"Yes. And they were interested. They took the syringe and ran some tests." He beamed. "They thanked me for being such a good citizen."

Kilpatrick nodded. "Pass the witness."

It almost seemed too easy to chastise Quint for being a homeless wastrel or having a record. Like kicking infants. "Let's talk about your visit to the police station. Given your history, you must've had some qualms about setting foot in there."

"Um...what?"

He realized his mistake. "You must've had...you must've been worried about seeing cops."

Quint shrugged. "Yeah. A little."

"Were you hoping to get something for your information?"

"Is that so wrong? I scratch your back, you scratch mine."

"You asked for money, didn't you?"

"I thought the intel might be worth something."

"But they weren't willing to pay for it, right?" Because then the payment could be used to impugn his testimony.

"True enough."

"How did you react to that news?"

"I tried to leave. They stopped me. Said they'd arrest me for withholding evidence."

"So they forced you to surrender the syringe." He thought for a moment. Something wasn't right here. Quint clearly expected a reward from the cops. And he was in that particular trash bin at such an opportune time... "It sure seems like a coincidence that you happened to be searching my client's trash right after Detective Kakazu claims he found the name on the mirror. Did you target that trash bin?"

"I'm...not sure what you mean."

"When I talked to you earlier, you mentioned that the best bins to search were behind restaurants, but this neighborhood was a far cry from any restaurants. So why were you there?"

"I told you—"

"Isn't it true that you went to that trash bin specifically hoping to find something that could be used against my client?"

"How would I know that was the right trash bin?"

"Yes, exactly. I don't think your research skills could get you there. I think someone must've told you. And the most likely candidate would be the police. Isn't it true that the police sent you to Ossie's house?"

WILLIAM BERNHARDT

Quint's eyes darted to Kilpatrick. "Why...would they do that?"

"If the police searched that bin, it might be considered an unreasonable search without probable cause and I'd be up here arguing that they needed a search warrant. If a homeless guy does it, there's no state action and thus no constitutional violation."

"You're way over my head now."

"And if the syringe was planted, they would definitely want someone else to 'discover' it."

"I don't know what you're talking about."

"Let me simplify it for you. Have you run errands for the police in the past?"

Kilpatrick rose. "Objection. Relevance. What the witness did or did not do in the past doesn't relate to this case."

"I'm establishing that the witness is a regular police informant, your honor. Or...police flunky."

"What if he is?" Kilpatrick said. "The bottom line here is that the incriminating syringe was found outside the defendant's home."

"No. The bottom line is that the police targeted my client before they'd had time to conduct any meaningful investigation."

"Another objection," Kilpatrick said. "Your honor, may we approach?"

The judge nodded. Most judges would've pulled the lawyers to the bench a long time ago. These arguments were not evidence, but they could influence the jurors.

Stress was smeared all over Smulders' face. "So...what is it you object to, Mr. Kilpatrick?"

"The irrelevant suggestion that this witness is a police informant."

"Is it true?"

He hesitated only an instant. "It doesn't matter."

Dan jumped in. "You'll note that he is not answering your question."

"Because it doesn't matter."

"I think it does. I think the police targeted my client and sent this loser out to create evidence to back their case."

"They already saw his name—"

"Anyone could scrawl a name on a mirror. Just as anyone could drop a syringe in a trash bin and then send Oscar the Grouch to find it."

"He's attacking the police department. Standard shyster defense lawyer trick. I can't believe you'd stand for it, your honor."

Who was the shyster now? Kilpatrick was playing on the judge's naiveté.

"Well, I don't want any of that," Smulders said.

"Good. Shut down this line of questioning."

The judge drew in his breath. "I don't think we need questions about what happened in the past. Let's stick to this case."

The lawyers left the bench. Dan continued questioning. "In this particular case, Mr. Quint, did anyone suggest that you should search the trash outside my client's home?"

He could see Kilpatrick thinking about another objection, but he kept his seat.

"Well...yes."

"And when was this request made?"

Another glance at Kilpatrick. After a few beats, Quint answered. "Early. Some cop found me under a bridge and woke me. Wasn't even light out yet."

At that point, most of the public didn't know about the murder yet. And the police hadn't had time to investigate much or to question any suspects. "How long did it take you to get to the trash bin?"

"A couple of hours."

"So the police had plenty of time to get there first. And put anything in it they wanted."

Kilpatrick shot up. "Objection! Your honor, this is exactly the kind of reprehensible tactic I warned you about."

Dan stepped toward the judge, jaw set. "I am entitled to question police conduct during a criminal trial. It's the court's job to make sure the police respect the constitutional rights of individuals." He paused. "You probably recall hearing something about that in Constitutional Law class, right?"

Judge Smulders drew in his breath. "Yes. I do."

"If my client was being framed by cops who decided he was guilty before they had any evidence just because he was the obvious suspect..." He paused. "Or because someone rich and powerful wanted Ossie out of the way...that's exactly what—"

Kilpatrick went into full-out aggro mode. "This man's paranoia is so thick you could cut it with a knife. The jurors are not stupid. They won't buy this fantasy. Mr. Pike wants everyone to believe that our boys in blue, the ones who risk their lives to keep us safe, are criminals. I reject this cynical liberal notion."

"If you're finished with your drama-queen scene, maybe we could return to actual legal argument."

Kilpatrick pounded the edge of the bench. "Outrageous."

"I agree with one thing he said, your honor. The jurors are not stupid. They can weigh evidence for themselves without all this shouting and bellyaching. If what I say has no value, they won't give it a second thought. But if they are concerned that the police may have pursued a particular suspect for reasons that have nothing to do with the evidence, that should rightfully play an important role in their deliberations."

A long pause ensued.

After a significant period of silence, Judge Smulders seemed to realize it was his turn to speak. "So...did you want me to...do something?"

His clerk muttered from behind the hand covering her face. "Rule on the objection."

"Oh, well, sure. I...don't think we should be dissing the police officers. Especially since they aren't even on the stand to defend themselves."

Kilpatrick leaned in. "You're sustaining my objection?"

"Um, yes. That's right."

"And strike the irrelevant business about police misconduct from the record?"

"Sure. Did the court reporter get that?"

Over in the corner, Bertha nodded. Dan didn't care. They could do anything they wanted to the record. The jury would not forget what he'd said.

"Anything else?"

He decided to end the cross. He'd done what he wanted— planted the possibility of a police conspiracy to frame his client. He'd pick up the thread again later. "Nothing more, your honor." He took his seat at the table.

Both Maria and Ossie looked pleased.

"You knocked the ball out of the court, slugger," Maria whispered.

"Technically, I did nothing. The syringe is still coming in. And it is incriminating."

"Till you get your hands on the next prosecution witness."

Ossie seemed more concerned than elated. "Why would the police want to go after me?"

He shook his head. "I'm not sure. But we're going to find out."

CHAPTER THIRTY-EIGHT

KILPATRICK CALLED HIS DNA EXPERT, DR. HARRIET VICTOR, TO the witness stand. Most of what she said was non-controversial. Ossie's DNA report indicated that he could be related to Zachary Coleman, but it did not prove conclusively that he was. But the DNA traces found in the bathtub proved that Harrison Coleman was the victim who was washed down the drain. "We were able to ascertain that the DNA came from Harrison Coleman with an almost 93% certainty," she explained.

"He probably bathed there. Couldn't he have left DNA on a previous occasion?"

"He could have, but it would've been obliterated by the bio-cremation process. There were barely traces of the victim. No one else's DNA could've survived."

"Where did you find a DNA sample for matching?" Kilpatrick asked.

"Harrison left genetic material with a company called Past Lives. They use it to provide ancestry reports. Apparently Harrison wanted to know more about where he came from."

"Can you explain to the jury how the body was destroyed?"

"Yes. It's not that complicated, and it could be done with

common materials easily obtained at most home and garden stores."

"Was it dangerous?"

"Somewhat. The killer probably wore a chemical retardant suit. And stripped the corpse naked."

"Where did the clothes go?"

"I can't be sure, but in all likelihood, the killer hung them up and put them in the closet where Harrison kept several other outfits. The killer used lye in concentrated powder form. He likely let the water in the tub get very hot, till the skin turned red. Then he'd toss in several scoops of the lye. Let the water run till the tub was almost full. Then he must've covered the tub."

"With what?"

"Some kind of drape. Maybe a rubber sheet. That would be the best thing and not hard to find or carry. He would need to seal the tub shut, perhaps with duct tape. We did find adhesive residue on the tub." She drew in her breath. "At that point, all the killer had to do was sit back and wait. The bio-cremation would break down everything—skin, muscle, tissues, even the teeth. At a cellular level."

"How long would that take?"

"Maybe fifteen, sixteen hours."

"The killer stayed that long?"

"Or left and came back. I can't say. The process would leave a green, or possibly brown residue that we didn't observe in the tub, though we later detected a little of it chemically. Presumably the killer drained the tub and washed away the residue. The only remains would be a bleached powder. You could crush it in your fist. Pound it to dust."

"Did you find any of this dust?"

"Yes. Scattered traces in the tub. The final remains of Harrison Coleman."

Dan watched the jurors' reactions. They were repulsed by the thought.

"Have you heard of anyone doing this before?"

"Yes. It's based on alkaline hydrolysis. Sometimes used in mortuaries and other places. But I've never seen it used by a private citizen to eliminate traces of a crime."

"No more questions. Mr. Pike?"

He didn't particularly want to cross and prolong the jurors' exposure to this subject, but a few questions needed to be asked. "Did you find any chemical traces on the syringe?"

"Yes. Ketamine."

Which apparently everyone had. Ketamine had been used in Camila's case as well. "What is that?"

"A tranquilizer. Can be used as a painkiller or anesthetic. Or in excessive doses, a paralyzing poison."

"How quickly would it take effect?"

"Almost immediately. At first, the victim wouldn't be able to move. Death would follow."

"Painless?"

"Far from it. The victim would feel as if he were burning alive from the inside out. He might not be able to move, but he would feel it, just the same. And once the body was immobilized —the killer would be able to do anything with him he wanted. Like place him in the bathtub. And chemically destroy his body. While he was still—"

"Please just answer the question. We don't need any embellishment." He changed the subject. "Were you present when Quint brought the syringe to the police station?"

"No, I was in my lab."

"Did anyone else have contact with the syringe before you did?"

"Or course. Many people. The admitting officer, the lead detective. My assistant. And of course, the killer."

"You don't know for a fact that the killer used the syringe, do you?"

"I found traces of—"

"But many people had contact with that syringe before you did, right? Like police officers?"

"True."

"Objection," Kilpatrick said. "Relevance."

Seriously? "I'm demonstrating that there is significant reason to doubt the story the prosecution is feeding the jury."

"Doubt?" Judge Smulders blinked. "That's important, right?"

"Very important, your honor. The defense is all about the doubt."

Smulders shrugged. "Then I guess I'll have to allow this one."

"Thank you, your honor. No more questions."

CHAPTER THIRTY-NINE

DAN FELT HE'D DONE A DECENT JOB SO FAR OF REMINDING THE jury that there were lots of possibilities and that no evidence pointed with absolute certainty toward Ossie.

The key words being, *so far*. If he could deal with the remaining evidence as effectively, they might stand a chance.

During the break between witnesses, he contemplated ditching his cane. He felt much sturdier. Maybe that was buoyancy emanating from a cross that went well—and maybe that was completely delusional—but he felt he could survive without it. His ribs still hurt like the blazes, but the cane wasn't helping with that, and he worried that the jury might suspect the cane was some sort of sympathy play. He decided to tentatively try crossing the next witness without it. He'd stay close to the table, just in case.

He noticed more of the Coleman clan sneaking into the courtroom during the break. Phil joined his father and Benny, though he didn't look like he wanted to be there. He wondered how anyone who had done two tours of duty in Afghanistan could stand Dolly's attempts to tell everyone around her what to do.

Before he looked away, Dolly motioned for him. Her version of a royal summons, he supposed.

He approached cautiously. "If you've come to see Ossie on the stand, you're early."

"No," Dolly said, "we've already heard his sad story. It won't be improved by the witness stand."

"Then what brings you here?"

"May I remind you, Mr. Pike, that this trial concerns the violent death of a member of our family? We are very determined to see that justice is done."

"And a potential threat to your inheritance is eliminated."

She drew herself up. "*Justice*, Mr. Pike. Perhaps you've heard of the concept."

"Just didn't know you were all that fond of Harrison."

"I loved that boy," Zachary Coleman said, cutting in. "Can't believe he's gone. Losing two sons..." He shook his drooping head. "It's too much. Too much."

"I'm sorry. I didn't mean to suggest—"

"Everyone I love disappears," Zachary muttered.

"Not true, Papa." Dolly patted him on the shoulder. "You've still got Benny and me. We will not desert you."

Zachary looked at her but said nothing.

He tried to think of something to break the silence. "I'm afraid you haven't picked the most exciting day to attend. Primarily technical and forensic witnesses today."

To his surprise, Benny spoke. "I like tech. Thought about being a research scientist when I was younger."

He tried not to appear skeptical. "Indeed."

"Yes," Dolly murmured. "Till he discovered that it required intelligence."

Benny chuckled. "My wife is such a kidder."

"When he learned that," she continued, "Benny decided a better choice might be managing his father's estate. Since it doesn't actually require him to do anything—"

"I have to—"

"—that a child couldn't do."

He decided to make a hasty retreat to the defense table. These people were a thousand times nastier than the trial was likely to get.

Kilpatrick called a few more necessary if unexciting witnesses. A toxicologist to provide more information about the poison on the syringe. The lieutenant who was the first to arrive at the crime scene. Zachary Coleman wheeled to the front of the courtroom and testified about his net worth. None of it was in question—presumably Kilpatrick wanted to create a motive.

He didn't even cross. He'd save his ammunition for when it could really do some damage.

After the mid-afternoon break, Kilpatrick called the St. Pete PD's expert on dactylograms—fingerprints—to the stand. Dr. Brenda Palmer had testified on many previous occasions in a calm and matter-of-fact manner. Wire-rimmed spectacles. Small scar beneath her left ear. About a size six.

Fingerprint evidence wasn't nearly as certain as people thought it was from watching television, which he had gone to great lengths to prove last time he saw Palmer on the stand. He had a hunch that this time she would be much more careful about what she said.

Kilpatrick spent about five minutes establishing her credentials, then brought the witness' attention to the syringe, specifically, a three-quarter thumbprint found at the base of the syringe plunger.

"Could you describe the print in question?"

"Certainly. I found a near-full ten-point ridge match between the print taken from the syringe and the prints taken from the defendant after his arrest."

"Can you put that in layman's terms?"

"Sure. You probably already know that everyone's fingers have ridges on them, and the ridges vary significantly from one person to the next." He noticed that Palmer did not claim, as she had on previous occasions, that everyone's fingerprints were different. That was an old cliché that had never been proven, and he demonstrated during a previous trial that it was possible for prints from two different people to look quite similar, especially when only viewing a partial print. As here. "Our natural body oil causes an impression of those ridges to be left on a flat adhesive surface when touched. We have a system for reading those prints at strategic points. That's how we determine whether there's a match."

"And was there a match in this case?"

"There was. The print on the syringe matches the prints from the defendant."

"Any room for error?"

"No. The match is clear."

"Thank you. Pass the witness."

Was it his imagination that the witness tensed when she saw him approach? Had prior experience left her apprehensive? He'd like to think so. Better than thinking she was holding back laughter because he looked so silly trying to inch forward without his cane.

"You mentioned that you found a ten-point match, correct?"

"Yes."

"But the system you and most fingerprint analysts use to compare prints has twelve points, doesn't it?"

"That's correct."

"So two of the points didn't match?"

"Two of the points weren't present. As I said, this was a partial print."

"Since you didn't have all twelve points, the reliability of the match decreases significantly, wouldn't you say?"

"No, I would disagree with that statement. For the ten points available, the match is strong."

"But the fact that you don't have all twelve points increases the chance that you may have a false positive, right? That the two prints could be similar, but not identical."

"I find that highly—"

"In fact, doesn't the International Association of Crime Analysis advise against even offering an opinion on prints when you don't have twelve points?"

Her shoulders rose. "That organization tends to be rather conservative."

"It's the organization that lays out the ethical rules for your profession."

"Guidelines, not rules."

"And you're violating those guidelines by testifying."

She craned her neck. "I make my own judgments about when it's appropriate to testify, on a case-by-case basis. In this instance, I felt that the commonality on the ten points we had was sufficient to merit offering a professional opinion."

He took a step closer. "Did the DA weigh in on that decision?"

"I'm...not sure what you mean."

"The District Attorney very much wanted you to take the stand against my client, didn't he?"

"I would assume the prosecutor always wants his staff—"

"No, it's more than that. He told you he wanted you to testify. Am I correct?"

She hesitated before answering. "I...did have a conversation with the District Attorney about this case."

"And he instructed you to testify."

"He told me he hoped I could support the strong case they were building."

"And you did what he wanted. Even though it put you in conflict with the professional guidelines of your profession." He pivoted toward the jury box. "Once again, we see that the law enforcement community was intimately involved and extremely determined to build a case against my client."

"Objection," Kilpatrick said. "That's not a question. More like a summation."

"I'll withdraw it." Since the jury had already heard it. He plowed ahead. "When did you receive the syringe?"

Palmer glanced at her report, then announced the date.

"That was four days after it was recovered. Four days after my client was arrested."

"I believe that is correct."

"Do you know where the syringe was during those four days?"

"No."

"Do you know who had possession?"

"No. But we have strict chain-of-custody procedures at the department. We make sure everything is handled properly."

"I've already heard enough to call that statement into question. And of course, if the police are the ones behind the frame, putting the syringe in their custody is no protection at all."

"Objection," Kilpatrick said. He was becoming visibly incensed.

"I'll withdraw. But you will acknowledge, Dr. Palmer, that if a member of the police force wanted to get at that syringe during this four-day period, they probably could've managed it?"

She squirmed. "Possibly..."

"Probably. And they fingerprinted my client almost immediately after he was arrested, didn't they?"

"That is standard procedure."

"So someone could have reproduced that thumbprint from the exemplar taken from Ossie. Could've pressed it onto the base of the syringe."

"Objection," Kilpatrick said. "There is no evidence—"

This time he stood his ground. "I didn't ask the witness if it happened. I asked if it was scientifically possible."

"Then—he's calling for speculation."

"Which I can do, given that this is the cross-examination of an expert witness. You are capable of offering an opinion as to whether a fingerprint could be reproduced on another surface in four days' time, aren't you, Dr. Palmer?"

Despite the pending objection, she answered. "Yes. It could be done. It's essentially what we do in the lab to run our tests. We don't tamper with the original. We copy the print to a surface we can safely run through analysis."

"Are you the only person on earth who knows how to do that?"

"Of course not."

"My point exactly. Thank you. No more questions."

CHAPTER FORTY

AFTER A BRIEF TEAM MEETING, DAN RETURNED TO HIS BOAT. HE thought he'd had a good day in court, but he also knew this was an uphill battle. Regardless of what the judge told the jurors, he did have a burden of proof—the burden of convincing the jury that everything the prosecution said was wrong. So far, he had batted down most of the evidence, but it was about to get much worse, and at some point, jurors start to think that where there is so much smoke, there must be fire.

Tomorrow he would have to confront the man who put his father in prison. Just the thought made him sick. Made him want to rip the man's head off. But in the courtroom, he had to stay calm and do his job. Even when it was tearing him apart.

He'd felt bad all afternoon. He was probably working too hard, too soon. He'd felt a sharp tremor rip through his body the second he approached the boat. The sight brought back too many memories. The three men. The little bastard with the tire iron. How they had...damaged him. Violated him. How they took him apart piece by piece.

Maybe that was the real reason he came back here alone. He had to prove to himself that he still could.

Mr. K had security everywhere, of course. Several security officers watching the boat, the courthouse, plus plainclothes officers dogging his footsteps. He didn't know who they were. Mr. K thought it best they remained undercover, unknown even to the man they were protecting. Camila had offered to come over tonight, but he turned her down, claiming he had too much work to be a good boyfriend.

He didn't need a babysitter. This was who he was and what he did, right?

But anxiety still clutched at his chest. His fight or flight instinct told him to run—but for some reason he didn't listen.

He'd like to call that bravery. But he suspected it was just stubbornness. Possibly stupidity.

He knew he wouldn't sleep much tonight, not that he ever did while a trial was in progress. He'd spend the night rehearsing witness examinations, strategizing, trying to solve the deepening mystery of Ossie Coleman, who he was and why so many people were out to get him.

And trying to convince himself that he was not scared. Even though he knew better.

WHEN HE ENTERED THE COURTROOM THE NEXT DAY, HE SPOTTED Bradley Ellison in the gallery, ready to roll. He nodded politely but kept walking, suppressing his thoughts. *You've already ruined one man's life. Now you're gunning for someone else.*

A few minutes later, Kilpatrick called his next witness.

Terry Dodgson was the hiker who first stumbled onto the now-famous cabin in the wilderness with the yellow triangle. Lean, wiry. Big bushy beard. Unkempt hair. Red ring on his right hand. Good that Dodgson preferred the great outdoors, because his social skills, not to mention grooming skills, were not highly advanced. He looked hardy and earnest, but no one you'd hire to run your corporation.

Dodgson explained that he loved the Florida outback. He hiked almost every day. He made a living, if that was the word, by contributing articles to an online outdoor-adventures website. He lived in a house his father had left him. He didn't shop, didn't have a wife, and didn't have children—so his needs were relatively small.

"I couldn't believe it," Dodgson said. "I'd hiked all over this area. Slow going. Lots of brush, no trails, no roads. Never saw another person. Much less a cabin."

"What did you do when you found it?"

"At first, nothing. Didn't want to intrude. Anybody who went to the trouble of building something way out there clearly did not want company. Then I noticed the triangle."

"The yellow triangle on the gable?"

"Right. I read the news online every morning. Helps me get ideas for things I might write about. So I knew about Ossie Coleman, the kid with no memory of the last fourteen years except a cabin with a yellow triangle."

"What did you do next?"

"I waited outside for a while. Didn't see anyone. I slowly walked to the front porch. No windows. I knocked on the door. No one answered. The door was open slightly."

"And then?"

"I stepped inside. And saw the corpse. The old man on the floor. Smelled him, too. I think he'd been there a long time."

"And then?"

"I decided it was time to call in the professionals. But it took two hours just to get to a cell signal, and two more hours before I met the police officers."

"What happened after that?"

"I showed them what I found."

"Let me ask you an important question. Did you see the defendant at or near that cabin?"

"No, I didn't see anyone. Alive."

"Did you see any traces that the defendant had ever been there?"

"No."

"You found the cabin. Is it possible someone else could have done the same?"

"Sure. It wasn't really hard to get to—just remote."

"Thank you. Nothing more."

Dan didn't cross. The primary reason Kilpatrick put this witness on the stand was that he didn't want someone else to suggest that he was trying to hide evidence supporting Ossie's story. But it had no bearing on whether Ossie was a murderer.

Kilpatrick's next witness was Sergeant Enriquez, the officer who took control of the crime scene once Dodgson got them there. He made sure the proper crime-scene protocols were implemented. They cordoned off the property—not that they expected anyone to wander by. They called the medical examiner's office to take charge of the body. And they systematically sent in crime-scene techs to search for evidence.

"Were there any indications that anyone other than the deceased lived in the cabin?"

"None. No clothes or personal belongings other than those attributable to the old man, who still has not been identified."

"What about outside?"

"There was a shack…with chains. It appears they were used as restraints. Presumably for the victims before they were…mummified."

"Did you find any fingerprints?"

"Unfortunately, no. The place was in bad shape. The man had been dead a long time, and I think it's safe to say the cleaning crew had stopped coming in. A dusty, dirty, filth-ridden environment is not an incubator for forensic evidence."

Slowly, and with great reluctance, Enriquez described the mummies, the corpses of young boys who had apparently been tortured before being killed and preserved and arranged in staged tableaus. And the pharmaceutical cabinet.

"Can you describe what drugs you found in the cabinet?"

"It would be easier to describe what wasn't found. This guy had everything. It was all legit—assuming he had a prescription. No street drugs."

"Any ketamine in the cabinet?" That was, as the jury would recall, the poison found in trace amounts on the syringe.

"Yes, that was on the list."

"Someone could have found the cabin, just as you did, noted the yellow triangle, acquired the poison and a syringe, then left."

"Objection," Dan said, rising to his feet. "Who's speculating now?"

Kilpatrick shrugged. "I'm posing a hypothetical."

The judge appeared baffled.

"If Pike can do it—" Kilpatrick took a breath, then tried a different approach. "I'm just establishing that a killer could've obtained the poison from this cabin."

"Oh." The judge extended his lower lip. "Well, that's okay, I think."

His clerk nodded subtly.

"Any idea where these drugs came from?" Kilpatrick asked.

"No idea. The man must've gone into town periodically for food and supplies. Looks like he had a source that hooked him up with drugs, too. A physician, maybe, or a Canadian pharmacy that didn't care whether he had a prescription. Hard to know."

And with that, Dan realized, the prosecution added the last element needed to complete its prima facie case—an explanation of where Ossie got the poison and perhaps the syringe. No signs that he lived in this cabin, much less for fourteen years.

But a strong suggestion that he might've dropped by and acquired the murder weapon.

And there wasn't a thing he could do about it. Because he knew every word the witnesses had spoken was true.

CHAPTER FORTY-ONE

As Dan expected, the last witness of the day was Bradley Ellison, the ex-cop cold-case expert. The man who put away his father.

Ellison eased into the witness stand as calm as could be. In a few brief strokes, he established that he was a retired member of the local police force, a former homicide detective, that he retired at the rank of captain, that he had testified in court on many previous occasions, and that he now acted as a private investigator.

"Do you get paid for this work?" Kilpatrick asked.

"Sometimes. Not always. I'm fortunate to be financially secure at this point in my life, so I don't worry about that too much. I focus on cases with unusual or intriguing aspects."

The Sherlock Holmes of St. Pete. Except Sherlock was never wrong.

"Have you investigated the Ossie Coleman case?"

"Yes. For years."

"What were the unusual aspects that attracted your interest?"

Ellison turned slightly, drawing the jurors into his line of sight. He was a good, experienced witness. He knew how to include the jury without making it seem as if he were putting on a performance for them. "I remember when the boy disappeared, fourteen years ago. I was on the force then. I didn't work that case, but I knew about it. And it was never solved, despite all the manpower put into it, and all the money the Coleman family spent trying to locate the lost heir."

"Are you familiar with the latest developments in the case?"

"I'm aware that a young man has come forth claiming to be Ossie Coleman." He pointed. "The defendant."

"And do you have an opinion on whether that claim is accurate?"

Dan rose. "Objection, your honor. There is a civil suit pending on this issue, a declaratory judgment suit filed by the Coleman family. This testimony might be relevant there, but it isn't here. This is a murder trial."

Judge Smulders nodded thoughtfully. "This *is* a murder trial. That's for certain. Right?"

Kilpatrick stepped toward the bench. "Nonetheless, this is relevant, your honor. It goes to motive."

The judge was still nodding. "Motive. Also…important."

"It's crucial," Kilpatrick added. "Even Mr. Pike would agree—"

"I do not agree. Motive is not an element of any of the crimes with which the defendant has been charged."

"Motive may not be an official element," Kilpatrick said, "but it's almost impossible to get a jury to convict without one. Let me explain why the defendant committed this crime."

"He already has. The jury knows there are zillions at stake. They probably knew before they got to the courthouse. If that's all this is, it's completely unnecessary."

"That's not all it is," Kilpatrick said, "as will be clear very soon. May I proceed, your honor?"

Judge Smulders pursed his lips. "Let's put a pin in that objection and…get on with the trial."

Did that mean "Overruled?"

Kilpatrick continued. "You were about to offer your opinion regarding the defendant's claim."

"Yes. It's my opinion, based upon careful investigation, that the claim is without merit."

"Meaning…?"

"Meaning the young man sitting over there in the nice suit is not Ossie Coleman."

"You think it's unlikely?"

"I think there's no possibility. His story does not hold water. Maybe he's just delusional, but I have strong reason to believe he's actively trying to swindle money from the Coleman estate."

"Could that swindle include murder?"

That was beyond the pale. "Objection."

"Never mind. I'll withdraw the question." Kilpatrick flipped a page in his outline. "Why do you say the story doesn't hold water?"

"Common sense, for starters. Think about it. Where did Ossie Coleman go after his mother killed herself? How would he get to a cabin in the middle of a swamp? A boy that age couldn't take care of himself. Who did? Plus the defendant looks nothing like the boy who disappeared."

"Can you explain what you mean by that?"

"We have photographs of Ossie Coleman taken before he disappeared. Not as many as I'd like, and the quality isn't great. His mother doesn't seem to have cared much for snapshots, and this was before everyone had a cellphone with a fabulous camera in their pocket."

Kilpatrick turned on the video screen facing the jury. He rambled through the procedure for admitting exhibits. "Can you identify this photograph?"

"Yes. That's one of the best of the handful of photographs we have of Ossie Coleman before he disappeared. It was taken at his fourth birthday party."

"Have you performed any kind of analysis with this photograph?"

"Yes. I've used a program called FaceApp, which uses artificial intelligence to age people, using common points of reference. Police often use programs like this to produce a portrait of a suspect who hasn't been photographed for many years. The program takes into account the natural shape of the young face. Prominent cheekbones remain prominent, big eyes remain big. But the features spread, weight is gained, the face lengthens. The program duplicates the natural aging process."

Kilpatrick put another photograph on the screen, a shot of a much older boy. After allowing the jury to see it by itself, he put the two photos side by side. "Can you tell the jury what the second photo is?"

"That's the photo my software program created. It's basically a portrait of the real Ossie Coleman—but fourteen years older. And as you can see, it is far from identical to the defendant. No one would look at that photo and ID the man sitting at the defendant's table."

Dan scrutinized the photos carefully. He'd looked at these on many previous occasions, of course, but this was the first time he'd seen them on an enlarged, backlit screen. What Ellison said was true—this was a reliable software program. He'd used it himself in the past. And the aged-photo face was not identical to his client, though he did not think it was so far different that it blew Ossie out of contention.

Kilpatrick let the jury gaze at the photos. "Do you have any other reasons for disbelieving the defendant's story?"

"Yes. He came to see me at one point. Tried to get me to back his claim."

Dan sat up. Ellison hadn't mentioned this when they talked before. And Ossie hadn't mentioned it either.

He turned toward his client, scribbling on the legal pad between them. TRUE?

Ossie hesitated a moment. I SAW HIM.

Great. Nothing like a big surprise to make a murder trial more challenging.

"When did this happen?"

"A few days after the police found him. You'll recall he claimed he'd lost his memory for the most part—but somehow remembered his name was Ossie Coleman. He was placed in a foster home. He actively sought out people he claimed were his relatives—including Harrison Coleman."

"Yes," Kilpatrick said. "We've had testimony putting the defendant at the theater where Harrison worked."

"Objection," Dan said. "That testimony was unreliable and highly disputed."

"I object to that objection," Kilpatrick growled.

Judge Smulders pressed a hand to his forehead. "This is getting very confusing."

Kilpatrick almost rolled his eyes. "For the sake of simplicity, I'll withdraw the statement. I'm sure the jury remembers what they've heard." He turned back to the witness. "The defendant sought you out?"

"Yes. He'd heard that I was a local expert on his case. He tried to persuade me that he was the real McCoy. Didn't seem like a bad kid, but I had to tell him I didn't for one minute believe he was the missing heir."

"How did he take that news?"

"Not well. He became angry. Accused me of trying to hurt him because he was black—which was absurd." Ellison took a deep breath. "Then he tried to bribe me."

Dan felt a chill run up his spine.

"What exactly did he say?"

"He noted that if I backed his claim, he would come into a lot of money. He said he planned to be generous with that money."

Ossie grabbed the pencil. WASN'T A BRIBE!!!

Dan gave him a stern look. *Stay calm. Don't let the jury see you sweat.*

Ellison continued. "He mentioned that my house could use some repairs and my truck looked pretty shabby. Wondered if maybe he could help."

Ossie kept writing. STILL NOT BRIBE!!! Then he underlined it three times.

Kilpatrick cleared his throat. "So basically, his message was, back me and I'll slide some of the loot your way."

"That's how I understood it."

"And of course, if a man is willing to bribe a witness to get his hands on the money...he could be capable of doing anything. No more questions."

Dan pushed himself to his feet. He skipped the warmup and plunged right in. He didn't like this man, thought he was a lying son of a bitch, and wasn't going to pretend otherwise. "You suggested that you started looking into this case out of intellectual curiosity. But in fact, didn't someone pay you to look into the Ossie Coleman case?"

"I have been compensated for my work."

"By whom?"

He raised his chin. "I prefer to keep my clients' confidences. Just as you do."

"The attorney-client privilege does not extend to dilettante investigators. Who paid you?"

"There is a privilege for private investigators who—"

"Are you a licensed PI?"

Ellison exhaled heavily. "No."

"One more time. Who paid you to look into this case?"

Ellison frowned. "Conrad Sweeney."

"And Sweeney is closely tied to the DA and local law enforcement, isn't he?"

"I believe that is an accurate statement."

"So in truth, you were hired to debunk my client's claim. Which you didn't mention to the jury."

"I was hired to look into the case. I reached my own conclusion about it. I would've reported the truth, whatever I thought it to be."

"It was just a coincidence that you ended up telling them exactly what they wanted to hear?"

Kilpatrick rose. "Objection."

"Sustained."

Wow. Not even Judge Smulders had to be coached on that one. "You've worked with Sweeney before, haven't you?"

Ellison gave him a penetrating look, as if to say, did he really want to go there? "Yes."

No, you bastard, we aren't going to discuss the lies you told to put my father away. "And Sweeney is an influential man in this community, right?" Out the corner of his eye, he could see Prudence in the gallery, looking extremely unhappy, scribbling notes onto an iPad.

"He's a successful tech businessman and philanthropist. He's probably done more for this town than anyone else alive."

"And the only way he can have influence is by having power. The power to manipulate people to get what he wants."

"I have not been manipulated. I've been hired. There's a huge difference. And I don't think you should malign one of the most prominent—"

He couldn't stand to listen to this and didn't have to. "Let's talk about the computer-generated photograph. What information did you give the software program before it aged the original photograph?"

"Only the number of years involved. I did nothing that would bias the result."

"Or make it more accurate. Do you think diet influences the development of the face?"

"Of course."

"Your photograph has a full, healthy appearance. But of course, if you've been out in the swamp eating irregularly or unhealthily for years, and then you get thrown into jail, you might not have the flushest face."

"True."

"What about abuse? Can that affect someone's appearance?"

"I would assume so."

"Exercise? Sunlight?"

"Of course, but—"

"There are many factors that could influence the development of someone's face. And your program didn't know about any of them."

Ellison hesitated. "I would maintain that although environment may be a factor, ultimately, genetics dominate."

"But you can't always predict genetics, can you? Sure, you can take an educated guess. But you can't tell this jury your photo represents the only possible way that four-year-old face might evolve, can you? Beyond a doubt?"

Ellison pursed his lips. "No. I can't say that."

He didn't skip a beat. "You called Conrad Sweeney a philanthropist."

"A great one."

"He's donated to the police retirement fund."

"I'm not surprised."

"And you acknowledged that he paid you to investigate."

"True."

"Does that mean he was bribing you?"

"Of course not."

"It's possible for someone to contemplate helping someone without intending it as a bribe."

"Well..."

"Like you just said about Sweeney."

Ellison took a deep breath. "I suppose it's possible. But when the boy started talking about my truck—"

"If he paid you for your expert opinion, would that be a bribe?"

"Well, no…"

"Is the DA's office paying you for your testimony today?"

"I'm being compensated for my time."

"So you were bribed."

"Absolutely not."

"Did the money influence your testimony?"

"Of course not."

"Seems like you only see a bribe when you want to see it." He paused. "Or when Sweeney wants you to see it."

Kilpatrick shot to his feet. "Objection!"

He waved it away. "Withdrawn. This witness is a complete waste of my time. I have no more questions."

CHAPTER FORTY-TWO

DAN CAUGHT HIS REFLECTION IN THE MICROWAVE OVER THE stovetop. Who was that guy staring back at him? He'd spent so much time worrying about who his client really was—who was that guy in the reflection? A scrappy courtroom brawler?

Or, as Ellison suggested, a scared little boy who desperately wanted his daddy to come home and go swimming with him.

And why couldn't he shake the feeling that his father had been trying to tell him something? Recently?

He scooped the polenta into bowls, then poured the mushroom ragu over it. A dose of specially prepared crema, a bit of lemon zest, and a sprinkling of Maldon sea salt. *Voila!* He carried plates to his partners as they gathered around the kitchen table. Like it or not, they needed to discuss the case. Kilpatrick said he planned to wrap up the prosecution tomorrow.

"Who do you think Kilpatrick will call for his grand finale?"

"No way of telling," Garrett answered. "Another advantage of the hired gun. Someone like Jazlyn has to worry about her long-term relationship with fellow members of the bar. This guy is free to alienate everyone in town. He doesn't care. He'll collect his fee, blow town, and never see any of us again, in all likelihood."

"Another reason for the DA to bench Jazlyn, I guess," Jimmy said.

"I personally don't think he wants Jazlyn to succeed him," Dan said, "so he didn't want her getting a big publicity coup on the cusp of election season."

"Really?" Maria said. "You think this is politically motivated?"

"I think it's Sweeney-motivated."

"Which is politically motived."

"Because everything is politically motived. Got a fix on the jury? Any problems?"

"Our consultant is worried about the skinny guy on the front row. He scowls almost every time you speak."

"Wonderful."

Jimmy tried to calm him. "One rogue juror isn't enough to convict."

"It might be," Maria suggested. "He looks pushy. If he's chosen foreperson, he'll lead the discussion. He won't be shy about telling people what to think."

"Doesn't mean everyone will listen," Garrett said.

"Yes, we'd all like to think they will all stick to their guns and apply the standard of 'beyond a reasonable doubt' as instructed. But sadly, even for adults, peer pressure is a powerful influencer. It's much easier to go with the flow than to chart an individual course. But I'm sure you can steer them in the right direction, Dan."

"Any other concerns?"

"Our consultant is somewhat confused about...what our defense case will be."

"Our strategy is clear. Blame the cops, the DA, and other highly placed muckety-mucks."

"Yes, but what witnesses will you call?" She gave him a stern look. "Truth is, you only have one, and historically, you've opposed calling the defendant to the stand."

"Because it's incredibly risky. But in this instance, we have no choice. No one can tell Ossie's story but Ossie. And there are parts even he can't tell, because he doesn't remember. Still, the jury needs to hear from him. I think all this nonsense about him swiping drugs and concocting elaborate murder schemes will disappear once the jury sees that he's basically just a kid trying to find his place in the universe." He paused. "Like all of us." He finished his bowl. "If we have nothing more to discuss, I'm heading back to the crib."

Maria popped up. "I'll walk with you."

"You will not. I'll be fine."

"You said that before."

"Mr. K has a squadron of people watching me. I spot them occasionally. They're good, but hardly invisible."

"Still coming," Maria said, grabbing her purse.

"Really no need…"

"Maybe I just want to get you alone."

"Not buying it."

"My Fitbit says I haven't met my steps quota."

"You're not wearing your Fitbit."

She pulled a face. "Damned nuisance, working with a guy who notices everything." She opened the front door. "I'm still coming. Race you to the curb?"

THE FOLLOWING MORNING, DAN FUMBLED WITH HIS CELL PHONE as he hustled to the courtroom. Normally he didn't talk and walk at the same time, but he decided to make an exception for his beautiful girlfriend who was also the mayor of the city.

"How did you sleep last night, cicada?"

He was honest. "I barely slept at all."

"Ribs still aching?"

"Some. I never sleep during trials."

"You know, I could help with that." There was a soft purr in her voice.

"You could try. Probably wouldn't work. But the attempt would be enjoyable."

"I thought maybe we could get dinner tonight."

"Sorry. I expect to spend long hours getting Ossie ready to go on the stand. He's already terrified of what Kilpatrick might do to him."

"Boo. Your girlfriend feels neglected. You need to carve out some quality time for her."

"After the trial. I don't expect our case will be lengthy. After Ossie, it's in the jury's hands."

"And the jury is in your hands."

"We'll see. Let's plan on dinner this weekend. Where would you like to go? Chez Guitano?"

"You know..." The purr returned to her voice. "My boyfriend is the best chef in the city. And his boat is extremely cozy..."

Well now. That was an offer he couldn't refuse. "Consider it a date."

Dan spotted several familiar faces in the courtroom gallery —the whole Coleman clan, Margaret Tully, Bradley Ellison, even Quint, the Dumpster diver. Could Kilpatrick be planning to recall a previous witness? Or was Quint just trying to get off the streets?

Phil Coleman, the youngest of Zachary's sons, slapped a folded piece of paper into his hand. "Discovery request. For the civil case."

"Seriously? Your bigshot lawyers couldn't do this the proper way?"

"I told them I was going to see you. Why waste money on a stamp?"

"We've already produced everything relevant."

"So you say. But if your client goes on the witness stand and says anything new, expect a major investigation."

"Why would you think that's going to happen?"

"Because you're a clever lawyer, and he's a kid pretending to have amnesia. If he has a sudden burst of memory at an opportune moment, we're going to be all over you like butter on a hot skillet."

He frowned. "You should never put butter on a hot skillet. Use olive oil. Healthier and tastier." He walked on past.

He almost collided with Jazlyn. Given the circumstances, he didn't expect to see her anywhere near. "Glad Kilpatrick allows you in the courtroom."

She gave him a smirk. "Only because he needed me to bring him a file. He's extremely territorial."

"Not surprised. His career is based on his reputation as a superstar. Superstars don't have assistants."

Jimmy leaned in. "Batman has Robin."

Jazlyn smiled. "Is Robin an assistant? More like a companion. Those two seemed very close."

"What are you implying?"

"Stay calm, Jimmy. I don't want to be Kilpatrick's Robin. Not a fan of the man's style."

Interesting. "And how would you describe his style?"

"Win at any cost."

"Is his fee dependent upon winning?"

"No. But the next fee might be. Superstars with poor records don't get hired."

"You think he's on Sweeney's payroll?"

"He doesn't need it. He's getting plenty of money through official channels."

"I know Sweeney's backing the DA's mayoral campaign."

"Yes. I so wish Camila would stay here forever. But it's too much to ask." She laid her hand on Dan's wrist. "The police are still investigating the attack on you. But so far, they've come up with nothing."

"I don't think the cops kill themselves trying to protect defense attorneys."

"There's probably some truth in that, but I don't think anyone knows anything. Whoever orchestrated this attack covered his tracks." She leaned closer. "And they may not be finished."

"Believe me, Jazlyn, if those three thugs had wanted me dead, they could've killed me."

"They didn't want you dead then. They hoped the attack would be enough. But you clearly haven't stopped, and if it starts to look as if this trial is going the wrong way..."

"I have people looking after me. I can take care of myself."

She squeezed his hand. "Except it's becoming increasingly clear that you can't. And I don't want to see you killed." She paused. "Esperanza would be heartbroken."

She turned abruptly and headed toward the door.

CHAPTER FORTY-THREE

KILPATRICK'S FINAL WITNESS WAS THE POLE DANCING PRODIGY, Vanessa Collins. She was dressed considerably more conservatively than when he'd met her before, but her manner was just as forthright and unapologetic. She established her identity, how she made a living, and her previous relationship with Harrison Coleman.

"When was your last contact with him?" Kilpatrick asked.

"The night he was murdered."

"You saw him?"

"Not at first. He was busy. I went backstage at the theater. I knew he liked to hole up on opening night, reading or playing chess with himself. But to my surprise, on this occasion, he was not alone."

"Who was with him?"

She pointed toward the defense table. "That boy. The one who claims to be Ossie Coleman."

"Do you believe he's Ossie Coleman?"

"I know Harrison didn't. He told many people that if anyone was in a position to know who deserved to inherit the estate, it was him. And this kid wasn't the one."

"So Harrison was a major obstacle to the defendant inheriting the money."

"I assume so. I had several reasons for visiting him that night. Found some of his clothes in the back of my closet I wanted to return. Plus I had a question I wanted to ask. Anyway, when I got to his office, I could tell immediately that he was not alone. The door to his office was closed, but I could hear people talking inside. Loudly."

"And when you say you could hear them—who did you hear?"

"Harrison. And the defendant."

"Could you make out what they were saying?"

"Perfectly. There was a lot of noise onstage, so maybe no one else heard, but when I pressed close to the door, it was clear as day."

"What were they talking about?"

"Money, of course. The kid wanted Harrison to back his claim. And he refused. Harrison called him an imposter. The kid offered him money to—"

"Objection," Dan said, rising. And here we go. Arguing a technical evidentiary matter of grave import to a judge who still wore training wheels. "This is hearsay."

"But clearly an exception to the rule," Kilpatrick said. "The declarant is deceased."

"My client is not. He can testify about what happened during this meeting."

Kilpatrick laughed out loud. "Yes, and I'm sure he'll include every word, warts and all. With respect, your honor, we're entitled to introduce another witness, one who has no stake in the matter. No incentive to lie. She's a completely objective observer."

There's no such thing. "The fact that she was present demonstrates that she's not completely objective. She had a relationship with the victim."

"But none with the defendant. She has no reason to invent incriminating evidence." Kilpatrick paused. "And this will be extremely incriminating."

Judge Smulders frowned. "I don't know..."

"Let me make it easier for you, your honor. Just let me introduce the recording. Then we'll see if there's a problem."

According to Vanessa, once she realized she was eavesdropping on something hot, she pulled her phone out of her purse and started recording it. He'd filed a motion to exclude on various grounds, but the judge had not granted it. Apparently electronic eavesdropping did not offend Smulders as much as it did him. "We completely object to that, your honor. On numerous grounds."

"But the recording eliminates the problem with unreliability," Kilpatrick said.

"It's wiretapping, your honor, which violates federal law."

"It's not like she tapped his phone. There was no opportunity to ask for consent."

"But the fact remains, she didn't obtain consent. Illegal recordings can't be used in court."

"Unless there are strong and valid reasons to do so. Like here. This is a murder case."

"That does not change the law. Nor does it change my client's constitutional expectation of privacy."

"What privacy?" Kilpatrick spread wide his arms. "Your honor, they were shouting so loudly they could be heard outside the door."

"That argument actually makes sense to me," Judge Smulders said. "We all know everyone on earth has a cellphone that can record conversations. If you're going to shout in a public place, you have no right to expect privacy. I'm going to allow the recording to be played for the jury."

"Exception. Permission to take an interlocutory appeal." He wondered if the judge even understood what he was saying.

"Whatever. We're not going to delay the trial for you." Which made it pointless. "Play the tape."

Kilpatrick used the same AV system that had displayed the photos. Although the jury wouldn't see any images during the playback, they would be able to read captions. Dan had reviewed the captions beforehand and agreed that they appeared to be accurate. He had also agreed, somewhat reluctantly, to post-production sound editing that removed much of the background buzz and made the recording easier to hear.

After some crackling static, the conversation gradually became comprehensible. Kilpatrick had edited it down to the parts he most wanted the jury to hear.

Ossie's voice was much higher pitched than Harrison's, so they were easy to distinguish. "You gotta back me on this."

"Sorry, son," Harrison replied. "That will never happen. I spent lots of time with Ossie. I loved that boy. And you are not that boy."

"Without you, I got no chance."

"Probably. The old man trusts me."

"Help me. I'll make you glad you did."

"Sorry, no."

There was a loud noise, as if furniture were being knocked over. "I won't ask again!"

"Break anything you want. It won't change my mind."

"Will this?"

They heard a loud sickening sound. Even without a visual image, it was obvious someone had just been hit. The cry of pain that followed cemented that impression.

"Get out of here!"

"I won't leave till you promise you'll help me."

"I will not—ever—"

Another crashing sound, louder than before. It sounded as if Harrison had been knocked to the ground.

"I'll—call someone."

"Not if I can help it. Do you think I'm going to let you ruin everything for me? Do you?"

Harrison's voice sounded weak. "I can't...tell..."

"I won't let you ruin my plans. *I won't!*"

The jurors' eyes widened. The looked from one to another, stunned, as if they had just heard a confession. If they could've voted then, he suspected, they all would vote to convict. And deliver the death penalty.

Kilpatrick switched off the recording and returned his attention to the witness. "What happened next?"

Vanessa looked distraught, as if she was hearing this for the first time. "I pounded on the door. Eventually, Harrison opened it. He assured me he was okay. I saw the defendant in there, glaring toward the door. I asked Harrison if he needed help, but he told me it was just a little disagreement and nothing to worry about." Her lips tightened. "I wish to God I'd called the police then and there. But I didn't. And look what happened."

"You shouldn't blame yourself. You had no way of knowing what would happen."

"I should've. I should've stayed with him. But I didn't. And now he's dead."

Kilpatrick nodded his head gravely. "No more questions. Mr. Pike?"

He knew he had to make an impression—fast—or this case was irretrievably lost. "I interviewed you shortly after I took this case, Ms. Collins. You never mentioned that you had a recording."

"You didn't ask."

"You knew I'd be interested."

"But you didn't ask. And the DA told you about it, so who cares anyway?"

"Were you hoping to get Ossie out of the way so you could inherit more of the estate?"

"Me? I'm not a beneficiary."

"But you claim you were the common-law wife of Harrison Coleman. You could use that claim to get a piece of the action."

"That's absurd."

"But you have made that claim, haven't you?"

"All I want is what the law says I'm entitled to have."

"I have to ask myself why you didn't come clean with me when we first talked. Were you working with the police?"

"I wanted them to catch Harrison's murderer, if that's what you mean."

"You said you saw my client in Harrison's office."

"That's right."

"How long did you see him?"

"Only a moment."

"Were the office lights on?"

"No. I think a lamp had been knocked over."

"How can you be sure who you saw?"

"I saw him and heard him. Voice analysis shows it was the defendant."

"On the tape. But how can you be sure who you saw when you peered through the door?"

"I saw the defendant."

"Have you talked to the District Attorney about your testimony?"

"Yes."

"What about Conrad Sweeney? Have you talked to him?"

"No. I don't know who that is."

"Why did you record the conversation?"

"He threatened to murder Harrison!"

"Did he say the word 'murder?'"

"It was obvious what he meant. Just listen to—"

"But you started recording before the alleged threat."

"The conversation was already threatening. Dangerous. I used to be a teacher, and I always caution students, especially young girls, to take precautions. When you're in a threatening

situation, get your phone out. Take pictures, make recordings. I was just taking my own advice."

"Of course, if you were that worried about it, you could have opened the office door earlier and intervened."

"And then maybe I'd be the dead one." She leaned forward, her voice forceful. "That man threatened to murder Harrison. And he said he'd done it before."

"That's not what Ossie—"

"This is not Ossie Coleman," she said, loud enough to be heard in the next courtroom. "He's a coldblooded killer. And I did not want to be his next victim."

She whipped her head around toward the jury. "Lock that man up. *Please!* For everyone's sake." Her voice trembled. Her hands shook. Several members of the jury were visibly disturbed. "No one will be safe until you do. Lock him up before he kills again!"

THE BEGINNING OF KNOWLEDGE

CHAPTER FORTY-FOUR

CONRAD SWEENEY SURVEYED HIS SURROUNDINGS.

The crowd gathered before the two-story brick building was impressive. He expected the media, of course. They came anytime anyone beckoned. But the other spectators—that was somewhat surprising and entirely pleasing. These were private citizens, people who could've been out playing with their children, or walking their dogs, or making love to their wives, people who instead opted to gather here today—because Conrad Sweeney issued an announcement.

That was a tribute to the reputation he had built in this town. When he spoke, people listened. When he acted, people paid attention. He was St. Pete's most prominent private citizen, a philanthropist and hero.

All he ever wanted was to be loved. Since he was a young boy. Blowing the lid off the achievement register while his parents reminded him what a disappointment he was.

No matter. The people in this town loved him.

Maybe not the mayor so much. But she was keeping her mouth shut today. She had too much at stake to cross him.

Pity her boyfriend didn't feel the same way.

"I want to thank you all for coming today," Sweeney said, once the cameras were rolling, "but this is not about me. I was the lucky one, the one who had the means and opportunity to help St. Pete emerge from a difficult period and become the city it was always meant to be. With Albert Kazan, we built the best park this town has ever seen. With Mayor Pérez, we built a dynamic series of women's shelters. And now, with the Athena Recovery Clinic, we will provide counseling and rehabilitative services to those who need them, regardless of their financial status, gender orientation, race, creed, or color. This facility is all-inclusive. This is for everyone. Because when our citizens are stronger, our city is stronger."

His words were met with tumultuous applause, which he modestly deflected. A series of meet and greets followed. He devoted time to as many people as he could, till he spotted Prudence giving him the slashed throat gesture. Time to move on.

Once he extracted himself from the well-wishers, he slid into the back seat of his waiting limo. Verity, his driver, started the engine.

Two other men were in back waiting for him. District Attorney George Belasco. And Paul Kilpatrick, the paid prosecutor currently handling the murder trial against the boy who claimed to be Ossie Coleman.

"I'm in a good mood, gentlemen," Sweeney said, popping open his briefcase. "Don't spoil it."

"We won't," Belasco said. His slender frame made his blue suit look baggy. "Far from it. Everything is going according to plan."

"You've got the trial locked up?"

"Certainly looks that way," Kilpatrick said. "I'd give us an 80% chance of success."

"I don't want to hear about percentages. I want to hear about certainties."

"No such thing, when you're talking about juries. I don't care how good you are, or how good a job you do. All it takes is one rogue juror with a forceful personality to throw every calculation off-kilter."

Sweeney shook his head. "Foolish man. Everything is predictable. Assuming you have sufficient data."

"I don't have the power to read minds."

"Or grease palms?" Sweeney smiled. "Not what I've heard. You didn't get that perfect win record by trusting fate." He turned to Belasco. "Are you paying this man enough?"

"I paid him everything we agreed on. More than our budget permitted."

"That's a problem for your successor to deal with. You need to focus on your mayoral campaign."

"I am."

"I need a mayor I can trust. Not a pain-in-the-ass crusader who thinks she knows better than everyone else. There is so much I could accomplish..."

"I'm your guy," Belasco said, cocking a thumb toward himself. "We've always worked well together in the past, haven't we?"

"I haven't always obtained the results I wanted."

"You will this time." The limo accelerated as they merged onto the highway, rocking him backward a bit. "That audiotape hit the jury like a ton of bricks. Not a doubt in their minds now."

"I hope you're right. But we both know Pike will do everything he can to stir up doubt."

"I don't think Pike's got the verve he had before," Kilpatrick opined. "Seems like he kinda got the wind kicked out of his sails."

"Indeed." A small smile played on Sweeney's lips. "I wonder how that happened."

"Doesn't matter. We expect the kid to tell his sad story, but so what? No one believed it before. Why would they believe it now?"

"Maybe you should offer a deal. Life imprisonment. Just make sure the kid is off the street and doesn't inherit a dime."

"Look, I know you've lost to Pike before—"

Sweeney leaned forward, grabbing Kilpatrick by the collar. "I have never lost to him. I never lose to anyone."

"I—I didn't mean—"

"Others may have lost. Not me." Sweeney's teeth clenched. "Temporary setbacks only make me stronger."

"Sure. That's what I meant."

Sweeney loosened his grip, then slowly relaxed back into the padded seat. "You're being paid to make sure I'm not disappointed."

"Understood. You're worrying too much. This is gonna be a slam dunk."

"You'd best be right."

Kilpatrick hesitated a moment. "You mind if I ask—why do you care so much?"

"Excuse me?"

"I mean—what's it to you? I saw that crowd. Those people love you. This town loves you. You're the most respected, most successful, most powerful person around. This is just a murder trial. A serious crime, sure, but in the big scheme of things— who cares? What difference does it make?"

"It matters."

"Because—"

Sweeney sprang forward like a cobra. "Everything hinges on the outcome of this trial. Not only money, but power. Influence. Secrets. Which, if revealed, could be extremely uncomfortable. So we're not going to let that happen. Are we clear on that?"

"Sure. Sure." Kilpatrick held up his hands. "One hundred percent."

"I've let Pike run free too long. Warnings don't seem to be enough with that man. If you can't put him down in the court-room—then I'll find some other way to do it."

CHAPTER FORTY-FIVE

DAN SLOWLY ROLLED OFF THE EDGE OF THE BED, HOPING TO shake the mattress as little as possible. Camila tended to be a sound sleeper, but you never could be certain, and he didn't want to deal with a chili-pepper temper this early in the morning.

He stretched, forcing the kinks out of his aching bones. His ribs still hurt. Not as badly as before, but more than enough to remind him, every minute of the day, what a beating he had taken. How much they hurt him.

How much he risked by continuing with this case.

He tiptoed into the tiny bathroom adjoining the so-called bedroom. Barely enough room for a sink and a mirror, but he had learned to make do. He reached for a shaving brush—

What was that noise?

He dropped the brush. The strength drained out of his arms. He felt his knees weaken.

What if it was them? The big man, and the UPS guy, and— what if they'd come back? What if their boss didn't like the way the trial was going and decided to—

He clenched his eyes shut. Get a grip on yourself, Pike.

He listened harder. There was no one there. It was just the wind in the sail, or the creaking of the timbers. Nothing.

Maybe it was time to stop pretending the attack had made no lasting impression.

They were still with him, every second of the day.

He splashed cold water on his face, breathing deep, drinking in the air. He wasn't even sure what question he should be asking himself. Do you have lawyer PTSD? What kind of crazy fool would continue with this case? Who are you trying to impress?

He grabbed a towel and dried his face, peering into the mirror. Who the hell are you, Pike? What are you doing here, with your life, with your client, with this woman in your bed?

For so long, he'd let his father's tragedy define him. He'd been on autopilot since he was a teenager. The government railroaded his father, so he wouldn't let them do it to anyone else. Fine. Except what did he ever do? Got a few people off the hook —and was well paid for it. But did he actually investigate his father's case? Even when he had a chance to talk to Ellison, the man directly responsible for his father's conviction, he avoided the subject.

Who are you? he asked the face in the mirror.

And why can't you solve this case? It shouldn't be that hard. A dead man, greedy relatives, a mysterious disappearance. Put it together already. Professor Plum in the Conservatory with the candlestick. Or something like that.

He heard a creaking door and fortunately did not jump. Camila shuffled behind him and pressed her warmth against his. "Pretrial jitters?"

"Something like that."

"You could come back to bed. It's not even light out."

Her hair was a mess, sleep in her eyes—but still gorgeous. "My mind is already at the courthouse." Bit of a lie, but it sounded good.

"Anything I can do?"

"Don't think so. Got any more PR events with Sweeney?"

"No, thank God. I've had as much of that man as I can take. But I can't afford to be rude, not when I'm fundraising."

"I understand. Don't like it, but I understand. I'm convinced that man is the puppet master pulling the strings in this case. And that he's using DA Belasco."

"There are ways we could deal with the district attorney."

He turned—not easy in this tiny alcove—and gave her a sharp look. "What do you mean?"

"We could have him taken care of."

He grinned. She was adorable when she pretended to be ruthless. "Just off him?"

"If he's on Sweeney's payroll, he deserves to be offed."

"I don't see you doing that."

She looked him in the eyes, wide and watery. "For you, I would do anything."

"Likewise." He pulled her close and planted a kiss on her lips, lingering a long time. "Here's an alternate plan. How about I win in court?"

She pressed harder against him, placing her hands in completely inappropriate places. "Are you sure you don't have time to come back to bed? Clear your head? Relieve some stress? It would be therapeutic. Really, I'm only thinking of you."

"Is that a fact."

"I am your mayor. That makes me the city's foremost service provider." She wrapped her hands around his waist. "I aim to provide service."

CHAPTER FORTY-SIX

KILPATRICK GREETED DAN AT THE COURTROOM DOOR, AND NOT just to be friendly. To his surprise, the man offered him a deal.

"Life. No chance of parole," Kilpatrick said, arms folded across his chest.

"You call that a deal? I call it your best-case scenario."

"Have you been watching those jurors, Pike? Because I have. They're ready to convict."

"I haven't put on my case yet."

"From where I sit, you don't have a case. You'll put the kid up there to tell the same cockamamie story he's been peddling since he appeared out of nowhere. No one bought it before, and no one will buy it now."

"We'll see. We might have a few surprises."

"We have multiple witnesses putting him at the scene of the crime. His name was on the mirror. His prints were on the murder weapon. He threatened—"

"I don't need a summary. I'll take your offer to my client. But he'll turn it down."

"How can you be sure of that?"

"Because he didn't do it." He turned away and, as he did,

noticed that the two remaining Coleman brothers, Benny and Phil, were seated together. For once, Dolly wasn't hovering about telling everyone what to do. Zachary wasn't with them, either.

Benny nodded amiably. "Morning, Pike." He could be a decent guy, it seemed, when his wife was absent. \Phil's fingers were pressed against his forehead.

"You feeling all right?"

"Migraines," Phil replied. "Stress always makes them flair up. I could barely move this morning."

"Sorry to hear that. How's your father doing?"

"Not well. This trial has been hard on him. But he'll never admit it."

Benny agreed. "The man is dying." He drew in his breath. "But when this trial ends, he's planning a bioluminescent kayak trip. Ever done that, Pike?"

"I've always wanted to. Where's your father now?"

Phil answered. "Said he had to take a phone call. Must be something brewing. He was up late last night."

Benny turned his head. "I thought I heard something."

"Probably me. I never sleep well. Haven't since Afghanistan."

Dolly entered the courtroom and he tried to disappear, but didn't move fast enough.

"Are you having an unauthorized meeting with my brother-in-law, Mr. Pike? I should report this to the Bar Association."

"We're not discussing the case."

"Nonetheless, all three of us are listed as prosecution witnesses."

"But you didn't testify."

"You've got an excuse for everything, don't you? That's how you slick lawyers work. Legal ethics are legerdemain."

"Unlike the world of business, where decisions are made based upon the common good and the betterment of mankind."

She smiled, in a lopsided way. "That was actually funny." She took a step forward, swinging her enormous purse between them. "You know, once this case is over, we should get a drink. We might learn to like one another."

That sent more shivers down his spine than the man who attacked him with a tire iron. "Would we invite your husband?"

"Why? Do we need someone to clean up afterward?"

Ouch. "I don't think we're compatible, Dolly. I did see the quarterlies in the paper this morning, though. Looks like your father-in-law's business might be hitting a rough patch."

She waved a dismissive hand. "Just a momentary setback. Happens all the time. We've had glitches before. It's part of the process."

"If you'll excuse me—"

"Of course." She winked. "Don't forget what I said. The mayor may be cuter. But there are times when a real woman has...advantages."

He wondered what her husband thought about this banter. Didn't matter, he supposed. Because that was never ever *ever* going to happen...

DAN FOUND OSSIE SEATED AT THE DEFENSE TABLE. HE LOOKED nervous, but that was to be expected. Anyone who wasn't nervous before he went on the witness stand to plead for his life was either completely amoral or too experienced to be innocent. Ossie, on the other hand, was completely innocent and scared to death.

"You ready to do this?"

"Sure." He took a deep breath, then released it. "I wish I could remember more."

"Just tell them what you know. No one can blame you for not remembering everything. And no one is going to catch you doing anything wrong as long as you stay honest."

"But what if they don't believe me?"

He laid his hand on the boy's shoulder. "Give the jury some credit. Too often, public cynicism about lawyers spills over to juries—and that's unfair. In my experience, juries work hard and try to do the right thing, despite the difficult situation presented by a keenly flawed system. They're better at figuring out who's telling the truth and who's lying than you might imagine." He smiled. "You just tell your story. They'll do the rest."

DAN TOOK HIS TIME WITH OSSIE'S TESTIMONY. HE KNEW THE JURY had been waiting for this and had been hoping they'd hear from the defendant—far from a certainty in a criminal prosecution. There was no substitute for getting up close and personal with the man accused of committing the crime.

Normally, he would spend the first ten or twenty minutes establishing the witness's background, but that was difficult in this case, because Ossie was so young and because he remembered so little. He hoped it wouldn't matter. If the jury didn't believe Ossie suffered from memory loss, they were sunk.

"Do you remember anything that happened prior to the police finding you on the street?"

"I get flashes—" Ossie's face twisted, as if he were struggling for memories he could not retrieve. "But it doesn't come together. I can't place it. I can't put it into context. It's like a movie montage sequence—except I haven't seen the movie." He thought another moment. "I know I was alive before I was found in St. Petersburg. My movie didn't begin there. But I can't put complete scenes together."

"Do you remember when the police came?"

"Yes. It's my first clear memory. And I recall being taken to the hospital. Then the police station. Then the foster home. My clothes were torn. For some reason, I kept thinking about dogs. War dogs."

"War dogs? Like Doberman Pinschers?"

"I don't know. My ears were ringing. My vision was blurry at first and I couldn't think straight. The only thing I could remember with any clarity was my name—Ossie Coleman."

"Did you tell the police who you were?"

"I told everyone. Doctors, nurses, cops. The guy who brought my food on a tray. Eventually word leaked out that the missing heir had been found. And soon the press was all over it. Everyone wanted an interview. Which I declined—leading to some nasty stories suggesting that I must be a con artist."

"Did you know about the Coleman family fortune?"

"Didn't have a clue. Till someone told me."

"How did you feel about that?"

He shrugged. "Mixed. I liked the idea of having a family, being a part of a family. Very much. The only person I remembered was Joe, back at the cabin—and I didn't consider him family. And everyone dreams about suddenly inheriting a ton of money. But I also knew that some people would think I was faking to get my hands on the cash. And then when I met the family for the first time—boy, did that turn out to be correct."

Ossie was telling his story calmly, evenly, honestly. There was no way to know if the jury was buying it, but they were listening.

He was worried about the man on the front row, the one the jury consultant targeted. That guy looked skeptical about every word. He wished the juror would do something outrageous so he could remove him—but that was a daydream.

"How did the Coleman family react?"

"My grandfather—Zachary—wasn't so bad. I could tell he was skeptical—but I could also tell he had loved his grandson and wanted more than anything to be reunited with him. Before it was too late. He didn't believe me yet, but he was open to the idea. With time, I think he would realize I wasn't lying. But his daughter and her husband—Dolly and Benny—they were outright hostile. Called me names I won't repeat in court, if that's okay with the judge."

"We get the general idea. What about the younger brother, Phil?"

"He was quieter. I wasn't sure how to read him. My hunch was that he would go with the flow, follow the others. But Dolly was never going to be convinced. She didn't want any more heirs in the mix."

"And Harrison?"

"He wasn't there when I met the others. Had a rehearsal or something. We arranged to meet at another time."

"Did you?"

"Yes." He glanced at the jury. "That was the night he was killed, I guess. I didn't know till later."

"But you were at the theater that night?"

"Yes, I was."

"You told the police you weren't."

"I know. I—I was scared." He took a deep breath. "So I lied. If I'd had more time to think about it, I would've realized what a stupid choice that was. I know lying is wrong, but surely you can see why I did it. The police came after me, chased me, called me names. I didn't know anyone had seen me at the theater. I was just trying to keep myself out of trouble."

"But that backfired on you."

"Big time. Lesson learned. No more lying."

"How did the conversation with Harrison go?"

"Not well. I probably came at the wrong time. Interrupted. He was playing chess."

"With himself?"

"Yes. He switched sides. I watched him. He was a serious Brainiac. I asked him to speak on my behalf. I thought if I could get the eldest brother to back me, the others would follow. But he wouldn't do it."

"He didn't believe you were Ossie Coleman."

Ossie hesitated a moment. "He said that, later. You heard it on the recording. I think he was trying to convince himself, so he could feel better about the choice he was making. But at first, he just said he didn't want to come forward. He thought it was dangerous. He said he thought people were after me. And he was afraid they might come after him."

"What did he recommend?"

"Lay low. He said that several times. Lay low. Be patient."

"What did you think about that?"

Ossie sighed. "I was a fool. I didn't want to wait for anything. I wanted everyone to know who I was. I wanted all this... turmoil to be over. I pushed him and pushed him. Got mad. Even threatened him a little."

"You heard the audiotape played in court."

"Yes. If you'd heard the entire conversation, it wouldn't sound so bad. That recording seems to have been edited down to the worst parts."

"But you admit you were there. Did you kill Harrison?"

"No, of course not. I liked him. He wouldn't do what I needed, but I don't think he disliked me. In fact, I think he liked me more than my other relatives. I think he was genuinely concerned about me, and in his own way, he was trying to help me."

"Did you take a syringe to the meeting?"

"No."

"Did you poison him?"

"No."

"Did you take chemicals to destroy his body?"

"Absolutely not."

"But you were spotted wearing a backpack."

"My foster mom gave it to me for schoolbooks. Not killer

chemicals. After our conversation ended, I ran out of the room and never came back."

"And you also spoke to Bradley Ellison?"

"Yes. Still looking for someone who would back me. I needed a friend."

"But he didn't think you were really Ossie Coleman."

"You know—he never once said that to me. He just refused to help. He said his employer wouldn't like it."

"Meaning Conrad Sweeney. The man who was paying him to investigate the case."

"He didn't say. But that's why I offered to help him—you know, with the truck and stuff. Sounded like someone else was bribing him to speak out against me. I offered to help him if he would tell the truth. I know I shouldn't have done it, but—I was desperate."

"Thank you, Ossie." The kid had told his story well. Convincingly, with no wasted words. He wasn't going to prolong it. He just hoped it would be enough. "Your witness."

Kilpatrick made a slow approach, probably deliberately trying to unnerve Ossie. He could see Ossie's demeanor change, even before Kilpatrick spoke. He had never been at ease, but now he was visibly apprehensive.

"You admit you're a liar, right?"

Ossie looked hurt. "I admit that I lied to the cops about being at the theater."

"You only fessed up after you got caught lying."

"I made a mistake. And I regret it."

"Now that you've been caught. But the fact remains—you lied."

"That is true."

"And for all we know, you're lying now."

"I have not lied today."

"We have no way of knowing. It might just be that you haven't gotten caught yet."

Ossie's unease appeared to grow. "I'm not lying."

"Why was your name written on the bathroom mirror?"

"I don't know."

"How did the syringe get in the trash bin outside the home where you lived?"

"I don't know."

"No idea?"

He squirmed a bit. "My roommate in the foster home may have put it there."

"Why would he do that?"

"I've seen him come home with red eyes and a funny smell. I think he may have a drug habit."

"Did you shoot him up?"

"Of course not."

Kilpatrick sprang forward. "Then how did your fingerprint get on the syringe?"

Ossie stayed calm. "I'm not convinced it was. I think your fingerprint expert saw what she wanted to see."

"Seriously?" Kilpatrick laughed out loud. "You think you know more about fingerprints than the expert?"

"The expert admitted she had only a partial print. I think my attorney showed how uncertain her testimony was."

Kilpatrick turned toward the judge. "You honor, I move that this response be stricken from the record."

Dan rose. "The prosecutor asked a question and the witness answered it. He can't object because he didn't like the answer."

"I object because this witness is not an expert."

"Then you shouldn't have asked him what he thought."

"I object again! This is outrageous!" Kilpatrick was getting heated—which gave Dan a pleasant buzz.

Kilpatrick continued. "Not one of these people is qualified to question the integrity of an expert witness."

"Could we just move along?" Judge Smulders said. He

lowered his voice. "I was hoping to get home in time for supper."

Kilpatrick turned back toward Ossie. "When the police came to your home—you ran."

"I was scared. I didn't want to be locked up. Does anyone?"

"But you ran from the police."

"To get my lawyer."

"Did you think the police were going to hurt you?"

"I thought it was a distinct possibility. Especially after one of them used the n-word."

Kilpatrick fell silent for a moment. "According to you."

"He used several other terms that...were about my skin color. Called me 'murdering lying black trash.'"

Several of the jurors reacted with creased foreheads and squinted eyes. He could tell this mattered to them. And they would surely notice that Kilpatrick was not denying it.

"I've been doing this job for a long time," Kilpatrick said, "and if there's anything I know for certain, it's this. Only one kind of person runs when the police come calling. The guilty kind."

"You say that because you're white. White and rich. College educated. If you spent a day with me, or any of the kids in my foster home, you'd see the world in a different way. A far more dangerous way."

"Stop trying to distract the jury. You ran as soon as you saw the police outside your house. You had no reason to mistrust them at that point."

"They'd been treating me like a liar since they found me. The first officer who took my statement said, 'Ossie Coleman, huh? Sure. Guess you're tired of living in the ghetto.' Another one muttered, 'Another colored kid looking for a handout.'"

"Your honor, this is outside the scope—"

Dan rose. "The prosecutor asked a question and Ossie answered it, in the most honest way possible."

"He's trying to erect a smokescreen."

"He's trying to get to the truth, your honor. Pretending the police are never at fault is the smokescreen. Reports of police brutality toward people of color make the news almost every day. An unarmed man shot in his own backyard. A teenage girl attacked at a party. How long are we going to pretend the police are colorblind when it's obvious they aren't?"

"This is way off topic. Your honor, I—"

To everyone's surprise, Ossie cut Kilpatrick off. "You're trying to silence me. But I will not be hushed." Ossie rose to his feet. "No disrespect, your honor. But the police have been out to get me from the first moment I showed up. And I don't think it's just because I'm telling a wild story and I can't prove who I am. I think a white boy telling the same story would get far more respect. But I'm not white. And that makes all the difference."

CHAPTER FORTY-SEVEN

CLOSING ARGUMENTS DID NOT TAKE THAT LONG. DAN SENSED that everyone had said everything they had to say and the jury was ready to get on with it. Kilpatrick gave a predictable summation with no surprises. When it was Dan's time to speak, he made a point of keeping it brief. He wanted the jurors to understand that he trusted them.

"When we began this trial together," he said, "my worthy opponent said he wouldn't lie to you. Well…I don't know if he lied, but he definitely did not present the whole picture. I tried to give you a peek behind the curtain. I wanted you to under-stand what's really going on here. And I think I exposed a few lies along the way—or misrepresentations, at the very least.

"My opponent also said he wouldn't waste your time…and I didn't. When I had no objection to the prosecution testimony, I kept my mouth shut. The only time I spoke was when I thought someone was trying to mislead you, which sadly happened far more often than it should. I let you hear from the accused, but I didn't drag it out forever, because I thought you'd heard enough to reach a verdict. I think it must be clear to every one of you that someone wants my client out of the way."

He paused, casting a glance first out to the gallery, where the entire Coleman family sat, then back to Kilpatrick, who appeared distinctly unhappy. "Who's pulling the strings in this case? The DA? The police? The Coleman clan? Or some other powerful figure lurking behind the scenes? Fortunately, you don't have to figure out that puzzle. All you have to do is decide whether my client has been proven guilty beyond a reasonable doubt. I don't think this is a hard call. What evidence of guilt do you have? Ossie was in the wrong place at the wrong time, true, he's admitted that. It gives him opportunity but hardly proves he acted upon it. The fingerprint evidence was not conclusive, the DNA evidence was not conclusive, and that syringe—don't even get me started. The skeeziest of paid ratfinks finds exactly what the police want him to find and brings it to them. Sure. Nothing suspicious there, huh?" He shook his head. "They can't even prove that syringe was used to kill the victim."

He paced alongside the jury box. "Even if you believe that evidence was legit—so what? We don't know how Harrison was killed, so the trace of what might be poison means nothing. Ossie explained there was a drug user in his house, and the prosecution did nothing to disprove that. Ossie's name was scrawled on a mirror, but anyone could have done that—to frame Ossie for someone else's crime. Yes, Ossie had a financial motive—but so did about half the people sitting in this courtroom. That isn't proof. Frankly, ladies and gentlemen, I don't even think you have a good reason to *suspect* Ossie—much less to convict him."

He leaned hard against the rail. "Here's what I know for certain. This case matters. It matters to you, to me, to everyone here today—and of course, to Ossie. You've been charged with an important—I would even say sacred—duty. You will probably never sit on a murder-trial jury again. I hope not, for your sake. You will remember this case for the rest of your life. You will be telling people about it for decades." He tried to make eye contact. "Let's make sure this story has the right ending, okay? One you can be proud of. Because this case will never let go of you. If you send an innocent man to the gallows—you will never shake that out of your soul. It will needle you and punish you till your dying day. Follow the judge's instructions, please. Guilt has not been proven beyond a reasonable doubt."

He knew he should probably end it there, but something compelled him to push just a little harder.

"You know—comes a time in all our lives when we have to decide who we are. Who we *really* are. Except maybe, maybe that's about deciding who we want to be. What drives us. And maybe this is one of those defining moments for you—and for me. I'm not arguing this case because I need to—but because I want to. I didn't represent Ossie because I had to. I did it because I could see he needed help, as we all do at one time or another. This young man was being treated wrongly, unfairly, with prejudice and contempt, and someone needed to do something about it. We live in complicated times, and now more than ever we all must be willing to take a stand and let our voices be heard.

"Now you need to decide who you want to be. Do you really believe this boy committed this atrocious crime? Did you ever? Or did you take one look at him and think—this doesn't feel right? Cold-blooded murder? Brutal chemical dissolution of the body? *This kid?* When you heard that, didn't some part of you think—I'm not going to be the kind of person who is manipulated by invisible fingers. When I can tell the fix is in, I'm not going along with it. I will resist. I will say the emperor has no clothes. I will rise and be counted. I will be the kind of juror who does what the judge asks, who looks at the evidence and says—this boy's guilt has not been proven beyond a reasonable doubt. I will do that even if it brings scorn and condemnation. Because that's who I am. Because that's the person I want to be."

CHAPTER FORTY-EIGHT

DAN CHECKED HIS WATCH. JUDGE SMULDERS WOULD BE
disappointed. Jury deliberation was continuing long past
dinnertime.

"What's taking so long?" Dan asked, pacing in the hallway
outside the courtroom.

"It's only been three hours. That's nothing," Maria assured
him. "The jurors will feel like they have to talk about it a little
bit just to show they took their job seriously. Especially after
that closing you gave them."

"True. And not remotely reassuring."

"Once they've reviewed the evidence, they've got to vote.
Most will want to speak, just to show that they've been paying
attention. Someone will make fun of Quint. Someone will claim
they always thought there was something dubious about the
fingerprint evidence. Someone—"

"Yes, I get the idea. But it doesn't help."

She placed a hand on his shoulder. "You did everything you
could. Especially under the circumstances."

"I don't know what that means."

"I think you do." She walked close, then pressed a hand against his cheek. "Your father would be very proud of you."

Ossie appeared in the doorway. "The bailiff just brought me a note. He says the jury is returning."

"With a question?"

He shook his head. "With a verdict."

———

"*NOT GUILTY ON ALL COUNTS!*"

Ossie swept Maria into the air. "*Yes!*"

Dan heard a cheer rise up from the gallery. Probably mostly Jimmy, but it sounded like everyone present, even though he knew that couldn't be true. He had a strong hunch, for instance, that the Coleman family was not celebrating. Dolly was already on her feet, looking disgusted, helping Zachary into his wheelchair.

Ossie pressed his hands against the table, breathing heavily. "I was so worried. I know you put on a good case, but—"

He nodded. "But it's not the same as hearing 'not guilty' from the jurors' lips."

Judge Smulders pounded his gavel, possibly for the first time in his life, calling for order. He thanked and discharged the jury, then added, "The defendant is free to go."

Dan patted Ossie on the back. "Congratulations. Justice prevails."

"Only because of you. You and your team."

"You should thank the jurors, if you get a chance. They showed a lot of courage and followed their consciences, not the party line."

"I will. Speaking of the party line—" He pointed.

Kilpatrick stood behind him, hand outstretched. "Congratulations, counsel. You put another murderer back on the street."

He gave the man a questioning look. "You're not still

pretending you think Ossie committed this murder, are you? This prosecution was bogus from the start. Ossie was framed. Admit it."

"I'm not even admitting your client is Ossie."

"Aw, don't be a sore loser. He's completely innocent."

"For your sake, I hope you're right. If he kills again—it's on your conscience."

What a buzzkill. "I'm confident that won't happen. And please take a message to your boss. Tell Belasco I know what he did—and I'm coming for him."

"Is that a threat?"

"Nope. A guarantee. By the way—is this really the first trial you've ever lost?"

Kilpatrick sighed heavily. "It is. And once this hits social media..."

"You'll have to reduce your astronomical fee?"

"Among other things." Kilpatrick smiled. "Still better than taking orders from some anonymous puppet master whose motives are completely unknown, moving his little lawyers around like pawns on a chessboard."

"I'd rather be directed by a grandmaster whose endgame—" He stopped short.

His eyes darted back and forth. Something was teasing him, something he knew was missing but couldn't nail down. Something that had been darting back and forth on the rim of his subconscious but never quite announcing itself...

Architect. Astronaut. Med school.

No, that wasn't it exactly. But something...

Small scar. Syringe. Civil suit.

Something, some idea, some observation, was waving its arms, trying to get his attention. But he just couldn't zero in...

Pole dance. Cold case. Two tours. I take what I'm owed...

"Oh my God. Oh my God."

Kilpatrick tilted his head. "You okay, Pike?"

"I'm fine…I think…"

"Because you look like you're having a brain seizure."

"Something has seized my brain all right. Something that should have seized it a long time ago. Good luck with your life, Kilpatrick. Hope I never see you again."

He whirled back to his table. "Maria, can you take care of Ossie? Collect his belongings and get him out of the jailhouse?"

"Well, sure, but—"

"I don't think he should go back to the foster home, at least not right away. Put him up at our office. Buy him whatever he needs."

"What are you going to be doing?"

He grabbed his backpack and raced toward the door. "Something I should've done a long time ago."

"But—"

"Because if I'm not mistaken, the murderer is about to strike again."

CHAPTER FORTY-NINE

DAN RACED TO THE FRONT DOOR OF THE MANSION AND HESITATED barely a second. He wasn't sure if he should ring the bell or just burst inside. Entering uninvited, of course, was technically trespassing. Plus it could lead to someone shooting him in the face. And then bio-cremating the body.

But if he didn't hurry, someone else might die. And that's what he had to prevent.

He tried the door. Unlocked. He ran inside. "Zachary? Where are you?"

He found them in the library, the patriarch, Zachary Coleman, plus his two sons and daughter-in-law. Benny and Dolly sat on the sofa. Phil leaned against the mantle where a completely unnecessary fire blazed. The old man sat in his wheelchair, holding a brandy snifter.

Phil was the first to speak. "Pike? What are you doing here?"

"Averting a tragedy."

"I'm calling our lawyers. This is completely inappropriate. You have no right—"

"Every citizen has the right to prevent a murder."

Zachary set down his glass and wheeled forward. "Pike, I am sick and tired of your insinuations."

"I'm sure they have been inconvenient."

"I came to you, initially, because I thought you were an honorable man and I didn't want that boy to get hurt. You got him acquited. Fine. What do you want now?"

"The truth."

"You wouldn't know the truth if it slapped you in the face."

"If by that you mean I've been slow on the uptake—you're right. Embarrassingly so. I've had a lot on my mind. But once I got that trial out of my head, I managed to have a moment of clarity."

"So now that your client is off the hook, you're coming after me?"

He stood his ground. "You've been lying for a long time, Zachary. About many things. Going back for years."

"I loved my son. I love all my sons."

"The sad thing is, I think that's true. You like them all, even…" He gestured toward the two other men in the room. "But every parent has a strong attachment to their first and eldest. Which is why this has all been so hard on you."

"You don't know what you're talking about."

Phil stood behind his father's chair. "This is harassment, Pike, and I won't stand for it. First I'm calling our lawyers. Then the police." He pulled his phone out of his pocket.

"You can do that—but I think you'll regret it."

Phil hesitated.

Dan returned his attention to the patriarch. "You didn't approve when your eldest son—Carl—married, did you?"

"That woman was trash. Poor and simple. Gutter trash. Couldn't even speak proper English."

"Was she evil?"

"Ruby lured my son into marriage. The way women usually do."

"Was she a bad mother?"

"She didn't know what she was doing. She wasn't worthy of the family name."

"But she handled your son. For a time. She knew the truth about him—just as you did. But she didn't leave him, didn't report him. And for a while, she kept him under control." He paused. "Until no one could keep him under control. Not even you."

"What's he talking about, Papa?" Phil asked. "Why is he talking about keeping Carl under control?"

Zachary glared at Dan, daggers shooting from his eyes. "There is no cause for this."

"I think there is."

"It's over. Ancient history. You're digging up the past for no good reason."

"You made it necessary." He waited, but Zachary said nothing. He looked tired. Given the man's poor health, he didn't want to push him too hard. But it had to be said. "When did you find out? Truthfully?"

Zachary said nothing for a long time. And then, all at once, it was almost as if scales had lifted from his eyes. His shoulders sagged, not so much in resignation as...release. "Carl was always...unusual. Even as a boy. Liked to start fires. First down in the sewers. Then closer to home. When he was ten, he started a blaze in the basement that threatened the whole house. Then he started killing small animals. Turned out he was torturing them, only killing them when he was done playing."

Phil's face paled. "Is that what happened to Snowball?'

Zachary pursed his lips. "And every other pet. Finally had to tell the kids they couldn't have any more animals. But I didn't know what to do about Carl. I worried that...in time, animals wouldn't be enough to satiate him. Sent him to a teen military academy. That gave me some rest. But it didn't change him.

When he got out...he was just the same. Only stronger. And soon after that, he met Ruby."

"You probably could've stopped his marriage," Dan said. "Or had it annulled. But you didn't."

"Ruby was completely unsuited to be a member of this family." He sighed. "But..."

"You hoped marriage might change Carl. That she might be a good influence. Might direct his energy in a less...cruel direction."

"I did. But it didn't work, of course. Nothing worked."

"Turned out he liked young boys, didn't he?"

Zachary clenched his teeth. "Not in the disgusting way you're suggesting."

"He wasn't drawn to them sexually. He was drawn to them murderously. He liked to torture. And maim. And kill. And at some point...mummify. Make death masks. When did you learn he'd advanced to human victims?"

"There was an...incident. Out near Sawgrass Lake. I had to spread a lot of money around to keep it quiet. But after that, I told Carl to get the hell out. Didn't want to see him again. Gave him some money and told him to go."

"Did he agree?"

"Given what I knew, and the fact that I controlled the money...he had no choice. A word from me and he would've been behind bars for the rest of his life."

"How did he take it? Being expelled from the family."

"Not...well. He swore he'd get even with me." Zachary's eyes looked as if they were heavier than stone. "And he did."

Phil stared at his father, uncomprehending. "You told everyone Carl died. That he—he had an incurable illness."

"That he did." Zachary averted his eyes. "But it didn't kill him. Unfortunately."

"You had records forged or destroyed to support your lie, to convince the world that Carl was dead. Probably used Sweeney to help pull that off. Except he did it a little too well, didn't he? When Carl's records were destroyed, Ossie's were lost as well."

Zachary did not reply.

Dan glanced at his watch. He needed to keep the man talking. "He used the money to build that cabin, right? Or buy it. He set up shop in a remote location. Off your radar."

"Looks that way."

"Once he supposedly died, disappeared, you tried to take Ossie from his mother."

"That woman couldn't raise my heir. She had no idea what it meant to be a member of this family. We argued, fought—physically. She hurt me, and I'm afraid I hurt her."

"So she ran. She loved her boy and wouldn't let you take him from her. She left that note for you—*You will never find him.* But she couldn't get far enough fast enough. You sent people after her. The police think she killed herself...but I don't. Not while her son was still alive."

"There was a...mistake." Tears began to seep from the elderly man's eyes. "One of my men, Derrick, got himself killed. After that, Ruby got desperate. She ran to a motel, but my men found her. One of them burst into the room. She fired a gun, wounding him. There was a struggle. She ended up dead. I didn't want that. I never wanted her dead! Just...gone. I never told them to kill her."

The silence hung like a blanket for several seconds. "And during the struggle...Ossie disappeared."

Zachary's head and shoulders drooped. "I looked everywhere. Tried everything. Spent millions. Couldn't find him."

"You didn't know he was with his father. Though I wonder if you didn't suspect. You knew Carl was still around. I wouldn't be surprised if he came to you every now and again for money."

Zachary stared up at him, tears streaking his face.

"I won't ask you to admit it. What could you do? Paying a little go-away money probably seemed the simplest solution."

"Carl must've been shadowing Ruby the day she was killed. Maybe she contacted him somehow. I don't know."

"But when she was killed, Carl realized the best possible way he could get even with you. To torture you. Take your beloved grandson and disappear. Let you spend a lifetime searching for someone you would never find. Which technically, he had the legal right to do. He wasn't just a random serial killer, after all. He was the boy's father."

"If I'd had any idea," Zachary said, his voice choking. "If I'd only known..."

"So Carl continued as before, low profile. Going into town for food and young boys when he needed to, but never harming the son he raised. Probably didn't explain that he was the boy's father, at least not at first, given that Ossie called him 'Joe.' Brought back supplies, even books. Homeschooled the boy, in his own twisted way."

Dan had noticed that Ossie had a superb vocabulary—and now he understood why. He'd been educated by Carl, who had been given a first-rate education by his father, Zachary, who was determined to eradicate all traces of his poor origins. The atypical way the whole family spoke should've been his first clue to solving this puzzle.

"I hope to God Carl kept his side activities out of Ossie's line of sight. Though he did make a life mask of Ossie, so..." Dan drew in his breath. "I don't know exactly what brought it to an end. But I like to think Carl knew he was sick. About to die. Maybe he had some mini-strokes. And he didn't want to leave his son untended. So he told the boy who he was and reached out to Harrison."

Benny stared at them, eyes bugging. "No."

"We know there was some kind of struggle. Ossie suffered a

huge blow to the head, back at the cabin, probably during a struggle with his father. I know he had been poorly fed, isolated, mistreated, lied to. Imagine it—the emotional trauma, losing the man who raised him, being alone with a corpse. He had probably been malnourished for years, and a B-12 deficiency can induce memory loss, just like a blow to the head. Honestly, it's amazing Ossie's brain is as sound as it is."

"You don't know any of that," Dolly scoffed.

"No, I don't know it. But it makes sense. When Harrison got to the cabin, no doubt using some kind of detailed directions or GPS pin, he found Carl dead and his nephew untended. A huge mess he didn't know how to handle. He didn't want the police to know anything about the cabin and what Carl had been doing all these years. He didn't want Ossie tainted with his father's crimes. So he brought the boy back to St. Petersburg and left him to be discovered by the police. Maybe Ossie hurt himself then. It's not impossible that Harrison hit the boy, trying to knock him out, but causing or augmenting the memory loss."

"Harrison would never do that," Dolly said.

"Maybe. Ossie's brain was fogged but he knew who he was. His father and Harrison both told him who he was, and one of them left a card bearing his name in his pocket. And he vaguely remembered something about war dogs. Except it wasn't war dogs—it was dogs of war. Harrison was the Shakespeare buff, and he knew what he was setting in motion that night. Given the situation, I can totally imagine him quoting *Julius Caesar*. 'Cry havoc, and let slip the dogs of war.'"

Benny stared at him. "So that boy…really is my nephew?"

"Certainly looks that way."

"Then why did he go to see Harrison? The night Harrison was murdered?"

"I think he did it for exactly the reason he said he did. You can hear it in the audio recording. He wanted Harrison's support. He needed a friend. Maybe he was starting to remember that Harrison had been involved in his reemergence. Maybe he just thought Harrison was his nicest relative."

Dolly gave him a cold look.

"But it didn't work. He pushed hard, but Harrison had already stuck his neck out as far as he cared to go. He couldn't support Ossie without revealing what he knew about Carl—which would destroy his father, and probably the whole family. I think he felt bad about it and might well have changed his mind later. If he'd had the chance." He turned toward the fireplace. "That's what you had to prevent, isn't it, Phil?"

Phil looked startled. "I don't know what you're talking about, Pike."

"I can tell you're lying just looking at you, and I'll bet I'm not the only one. I don't need micro-expressions to read that much guilt."

"You're crazy."

"No, but I think you might be somewhat crazy—given what you did. Seems to run in this family."

Benny turned slowly. "What is he talking about, Phil?"

"I have no idea."

"Phil—"

"I said I have no idea."

Zachary looked as if he were about to explode. "I am sick to death of all this lying!" His entire body trembled. "For God's sake—let this nightmare end."

Phil wrapped his arms around himself and said nothing.

"Let me help you tell your family the truth," Dan said. "You're deep in debt. That's the real reason you sold your car and your house."

Phil shrugged. "Businesses take downturns."

"You're in so deep you'll never get out."

"Then I'll take bankruptcy. All the best people do it. Some do it repeatedly, and the world still supports them. No one cares anymore."

"Conrad Sweeney cares. He's not the kind of creditor you default on. He's the kind who sends thugs to beat the hell out of you—or kill you—when you don't pay up. I think the only reason you're still standing is that he knew your father had money. But he wouldn't wait forever. I think he sent his assistant Prudence to my office to learn more about the case— and how it might affect your ability to pay him back. What was it, some failed tech project? Garrett found a patent application online. Something about quantum computing."

Slowly, as if he were measuring each word, Phil spoke. "Sweeney and I were going to take it to the next level. He loaned me the money. I was supposed to create the product. Google has the edge on quantum computing. We were going to give the world bio-quantum. Computers that not only learn—but live. I'm not a scientist, but my background in chemistry and medicine gave me the authority to manage the project. But research on that level is astronomically expensive. So we partnered. It all started out fine—"

"Until you ran out of money. And had nothing to show for it. You made promises to Sweeney but couldn't deliver. You owed him a ton of money and couldn't pay him back." He paused. "Unless you got a huge intake of money. I think you need something like half a billion. Not just a fourth."

Benny turned and stared wordlessly at his brother.

"First of all, you had to make sure your father didn't change his will to make Ossie an heir. That's why you filed the declaratory judgment lawsuit. To put everything on hold for a long time—possibly forever, given the likelihood that your ailing father would die before the lawsuit was resolved. Once he was dead, he couldn't change his will, so it wouldn't matter whether Ossie was a true Coleman. I looked—Zachary's current will doesn't mention Carl or his heirs. Understandable given the circumstances. But was that enough? I got into the civil case and started pushing for a fast resolution—so you got worried again. Murdering Harrison and framing Ossie—that was perfection. Two heirs, two lines of inheritance eliminated with a single stroke. You stood to inherit half a billion." He paused, bringing his gaze back to the sofa. "Unless something tragic happened to Benny. Then you'd get it all."

Benny somehow pushed himself up on wobbly legs. "Were you planning to murder me, too?"

Phil looked angry. "Of course not. This is all bull. Don't you see what he's doing? Trying to get money for his client. He's probably got some kind of contingency fee arrangement."

Dan shook his head. "I think you found out what Harrison knew, which gave you one more reason to kill him before his conscience took control and he went public. I think your background with chemicals, and your military training with bombs and weapons in Afghanistan, helped you put the whole thing together."

Zachary looked frozen, paralyzed. "This isn't true, is it, Phil?" No answer. "*Is it?*"

Phil pushed away from the hearth. "I don't have to listen to this garbage."

Dan laid a hand on his collar, holding him back. "You're staying right here till I'm finished."

Phil struggled but couldn't get loose. "Let go of me!"

"Can't take me, can you? Not on your own. Which is why you hired those thugs to attack me. Twice. You didn't want to kill me. You realized the murder trial would be a referendum on Ossie's identity, and you wanted that stopped. You thought taking me out would delay the trial. By the time a new lawyer was appointed and ready to go, your father would be dead, never having changed his will. As you told me, Zachary is very ill, so if you could just gum up the wheels of justice for a while…"

Phil shook loose. "This is pure fantasy. Don't listen to this."

"You take ketamine for your migraines, don't you? That's why you had it on hand—and the syringe. A large overdose would kill Harrison."

"You have no proof of any of this!"

Dolly's lips parted. "Phil—you give yourself the migraine injections. I've seen you do it."

Dan nodded. "You went to the theater that night, after Ossie and Vanessa left. Maybe you'd already made up your mind, but when you learned Harrison and Ossie had been talking, you knew you had to act fast. Murdering both would be too obvious —everyone would suspect another member of the family, and Benny doesn't seem nearly as likely a suspect as the former soldier. So you came up with a plan that eliminated them both— in different ways. You killed Harrison, then destroyed the body to prevent anyone from figuring out how he was murdered. You left the syringe in the trash bin outside Ossie's house and sent Quint to find it, pretending to be a police officer. Since you were in the courtroom most days, I'm sure you now realize that was a mistake. You destroyed Harrison's body because you worried about the ketamine being traced to you, but Dr. Zanzibar found traces on the syringe. Unfortunately, by that time, the police were convinced Ossie was the murderer and weren't considering any other suspects."

Zachary rolled his chair close to his youngest son. "Phil—is this true?"

"Of course not. It's all lies. This shyster is probably hoping we'll pay him to stay quiet."

Dan shook his head. "I'm not the one who needs money. You are. You killed Harrison, planted fake evidence, and missed the real clue—the chessboard."

"What are you talking about?"

"I noticed when I went to the crime scene that the pieces had been arranged in a famous endgame position.

White has a rook and a pawn, but black has only a rook. If Black screws it up, White wins. That's called the Lucena position. But if Black forces a draw, it's called the Philidor position. *Phil*-idor." He smiled. "You probably had a gun to his head, but Harrison still managed to leave us a clue identifying his killer. Not on the mirror. On the chessboard."

"This is completely preposterous, farfetched nonsense. Who would know that?"

"Harrison. A chess grandmaster."

"You probably rearranged those pieces yourself."

"Detective Kakazu can tell you that I never touched them."

"This is outrageous! Crazy!" Phil screamed at the top of his lungs, spittle flying from his lips. "Have you all gone insane?"

"No," Dan said quietly. "But I think you have."

Benny took a step forward. "Mr. Pike...is there any way you can...let us handle this? It is a family matter."

"No, I'm afraid I can't. Because you see, Phil has been watching this trial very carefully. And as soon as Ossie was acquitted, after he spoke so convincingly on the witness stand, Phil realized he had to do something fast before your father changed his will." He pointed at the coffee table. "I'm willing to bet Phil put a heavy dose of ketamine in that snifter. Phil poured that drink for you, didn't he, Zachary?"

Zachary stared at the snifter. "Yes." He picked up the snifter and threw it at Phil. It smashed against the fireplace.

"Wish you hadn't done that. But there will be trace elements on the glass. That should be all we need to convict Phil of attempted murder. Then we can—"

"Shut up, you son of a bitch!"

Dolly stood—holding a gun. "I think everyone needs to stay calm and be quiet. I'll take charge of this situation. No one is going anywhere until I—"

Phil sprang on her. They struggled. Benny tried to get

between them, but Phil pushed him away. A moment later, Phil held the gun.

And pointed it at Dan. "I am going to make you sorry you came here tonight."

"And now we have all the proof we need," Dan said quietly.

"You think you're so damn smart? You're just a paid mouthpiece. You're a crook and your father was a killer."

"My father was a hero and a great man."

"Yeah? Well, you're about to be a dead man."

Dan stared at him but didn't move.

"You think I won't shoot?"

"Sadly, I think you will. You're far more afraid of Sweeney, and what he'll do if you don't pay him back, than you are of me. So do it already. Get it over with."

Sweat streamed down Phil's flushed face. His gun hand shook. His eyes were wild. "I will. I'll do it."

"Then do it already!"

"I will!"

"*Do it!*"

Phil pulled the trigger.

It made a loud noise—but nothing happened.

Dan walked forward and snatched the gun away. "I called Dolly before I got here, told her I suspected you—which she believed with impressive alacrity—and asked her to appear at the right moment with a gun. A gun with no bullets."

Phil stared at her. "You—you betrayed me."

Dolly shook her head. "You betrayed us all, Phil. Every single one of us. Starting with Ossie. If you needed money you should've told us."

"Why? So you could laugh at me? Remind me how inferior I am? So our father could hate me even more than he already does? Phil, the perpetual screw-up. You all treated me like a nuisance, not a member of the family."

Dan glanced at his watch. "The police are almost here. I'm

not your lawyer—and never will be—but I recommend that you keep your mouth shut."

"All I ever wanted was what was rightly mine." Phil crumbled to the floor. "All I want is what I deserve."

"Very glad to hear that." Red lights were visible in the window. "Because that's exactly what you're about to get."

CHAPTER FIFTY

SEVERAL DAYS LATER, IN THE LIVING ROOM OF HIS OFFICE, DAN sat opposite Ossie—with a checkered board between them. Jimmy was in the kitchen with Garrett. Maria and Camila huddled together, staring at Maria's phone.

"Just got off the phone with Mr. K," Garrett said. "He is very pleased with how this has worked out. He says we should all expect a handsome bonus this month, and that we should take some time off..."

"My kind of boss," Maria said, poking at her phone screen.

"...and then be back in the office Monday morning. Because he has another case for us."

Dan grinned. Sounded like business as usual in this crazy firm. He continued his lesson. "Okay, Ossie, those are the basics. Got it? Chess rules are pretty simple."

Ossie smiled. "Thanks for explaining it to me."

"It's fun, once you understand it."

"Fun? Really?"

"And good for developing valuable skills. Focus. Planning. Persistence. The rules are easy. Strategy is complex."

"I think I've got the movements down."

"The only complicated one is the knight."

"The horse."

"It's called a knight."

"Why? It looks nothing like a knight. The bishop looks more like a knight. This is a horse."

"Be that as it may—"

"For that matter, the rook looks nothing like a rook. It's a castle."

"But we don't—"

"When you switch it with the king, you call it castling. Why don't we just call it a castle?"

He bit his lower lip. "Never mind." He pushed the chessboard to the side. "Figured out what you want to do next?"

"Maybe..."

"You've been through a rough patch. Don't let it define your future. Start fresh. Make yourself into whatever you want to be. Didn't you tell me you wanted to be an astronaut?"

Ossie looked pensive, as if he were working up the courage to say something.

"You know you can tell me anything."

"I know." Ossie paused. "I've decided I want to be a lawyer. Like you."

His eyes widened. "You do?"

"I made up my mind during the trial. If I survived, I promised myself I was going to dedicate my life to helping others who need it. Just like you helped me."

He felt a strange itching behind the eyeballs. "Well...if you're sure."

"Problem is—college enrollment starts soon. And I have no academic record."

"Take the GED. You'll pass."

"I don't have a transcript."

"I think I may be able to help with that," Camila said from

the kitchen. "A letter from the mayor should get you into any college around here."

"Mr. K has promised to help, too," Maria added. "And he seems to be able to get anything done."

"Will he pay the tuition?"

"You don't need it." Dan paused. "Your grandfather has asked our firm to create a trust fund for you."

"What? He doesn't have to—"

"Shush. You've had a rocky start in life, which was in some part due to decisions and mistakes he and his family made. You deserve some assistance. The civil suit has been dropped and your grandfather has added you to his will. But even before the time comes to inherit your share of his fortune, you'll have access to enough cash to live on."

"You're kidding!"

"I've got something else for you." Camila walked over passed him an envelope.

Ossie opened it. "A party invitation?"

"Dolly Coleman is throwing a society ball. Fundraiser. For our new Athena Clinic."

Ossie put the invite back in the envelope. "Wow. Thanks. That sounds...really boring."

Camila laughed. "Yes. But the point is—the invitation came from Dolly. She's reaching out to you. She wants you to be part of the family."

Ossie's eyes suddenly looked very wet. "I—don't know what to say. This is all I've ever wanted."

"I know."

"I thought I was completely out of chances." He grinned lopsidedly, tears welling up in his eyes. "Guess I still had one more."

Dan clasped Camila's hand. "And that is exactly what the Last Chance Lawyers are all about."

LATE THAT EVENING, DAN AND MARIA SAT ON THE UPSTAIRS
balcony of their office, watching the ocean lap the shore as the
sun set, savoring a bowl of Dan's homemade vanilla toffee ice
cream.

"Dan," she said, "this may be your greatest achievement yet."

"The Coleman case?"

"No. The ice cream. Yum. But speaking of the case. There is
one minor detail that no one has focused on."

He laughed. "More than one, actually. Which are you talking
about?"

"Ossie." She paused. "If that is his real name."

He nodded slowly. "We have no proof. We're assuming Carl
wouldn't kill his own son. But that man was seriously, danger-
ously insane—a quality that appears to be prominent in that
family tree. Maybe he noticed a resemblance and tried to pass
off a kid he abducted as Ossie, using Harrison as a pawn. Carl's
final revenge against his father. There's no way we can know
and no one left to ask. Is the boy Harrison found at the cabin
the true heir?"

"Or just a Carl abductee who fortunately managed to outlive
his captor."

"I don't think 'fortunate' is the right word for anyone forced
into that nightmare."

"But still. Who can be sure about anything, given the state of
this boy's mind...assuming the memory loss hasn't been an act
from the beginning..."

He took another spoonful of ice cream and let it roll down
his tongue. "But whoever he is, he needs a family. And Zachary
wants to believe his grandson is alive. I know—that man made
some horrible choices so I shouldn't get too griefy about him.
But still. He's about to pass and he deserves some peace before
the end. I think this is the perfect resolution."

"I agree, but—does it make you feel like a failure? We didn't really figure out who that boy is."

"No. I feel like a huge success. Because I figured out who *I* am."

She squinted. "If you didn't know, you should've asked me. You're St. Pete's courtroom Jiminy Cricket—"

"But for the right reasons. Not because I have to be. Not because I'm defined by a tragedy in my past. Because that's who I *choose* to be. That's what my father was telling me—well, in a dream. Or a memory, who knows? I choose to be the guy who doesn't sit on his butt while the government—or anyone else—screws someone over. Aristotle said knowing who you are is the beginning of all wisdom."

Maria nodded. "You know who I am?"

"Um...super-smart, devastatingly attractive, social media maven?"

She laughed. "Just a young lawyer...who really likes working with you. No worries about Ossie—I will keep my big mouth shut."

"I know you will." He gazed out at the horizon. "I genuinely like working with you, too, Ms. Morales."

And together, they watched the palm trees dance in the darkness.

EPILOGUE

CONRAD SWEENEY SAT BEHIND HIS MAHOGANY DESK DRUMMING his fingers, staring at the two men seated on the other side. His face was calm, almost blank. His posture was straight. Only the fingers provided a clue to his inner state.

"This cannot continue."

"I know. None of us saw this coming, Mr. Sweeney."

"Doctor Sweeney. I've been patient. God knows I have. Bad enough to lose in court. Again. But this is a disaster."

"You'll bounce back, sir."

"The kid gets off. Phil goes to jail—which means he'll never be able to pay me what he owes. He'll probably be disinherited, so I can't collect against the estate. This is a catastrophic blow. The biggest loss I've taken in my entire career."

"I know. I know."

"And worse—Pike knows I'm involved. He used my name in open court. He knows he's hurt me. He may not know all the details—but given his talent for unraveling secrets, it's only a matter of time before he figures out the rest. Something has to be done."

The two men facing him—District Attorney George Belasco and Bradley Ellison—matched his somber expression.

"I tried to keep you out of it," Ellison said, "when I was testifying. Pike forced my hand."

"Pike's not as smart as he thinks he is," Belasco said. "He's not in your class. Not even close. He wants to be what you are."

"Not exactly correct," Ellison said. "He wants to fix his father's mistakes."

Sweeney steepled his fingers, still stoic as a rock. "He blames you."

"Yes. And now you."

Sweeney shook his head. "If he only knew."

"Maybe it's time he did."

"I can't do that. Fun though it might be."

"Imagine how that would screw him up. He's built his whole life around the belief that his father was wronged so he's going to spend the rest of his life playing Zorro."

"I know, I know. And I've let him have his little delusion. Even though we both know better. You testified that his father killed that man—because he did."

Ellison nodded. "And you know it's true—because you were there."

Sweeney turned to Belasco. "Did you bring the folder?"

"Yes." He opened his briefcase.

"What, no backpack?"

"I'm a lawyer, not a child." Belasco slid the file across the desk.

Sweeney picked up the file and thumbed through it. "This is good. Very good." He looked up. "You know I've been gathering information against Pike for some time. But waiting. Choosing the moment. I believe the moment has arrived." He tilted his head slightly. "But I don't think you're going to enjoy it very much."

DAN ROLLED OVER, BUT THE BED WAS SO SMALL THAT PUT HIM halfway on top of Camila.

"What's that racket?"

She blew hair out of her face. "Someone is at your front door. If you can call it that."

He immediately tensed.

"Relax, Dan. Murderous thugs don't knock."

Sound point. And they would've come in the dark. The sun was already rising. "Still weird." He grabbed a robe. "I'll see who it is."

"Right behind you."

"You don't have to—"

"Just in case you need the Kung Fu mayor to take them out."

A minute later he was topside. He opened the door—

Detective Kakazu stood outside.

"Jake? Kind of early. What's going on?"

He glanced at the two officers standing behind him, Enriquez and a cop he didn't know. "I'm surprised you were sleeping. We've been awake all night."

"That doesn't explain why you're bothering us. Look, if this is some crap Belasco put you up to, just take it home and leave me alone."

The officers looked at one another.

Kakazu drew in his breath. "It does involve Belasco. In a way. He's dead."

"What? The district attorney? When? How?"

"We're just beginning to unpack the details…"

Camila pushed forward. "This is an outrage. I don't know what you're doing, but it should have gone through the mayor's office first."

"That wasn't possible in this case, ma'am."

"And why not?"

"You couldn't be objective about your...paramour. And this involves you, too. Directly."

"Stop talking in riddles and tell me what you're babbling about."

The men glanced at one another. Kakazu shrugged. "You're going to find out soon enough. We received this by anonymous email. We've already checked to make sure it's authentic and hasn't been altered. Our experts say it's legit."

"Just get to the point. What is it?"

Kakazu pulled out his phone and played a recording.

It didn't take long before Dan realized he was listening to his own voice. His and Camila's.

"There are ways we could deal with the District Attorney."

"What do you mean?"

"We could have him taken care of."

"Just off him?"

"If he's on Sweeney's payroll, he deserves to be offed."

"You don't have to do that."

"For you, I would do anything."

"Likewise."

Kakazu withdrew a folded piece of paper and slapped it into Dan's hand. "This is a warrant. You're both under arrest. For the murder of District Attorney George Belasco."

PREVIEW OF TWISTED JUSTICE (BOOK 4 OF THE DANIEL PIKE SERIES)

Elena emerged from the water an inch at a time, first the top of her head, then her forehead, her face, her neck. She moved slowly, clinging to the ocean bed as if walking underwater came naturally, as if she were a mermaid who had suddenly discovered her legs. Her shoulders rose above the water line, then her arms, her breasts. She imagined herself as Botticelli's Venus emerging from a watery half-shell, hair slicked back, body on display for all to see.

"Mama, look! That lady isn't wearing anything!"

"Where did she come from?" another voice asked. "I've been on this beach all day."

"She's hurt! Someone do something!"

Elena heard the cries echo in the clouded reaches of her mind, but the meaning of the words did not register. She had been damaged and she had traveled so far, so fast. Each step was a struggle. She moved like a relentless sea nymph with nothing to hide, no cause for shame, each step a triumph only she understood. The sand oozed between her toes, slowing her, but the sun felt so warm on her body that she almost wanted to cry.

"Hey, kid! You need some help?"

For the briefest of moments, she allowed her gaze to drift. She was bruised and blood-blemished, on her arms, on her left thigh, on the side of her face. Venus should be immaculate, not battered and beaten. Barely alive. How much had she lost? How much more could she lose?

Someone ran beside her, a young man, a little older than she was. Bearded, bloated, hardly Michelangelo's David, but bearing a concerned expression. "You want my towel?"

She tilted her head slightly. Why would she want his towel? The sunshine was a delightful change, after so many days of darkness.

"You know. To cover yourself."

Her gaze intensified. A small crease formed between her eyebrows.

"Um, maybe you don't know, but…you lost your suit. And I think someone already called the cops."

Her suit? Did he mean her rags? Her slave clothes? She was glad to be rid of them.

"You should probably see a doctor, too. You're banged up pretty bad."

A doctor. A doctor. She thought she knew what he meant. Her brain was still muddy, like the sand beneath her feet. But she couldn't allow that. She couldn't bear to be trapped, confined, not again. She fought so hard to be free. Better to bleed to death than be a prisoner.

"Look, I don't mean to be pushy, but I know a guy. I could get you in to see him. And then maybe we could get you some clothes and a hot cup of coffee. You'll feel better in—"

She ran. Bolted away with all the speed she could muster.

She kept running until she reached a brown dirty strip surrounded by tall trees. Two more seconds and she found a sidewalk. A second after that, a street.

Cars zigzagged across her field of vision. She barely recognized them. It had been so long. But she had to make it across. She had to flee.

She darted into the street. Horns blared. Brakes squealed. She heard shouting in a tongue she did not understand. Keep moving, she told herself. Don't let them capture you.

Water flew off her hair and skin as she increased her speed. She heard a whistle somewhere behind her. "Stop! Hey, stop!"

No, no, no, no, no. She could not let it happen to her, not again. She would not be someone else's tool. She had to be free.

"Please stop! You're hurt!"

She knew she was injured, but she also knew she would get better. If only they would leave her alone. She looked around desperately, trying to find someplace to hide. Shops, restaurants, bicycles, boats. She didn't know where she was. She didn't know where she would be safe.

She heard rapid footsteps gaining on her. She crashed into people, trying to move faster. She hit a large woman full on, knocking her to the pavement. The woman shouted. Suddenly everyone was looking at her. Suddenly there was nowhere to run.

Someone tackled her from behind. She fell hard. Her bare knees scraped against the concrete. Blood rose to the surface.

"Miss, I'm taking you into custody for your own safety. Do you know where you are?"

He whipped her body around to face him. He wore a uniform. Glittering pieces of metal. She tried to struggle. He grabbed her fists and forced them down, pinning them between her breasts.

"I'm sorry, miss. You're not leaving me any choice."

A second later, he snapped cuffs around her wrists.

She screamed. It was a loud, keening scream, like something a banshee might release. Piercing and penetrating, sharing her pain with everyone who heard it.

A large crowd gathered around them. "Kid, please. I'm trying to help you. Are your parents around here?"

She did not answer. She did not know what to say.

"Do you have anyone? Anyone we could call?"

She tried to remember, tried to bring back the shattered remnants of what came before. But it was so hard. And part of her didn't want to remember.

"Can you at least tell me who you are?"

Something triggered inside her head. "I am the wave that aches for the shore. I am the fire that never burns cold. I am the lover who can never be kissed."

Holding her beneath the arms, the man raised her to her feet. Between the gash in her side and the bruises on her knees, she could barely stand. "Sure, whatever. But can you give me a name?"

"Izzy. *Izzy?*" She shrieked, and all the strength went out of her. Her legs buckled. But for the man holding her, she would've crumpled to the pavement. "Please...don't let them take me back." Her eyes closed and she could feel her consciousness fading.

"Save the others," she mumbled, her last words before the sleep came. "Before it's too late."

Dan stared through the Plexiglas screen, as angry as he had ever been in his entire life. And he had been plenty angry on many occasions. He'd spent years establishing his rep as one of the best defense lawyers in the city, maybe the state. He'd built up a sizeable bank account and a life that, on the whole, was a source of pride. He'd dedicated his life to protecting the innocent, to making sure his clients weren't railroaded by the government.

Who was riding that railroad now? He'd barely been able to acquire any details since his arrest, but he knew one thing for certain. Someone wanted him out of the way. He was on the express train to the electric chair.

He didn't like to admit it—but he was scared. He'd had people out to get him before, but never anything like this. Nothing so career-damaging. Nothing so potentially life-threatening. He hadn't slept since they locked him away. His hands were trembling and he didn't know what to do about it. The fluttering sensation inside his chest would not stop.

He had peered through this Plexiglas screen before, but from the other side, looking in. This was different. This was something all his keen observational powers and his courtroom bag of tricks could not save him from.

His partner, Maria Morales, sat on the other side. She'd claimed to be his lawyer so she could get in to see him. He leaned forward on his elbows so she couldn't see the trembling.

"Go ahead," Dan said into the antiquated phone receiver that allowed them to communicate. "Just say it."

Maria pursed her lips. "Orange is not your color."

DAN'S RECIPES

Want to try Daniel Pike's recipe for mushroom ragu with polenta? Only takes about 30 minutes to make. Delicious.

Ingredients (for two servings):
    button mushrooms (8 oz)
    grape tomatoes (4 ounces)
    2 scallions
    2 garlic cloves
    Italian seasoning (4 tsp)
    2 veggie stock concentrate packets (easy to find online)
    cornmeal (1/2 cup)
    2 slices ciabatta bread
    cheese of choice (optional)
    kosher salt
    black pepper
    olive oil
    butter (about 4 tbsp)

Instructions:
    1) PREP: Thinly slice the scallions, separating white from

green. Quarter the mushrooms. Halve the tomatoes. Mince one garlic clove, then halve the other.

2) COOK: Heat 1 tbsp butter and some olive oil in a large pan over medium heat. Once warm, add the mushrooms, then 2 tsp Italian seasoning, plus salt and pepper. Cook until tender and golden brown, stirring occasionally, probably about 5-7 minutes. Reduce heat.

3) RAGU: Add the tomatoes, scallion whites, and minced garlic to the pan with more olive oil. Cook until the tomatoes are soft, stirring occasionally, probably around 3-5 minutes. Stir in a veggie stock packet and 1/4 cup of water. Once simmering, remove the pan from the heat.

4) BREAD: Toast ciabatta slices until golden brown. Rub the bread with halved garlic cloves and drizzle with olive oil. Sprinkle with Italian seasoning. Add salt and pepper to taste. Halve bread on the diagonal (triangle shapes).

5) POLENTA: Add 2.5 cups of water, the other veggie stock packet, and 1 tsp salt to a medium pan. Bring to a boil, then whisk in the cornmeal. Reduce heat to low and cook until tender, stirring occasionally, probably around 8-10 minutes. If your polenta gets too thick to stir, add hot water, 1/2 cup at a time.

6) FINISH: Put the ragu pan on medium heat. Stir in 1 tbsp butter. Cook until warm, a minute or so. Add cheese (if you wish) and 2 tbsp butter to the polenta pot and whisk till melted. Add salt and pepper. Pour into bowls, then add the ragu on top. Sprinkle scallion greens over it. Serve with your garlic bread.

ABOUT THE AUTHOR

William Bernhardt is the author of forty-nine books, including *The Last Chance Lawyer* (*#1 Amazon Bestseller*), the historical novels *Challengers of the Dust* and *Nemesis*, two books of poetry, and the Red Sneaker books on fiction writing. In addition, Bernhardt founded the Red Sneaker Writers Center to mentor aspiring authors. The Center hosts an annual conference (WriterCon), small-group seminars, a newsletter, and a bi-weekly podcast. He is also the owner of Balkan Press, which publishes poetry and fiction as well as the literary journal *Conclave*.

Bernhardt has received the Southern Writers Guild's Gold Medal Award, the Royden B. Davis Distinguished Author Award (University of Pennsylvania) and the H. Louise Cobb Distinguished Author Award (Oklahoma State), which is given "in recognition of an outstanding body of work that has profoundly influenced the way in which we understand ourselves and American society at large." In 2019, he received the Arrell Gibson Lifetime Achievement Award from the Oklahoma Center for the Book.

In addition Bernhardt has written plays, a musical (book and score), humor, children stories, biography, and puzzles. He has edited two anthologies (*Legal Briefs* and *Natural Suspect*) as fundraisers for The Nature Conservancy and the Children's Legal Defense Fund. In his spare time, he has enjoyed surfing, digging for dinosaurs, trekking through the Himalayas, paragliding, scuba diving, caving, zip-lining over the canopy of the Costa Rican rain forest, and jumping out of an airplane at 10,000 feet.

In 2017, when Bernhardt delivered the keynote address at the San Francisco Writers Conference, chairman Michael Larsen noted that in addition to penning novels, Bernhardt can "write a sonnet, play a sonata, plant a garden, try a lawsuit, teach a class, cook a gourmet meal, beat you at Scrabble, and work the *New York Times* crossword in under five minutes."

ALSO BY WILLIAM BERNHARDT

The Daniel Pike Novels

The Last Chance Lawyer

Court of Killers

Trial by Blood

Twisted Justice

The Ben Kincaid Novels

Primary Justice

Blind Justice

Deadly Justice

Perfect Justice

Cruel Justice

Naked Justice

Extreme Justice

Dark Justice

Silent Justice

Murder One

Criminal Intent

Death Row

Hate Crime

Capitol Murder

Capitol Threat

Capitol Conspiracy

Capitol Offense

Capitol Betrayal

Justice Returns

Other Novels

Challengers of the Dust

The Game Master

Nemesis: The Final Case of Eliot Ness

Dark Eye

Strip Search

Double Jeopardy

The Midnight Before Christmas

Final Round

The Code of Buddyhood

The Red Sneaker Series on Writing

Story Structure: The Key to Successful Fiction

Creating Character: Bringing Your Story to Life

Perfecting Plot: Charting the Hero's Journey

Dynamic Dialogue: Letting Your Story Speak

Sizzling Style: Every Word Matters

Powerful Premise: Writing the Irresistible

Excellent Editing: The Writing Process

Thinking Theme: The Heart of the Matter

The Fundamentals of Fiction (video series)

Poetry

The White Bird

The Ocean's Edge

For Young Readers

Shine

Princess Alice and the Dreadful Dragon

Equal Justice: The Courage of Ada Sipuel

The Black Sentry

Edited by William Bernhardt

Legal Briefs: Short Stories by Today's Best Thriller Writers

Natural Suspect: A Collaborative Novel of Suspense

Made in the USA
Coppell, TX
07 August 2021